CW01635342

THE BOOK OF TIME

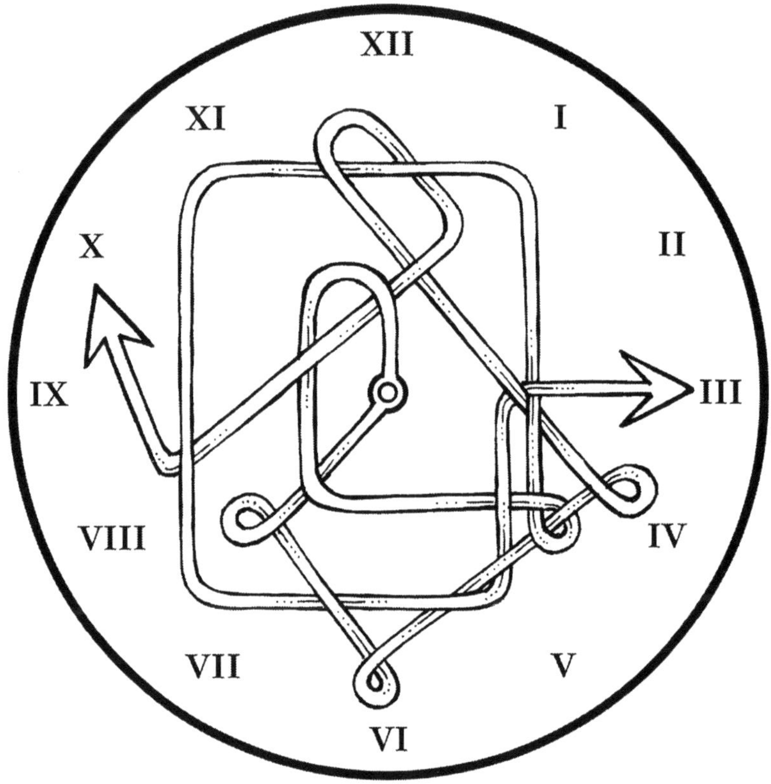

Introduction by

FENDER TUCKER

Illustrated by

GAVIN L. O'KEEFE

THE BOOK OF TIME

THE TIME MACHINE

THE GREY MAN

THE CHRONIC ARGONAUTS

by

H. G. WELLS

NEBOGIPFEL AT THE END OF TIME

12:01 P.M. 12:02 P.M. 12:03 P.M.

by

RICHARD A. LUPOFF

Surinam Turtle Press
2014

First published in 2011 by
Surinam Turtle Press
an imprint of
Ramble House
10329 Sheephead Drive
Vancleave MS 39565 USA

www.ramblehouse.com

First Revised Edition 2014

© 2014 Surinam Turtle Press

Introduction © 2014 Fender Tucker

'Nebogipfel at the End of Time,' '12:01 P.M.', '12:02 P.M.' & '12:03 P.M.'
© 2014 Richard A. Lupoff

Illustrations & Design © 2014 Gavin L. O'Keefe

ISBN 13: 978-1-60543-534-3
ISBN 10: 1-60543-534-1

All Rights Reserved
Printed in the United States of America

Surinam Turtle Press #23

CONTENTS

Preface

"The Chronic Argonauts" was first published by the Royal College of Science in 1888. That story is the precursor of *The Time Machine*, first published in serial form in *New Review*; "The Grey Man" chapter (omitted from book publications of *The Time Machine*) appeared in the *New Review* serial version. The first book publication of *The Time Machine* was by Henry Holt in the United States in early May 1895, followed later that month by the British edition published by William Heinemann (the present book uses the latter text).

"Nebogipfel at the End of Time" was first published in *Heavy Metal* in September 1978, and as a chapbook by Underwood/Miller in 1979.

"12:01 P.M." was first published in *The Magazine of Fantasy & Science Fiction* in December 1973; the story was included in the author's collection *Before...12:01...and After* (Fedogan & Bremer, 1996). "12:02 P.M." was first published in the January/February 2011 issue of *The Magazine of Fantasy & Science Fiction*, and "12:03 P.M." first appeared in the September/October 2012 issue of *The Magazine of Fantasy & Science Fiction.*

Illustrator's Note: The illustration appearing on page 16 is a 'treatment' of a page taken from *The Belton Estate* by Anthony Trollope (Crawford Brothers, Melbourne, undated reprint, p.24). *The Belton Estate* was first published in England in 1866, the year of H. G. Wells' birth.

Introduction

A Time For Ideas

Sometimes you read a book because of the wonderful style of the author. You relish the phrasing, or the timing, or the vocabulary, and keep on reading to find more of what you enjoy. Or if it's fiction you might get off on the plot, wondering what will happen next and if the hero will make it through the book alive.

These are all good reasons for reading books, especially modern books by authors who have been schooled in the art of making things swift and accessible. Authors who don't write swift prose are relegated to print-on-demand publishing and their books will probably never find themselves on the grandest altar of 21st century literary glory: the shelves at Wal-Mart.

H. G. Wells is an exception. His prose is as stodgy and slow as any of his contemporaries of the early 20th century but there's a chance that some of his books might be embraced by the Walton cartel. I'm thinking *War of the Worlds, The Invisible Man,* or *The Time Machine.* I wouldn't be surprised to see one of them at Wal-Mart because they are classics which occasionally get placed on the shelf next to the latest teenage vampire novel—and because movies have been made of them.

But the other author featured in the book you're holding now will, alas, probably never make the Wal-Martian pantheon, even though films have been made of some of his works, including a story in this book. Richard A. Lupoff writes like a modern man, recognizing that the reader doesn't have time to parse every complex sentence for its meaning, and doesn't engage in the "see-how-erudite-I-am" vanities of our great-grandfathers. He has a story to tell and presents it in a linear and mostly concise manner. In that respect he makes an odd bookfellow for H. G. Wells.

The Book Of Time is an anomaly in today's literature. It has both the old style of Wells and the modern style of Lupoff and each is represented by several examples. For Wells it's the immortal novel *The Time Machine*, and the short stories "The Grey Man" and "The Chronic Argonauts." For Lupoff we have the short stories "Nebogipfel at the End of Time," "12:01 P.M.," and its sequels, "12:02 P.M." and "12:03 P.M."

The Time Machine has been filmed twice and "12:01 P.M." three times. The first 'Time Machine,' with Rod Taylor (1960), had its charms but the second, with Guy Pearce (2002), was universally disappointing. We can be thankful that Hollywood hasn't considered "The Grey Man" and "The Chronic Argonauts" because you know they'd be bad.

"12:01 P.M." is another matter. The first version of it was a 1990 Hollywood short film, '12:01 P.M.', that captured the spirit of Lupoff's story of a "time bounce," where the world is caught in a loop, repeating the same snip of time over and over again. In 1993 two full-length films were made in Hollywood. The first, entitled '12:01,' was made with Lupoff's approval, but it was eclipsed by the second, a film with Bill Murray and Andie MacDowell called 'Groundhog Day.' No credit was given to Lupoff for the idea and although he and the producers of '12:01' complained of plagiarism, the big bucks of Hollywood prevailed. Nothing new about that.

What sets the two authors and their stories about time apart from the rest of literature and film is the originality of their ideas. In Wells' time, the idea of traveling through time at anything but the normal rate or direction was completely original. In Lupoff's time, the idea of a time bounce was completely his own. Both men were rewarded with published books and films—unequally, I'm sure—and now this Ramble House book places them together for handy comparison, along with their spin-offs.

Original ideas are not easy. They don't come very often but when they do, they are impossible to kill. Wells had his in 1895 and Lupoff had his in 1973. THE BOOK OF TIME has both of them and for an investment of a few hours of your time you can read them one after the other. And Ramble House guarantees that neither Hollywood nor Wal-Mart had anything to do with the words in this book. Take your time and enjoy. That's what time is for.

Fender Tucker
Vancleave MS
February 1, 2011

THE TIME MACHINE

I

THE TIME TRAVELLER (for so it will be convenient to speak of him) was expounding a recondite matter to us. His grey eyes shone and twinkled, and his usually pale face was flushed and animated. The fire burned brightly, and the soft radiance of the incandescent lights in the lilies of silver caught the bubbles that flashed and passed in our glasses. Our chairs, being his patents, embraced and caressed us rather than submitted to be sat upon, and there was that luxurious after-dinner atmosphere, when thought runs gracefully free of the trammels of precision. And he put it to us in this way—marking the points with a lean forefinger—as we sat and lazily admired his earnestness over this new paradox (as we thought it) and his fecundity.

"You must follow me carefully. I shall have to controvert one or two ideas that are almost universally accepted. The geometry, for instance, they taught you at school is founded on a misconception."

"Is not that rather a large thing to expect us to begin upon?" said Filby, an argumentative person with red hair.

"I do not mean to ask you to accept anything without reasonable ground for it. You will soon admit as much as I need from you. You know of course that a mathematical line, a line of thickness *nil*, has no real existence. They taught you that? Neither has a mathematical plane. These things are mere abstractions."

"That is all right," said the Psychologist.

"Nor, having only length, breadth, and thickness, can a cube have a real existence."

"There I object," said Filby. "Of course a solid body may exist. All real things —"

"So most people think. But wait a moment. Can an *instantaneous* cube exist?"

"Don't follow you," said Filby.

"Can a cube that does not last for any time at all, have a real existence?"

Filby became pensive. "Clearly," the Time Traveller proceeded, "any real body must have extension in *four* directions: it must have Length, Breadth, Thickness, and — Duration. But through a natural infirmity of the flesh, which I will explain to you in a moment, we incline to overlook

this fact. There are really four dimensions, three which we call the three planes of Space, and a fourth, Time. There is, however, a tendency to draw an unreal distinction between the former three dimensions and the latter, because it happens that our consciousness moves intermittently in one direction along the latter from the beginning to the end of our lives."

"That," said a very young man, making spasmodic efforts to relight his cigar over the lamp; "that … very clear indeed."

"Now, it is very remarkable that this is so extensively overlooked," continued the Time Traveller, with a slight accession of cheerfulness. "Really this is what is meant by the Fourth Dimension, though some people who talk about the Fourth Dimension do not know they mean it. It is only another way of looking at Time. *There is no difference between Time and any of the three dimensions of Space except that our consciousness moves along it*. But some foolish people have got hold of the wrong side of that idea. You have all heard what they have to say about this Fourth Dimension?

"*I* have not," said the Provincial Mayor.

"It is simply this. That Space, as our mathematicians have it, is spoken of as having three dimensions, which one may call Length, Breadth, and Thickness, and is always definable by reference to three planes, each at right angles to the others. But some philosophical people have been asking why *three* dimensions particularly — why not another direction at right angles to the other three?—and have even tried to construct a Four-Dimensional geometry. Professor Simon Newcomb was expounding this to the New York Mathematical Society only a month or so ago.

You know how on a flat surface, which has only two dimensions, we can represent a figure of a three-dimensional solid, and similarly they think that by models of three dimensions they could represent one of four—if they could master the perspective of the thing. See?"

"I think so," murmured the Provincial Mayor; and, knitting his brows, he lapsed into an introspective state, his lips moving as one who repeats mystic words. "Yes, I think I see it now," he said after some time, brightening in a quite transitory manner.

"Well, I do not mind telling you I have been at work upon this geometry of Four Dimensions for some time. Some of my results are curious. For instance, here is a portrait of a man at eight years old, another at fifteen, another at seventeen, another at twenty-three, and so on. All these are evidently sections, as it were, Three-Dimensional representations of his Four-Dimensioned being, which is a fixed and unalterable thing.

"Scientific people," proceeded the Time Traveller, after the pause required for the proper assimilation of this, "know very well that Time is only a kind of Space. Here is a popular scientific diagram, a weather record. This line I trace with my finger shows the movement of the barometer. Yesterday it was so high, yesterday night it fell, then this morning it rose again, and so gently upward to here. Surely the mercury did not trace this line in any of the dimensions of Space generally recognised? But certainly it traced such a line, and that line, therefore, we must conclude was along the Time-Dimension."

"But," said the Medical Man, staring hard at a coal in the fire, "if Time is really only a fourth dimension of Space, why is it, and why has it always been, regarded as something different? And why cannot we move in Time as we move about in the other dimensions of Space?"

The Time Traveller smiled. "Are you so sure we can move freely in Space? Right and left we can go, backward and forward freely enough, and men always have done so. I admit we move freely in two dimensions. But how about up and down? Gravitation limits us there."

"Not exactly," said the Medical Man. "There are balloons."

"But before the balloons, save for spasmodic jumping and the inequalities of the surface, man had no freedom of vertical movement."

"Still, they could move a little up and down," said the Medical Man.

"Easier, far easier down than up."

"And you cannot move at all in Time, you cannot get away from the present moment."

"My dear sir, that is just where you are wrong. That is just where the whole world has gone wrong. We are always getting away from the present moment. Our mental existences, which are immaterial and have no dimensions, are passing along the Time-Dimension with a uniform velocity from the cradle to the grave. Just as we should travel *down* if we began our existence fifty miles above the earth's surface."

"But the great difficulty is this," interrupted the Psychologist. "You *can* move about in all directions of Space, but you cannot move about in Time."

"That is the germ of my great discovery. But you are wrong to say that we cannot move about in Time. For instance, if I am recalling an incident very vividly I go back to the instant of its occurrence: I become absent-minded, as you say. I jump back for a moment. Of course we have no means of staying back for any length of Time, any more than a savage or an animal has of staying six feet above the ground. But a civilised man is better off than the savage in this respect. He can go up against gravitation in a balloon, and why should he not hope that ultimately he may be able to stop or accelerate his drift along the Time-Dimension, or even turn about and travel the other way?"

"Oh, *this*," began Filby, "is all—"

"Why not?" said the Time Traveller.

"It's against reason," said Filby.

"What reason?" said the Time Traveller.

"You can show black is white by argument," said Filby, "but you will never convince me."

"Possibly not," said the Time Traveller. "But now you begin to see the object of my investigations into the geometry of Four Dimensions. Long ago I had a vague inkling of a machine—"

"To travel through Time!" exclaimed the Very Young Man.

"That shall travel indifferently in any direction of Space and Time, as the driver determines."

Filby contented himself with laughter.

"But I have experimental verification," said the Time Traveller.

"It would be remarkably convenient for the historian," the Psychologist suggested. "One might travel back and verify the accepted account of the Battle of Hastings, for instance!"

"Don't you think you would attract attention?" said the Medical Man. "Our ancestors had no great tolerance for anachronisms."

"One might get one's Greek from the very lips of Homer and Plato," the Very Young Man thought.

"In which case they would certainly plough you for the Little-go. The German scholars have improved Greek so much."

"Then there is the future," said the Very Young Man. "Just think! One might invest all one's money, leave it to accumulate at interest, and hurry on ahead!"

"To discover a society," said I, "erected on a strictly communistic basis."

"Of all the wild extravagant theories!" began the Psychologist.

"Yes, so it seemed to me, and so I never talked of it until—"

"Experimental verification!" cried I. "You are going to verify *that?*"

"The experiment!" cried Filby, who was getting brain-weary.

"Let's see your experiment anyhow," said the Psychologist, "though it's all humbug, you know."

The Time Traveller smiled round at us. Then, still smiling faintly, and with his hands deep in his trousers pockets, he walked slowly out of the room, and we heard his slippers shuffling down the long passage to his laboratory.

The Psychologist looked at us. "I wonder what he's got?"

"Some sleight-of-hand trick or other," said the Medical Man, and Filby tried to tell us about a conjurer he had seen at Burslem, but before he had finished his preface the Time Traveller came back, and Filby's anecdote collapsed.

The thing the Time Traveller held in his hand was a glittering metallic framework, scarcely larger than a small clock, and very delicately made. There was ivory in it, and some transparent crystalline substance. And now I must be explicit, for this that follows—unless his explanation is to be accepted—is an absolutely unaccountable thing. He took one of the small octagonal tables that were scattered about the room, and set it in front of the fire, with two legs on the hearthrug. On this table he placed the mechanism. Then he drew up a chair, and sat down. The only other object on the table was a small shaded lamp, the bright light of which fell full upon the model. There were also perhaps a dozen candles about, two in brass candlesticks upon the mantel and several in sconces, so that the room was brilliantly illuminated. I sat in a low armchair nearest the fire, and I drew this forward so as to be almost between the Time Traveller and the fireplace. Filby sat behind him, looking over his shoulder. The Medical Man and the Provincial Mayor watched him in profile from the right, the Psychologist from the left. The Very Young Man stood behind the Psychologist. We were all on the alert. It appears incredible to me that any kind of trick, however subtly conceived and however adroitly done, could have been played upon us under these conditions.

The Time Traveller looked at us, and then at the mechanism. "Well?" said the Psychologist.

"This little affair," said the Time Traveller, resting his elbows upon the table and pressing his hands together above the apparatus, "is only a model. It is my plan for a machine to travel through time. You will notice that it looks singularly askew, and that there is an odd twinkling appearance about this bar, as though it was in some way unreal." He pointed to the part with his finger. "Also, here is one little white lever, and here is another."

The Medical Man got up out of his chair and peered into the thing. "It's beautifully made," he said.

"It took two years to make," retorted the Time Traveller. Then, when we had all imitated the action of the Medical Man, he said: "Now I want you clearly to understand that this lever, being pressed over, sends the machine gliding into the future, and this other reverses the motion. This saddle represents the seat of a time traveller. Presently I am going to press the lever, and off the machine will go. It will vanish, pass into future time, and disappear. Have a good look at the thing. Look at the table too, and satisfy yourselves there is no trickery. I don't want to waste this model and then be told I'm a quack."

There was a minute's pause perhaps. The Psychologist seemed about to speak to me, but changed his mind. Then the Time Traveller put forth his finger towards the lever. "No," he said suddenly. "Lend me your hand." And turning to the Psychologist, he took that individual's hand in his own and told him to put out his forefinger. So that it was the Psychologist himself who sent forth the model Time Machine on its interminable voyage. We all saw the lever turn. I am absolutely certain there was no trickery. There was a breath of wind, and the lamp flame jumped. One of the candles on the mantel was blown out, and the little machine suddenly swung round, became indistinct, was seen as a ghost for a second perhaps, as an eddy of faintly glittering brass and ivory; and it was gone—vanished! Save for the lamp the table was bare.

Every one was silent for a minute. Then Filby said he was damned.

The Psychologist recovered from his stupor, and suddenly looked under the table. At that the Time Traveller laughed cheerfully. "Well?" he said, with a reminiscence of the Psychologist. Then, getting up, he went to the tobacco jar on the mantel, and with his back to us began to fill his pipe.

We stared at each other. "Look here," said the Medical Man, "are you in earnest about this? Do you seriously believe that that machine has travelled into time?"

"Certainly," said the Time Traveller, stooping to light a spill at the fire. Then he turned, lighting his pipe, to look at the Psychologist's face.

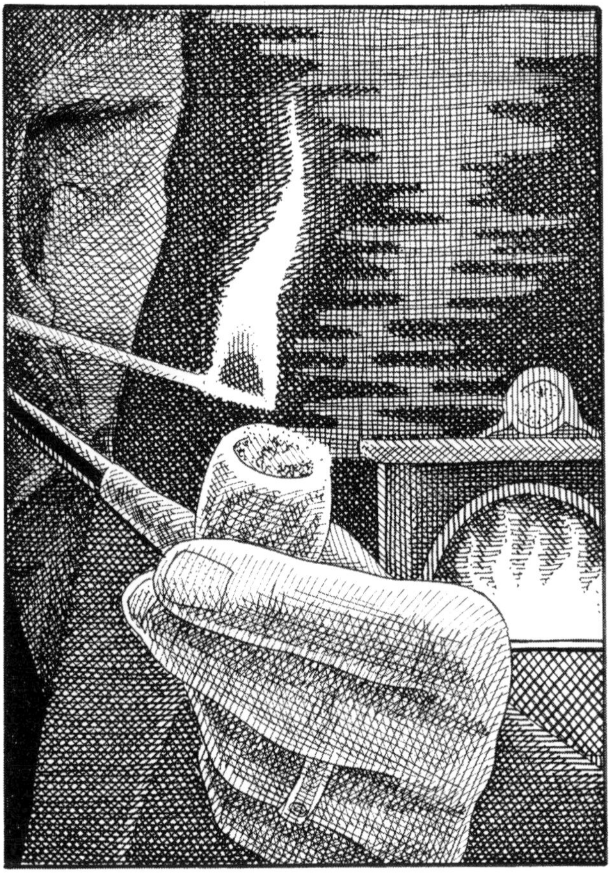

(The Psychologist, to show that he was not unhinged, helped himself to a cigar and tried to light it uncut.) "What is more, I have a big machine nearly finished in there"—he indicated the laboratory—"and when that is put together I mean to have a journey on my own account."

"You mean to say that that machine has travelled into the future?" said Filby.

"Into the future or the past—I don't, for certain, know which."

After an interval the Psychologist had an inspiration. "It must have gone into the past if it has gone anywhere," he said.

"Why?" said the Time Traveller.

"Because I presume that it has not moved in space, and if it travelled into the future it would still be here all this time, since it must have travelled through this time."

"But," said I, "if it travelled into the past it would have been visible when we came first into this room; and last Thursday when we were here; and the Thursday before that; and so forth!"

"Serious objections," remarked the Provincial Mayor, with an air of impartiality, turning towards the Time Traveller.

"Not a bit," said the Time Traveller, and to the Psychologist: "You think. *You* can explain that. It's presentation below the threshold, you know, diluted presentation."

"Of course," said the Psychologist, and reassured us. "That's a simple point of psychology. I should have thought of it. It's plain enough, and helps the paradox delightfully. We cannot see it, nor can we appreciate this machine, any more than we can the spoke of a wheel spinning, or a bullet flying through the air. If it is travelling through time fifty times or a hundred times faster than we are, if it gets through a minute while we get through a second, the impression it creates will of course be only one-fiftieth or one-hundredth of what it would make if it were not travelling in time. That's plain enough." He passed his hand through the space in which the machine had been. "You see?" he said, laughing.

We sat and stared at the vacant table for a minute or so. Then the Time Traveller asked us what we thought of it all.

"It sounds plausible enough to-night," said the Medical Man; "but wait until to-morrow. Wait for the common sense of the morning."

"Would you like to see the Time Machine itself?" asked the Time Traveller. And therewith, taking the lamp in his hand, he led the way down the long, draughty corridor to his laboratory. I remember vividly the flickering light, his queer broad head in silhouette, the dance of the shadows, how we all followed him, puzzled but incredulous, and how there in the laboratory we beheld a larger edition of the little mechanism which we had seen vanish from before our eyes. Parts were of nickel, parts of ivory, parts had certainly been filed or sawn out of rock crystal. The thing was generally complete, but the twisted crystalline bars lay unfinished upon the bench beside some sheets of drawings, and I took one up for a better look at it. Quartz it seemed to be.

"Look here," said the Medical Man, "are you perfectly serious? Or is this a trick—like that ghost you showed us last Christmas?"

"Upon that machine," said the Time Traveller, holding the lamp aloft, "I intend to explore time. Is that plain? I was never more serious in my life."

None of us quite knew how to take it.

I caught Filby's eye over the shoulder of the Medical Man, and he winked at me solemnly.

2

I THINK that at that time none of us quite believed in the Time Machine. The fact is, the Time Traveller was one of those men who are too clever to be believed: you never felt that you saw all around him; you always suspected some subtle reserve, some ingenuity in ambush, behind his lucid frankness. Had Filby shown the model and explained the matter in the Time Traveller's words, we should have shown him far less scepticism. For we should have perceived his motives: a pork-butcher could understand Filby. But the Time Traveller had more than a touch of whim among his elements, and we distrusted him. Things that would have made the fame of a less clever man seemed tricks in his hands. It is a mistake to do things too easily. The serious people who took him seriously never felt quite sure of his deportment: they were somehow aware that trusting their reputations for judgment with him was like furnishing a nursery with eggshell china. So I don't think any of us said very much about time travelling in the interval between that Thursday and the next, though its odd potentialities ran, no doubt, in most of our minds: its plausibility, that is, its practical incredibleness, the curious possibilities of anachronism and of utter confusion it suggested. For my own part, I was particularly preoccupied with the trick of the model. That I remember discussing with the Medical Man, whom I met on Friday at the Linnæan. He said he had seen a similar thing at Tübingen, and laid considerable stress on the blowing-out of the candle. But how the trick was done he could not explain.

The next Thursday I went again to Richmond—I suppose I was one of the Time Traveller's most constant guests—and, arriving late, found four or five men already assembled in his drawing-room. The Medical Man was standing before the fire with a sheet of paper in one hand and his watch in the other. I looked round for the Time Traveller, and—"It's half-past seven now," said the Medical Man. "I suppose we'd better have dinner?"

"Where's—?" said I, naming our host.

"You've just come? It's rather odd. He's unavoidably detained. He asks me in this note to lead off with dinner at seven if he's not back. Says he'll explain when he comes."

"It seems a pity to let the dinner spoil," said the Editor of a well-known daily paper; and thereupon the Doctor rang the bell.

The Psychologist was the only person besides the Doctor and myself who had attended the previous dinner. The other men were Blank, the

Editor aforementioned, a certain journalist, and another—a quiet, shy man with a beard—whom I didn't know, and who, as far as my observation went, never opened his mouth all the evening. There was some speculation at the dinner-table about the Time Traveller's absence, and I suggested time travelling, in a half jocular spirit. The Editor wanted that explained to him, and the Psychologist volunteered a wooden account of the "ingenious paradox and trick" we had witnessed that day week. He was in the midst of his exposition when the door from the corridor opened slowly and without noise. I was facing the door, and saw it first. "Hallo!" I said. "At last!"And the door opened wider, and the Time Traveller stood before us. I gave a cry of surprise. "Good heavens! man, what's the matter?" cried the Medical Man, who saw him next. And the whole tableful turned towards the door.

He was in an amazing plight. His coat was dusty and dirty and smeared with green down the sleeves; his hair disordered, and as it seemed to me greyer—either with dust and dirt or because its colour had actually faded. His face was ghastly pale; his chin had a brown cut on it—a cut half healed; his expression was haggard and drawn, as by intense suffering. For a moment he hesitated in the doorway, as if he had been dazzled by the light. Then he came into the room. He walked with just such a limp as I have seen in footsore tramps. We stared at him in silence, expecting him to speak.

He said not a word, but came painfully to the table, and made a motion towards the wine. The Editor filled a glass of champagne, and pushed it towards him. He drained it, and it seemed to do him good: for he looked round the table, and the ghost of his old smile flickered across his face. "What on earth have you been up to, man?" said the Doctor. The Time Traveller did not seem to hear. "Don't let me disturb you," he said, with a certain faltering articulation. "I'm all right." He stopped, held out his glass for more, and took it off at a draught. "That's good," he said. His eyes grew brighter, and a faint colour came into his cheeks. His glance flickered over our faces with a certain dull approval, and then went round the warm and comfortable room. Then he spoke again, still as it were feeling his way among his words. "I'm going to wash and dress, and then I'll come down and explain things. ... Save me some of that mutton. I'm starving for a bit of meat."

He looked across at the Editor, who was a rare visitor, and hoped he was all right. The Editor began a question. "Tell you presently," said the Time Traveller. "I'm—funny! Be all right in a minute."

He put down his glass, and walked towards the staircase door. Again I remarked his lameness and the soft padding sound of his footfall, and standing up in my place, I saw his feet as he went out. He had nothing on them but a pair of tattered, blood-stained socks. Then the door closed upon him. I had half a mind to follow, till I remembered how he detested any fuss about himself. For a minute, perhaps, my mind was wool gathering. Then, "Remarkable Behaviour of an Eminent Scientist," I heard the Editor say, thinking (after his wont) in headlines. And this brought my attention back to the bright dinner-table.

"What's the game?" said the journalist. "Has he been doing the Amateur Cadger? I don't follow." I met the eye of the Psychologist, and read my own interpretation in his face. I thought of the Time Traveller limping painfully upstairs. I don't think any one else had noticed his lameness.

The first to recover completely from this surprise was the Medical Man, who rang the bell—the Time Traveller hated to have servants waiting at dinner—for a hot plate. At that the Editor turned to his knife and fork with a grunt, and the silent man followed suit. The dinner was resumed. Conversation was exclamatory for a little while, with gaps of wonderment; and then the Editor got fervent in his curiosity. "Does our friend eke out his modest income with a crossing? or has he his Nebuchadnezzar phases?" he inquired. "I feel assured it's this business of the Time Machine," I said, and took up the Psychologist's account of our previous meeting. The new guests were frankly incredulous. The Editor raised objections. "What was this time travelling? A man couldn't cover himself with dust by rolling in a paradox, could he?" And then, as the idea came home to him, he resorted to caricature. Hadn't they any clothes-brushes in the Future? The journalist, too, would not believe at any price, and joined the Editor in the easy work of heaping ridicule on the whole thing. They were both the new kind of journalist—very joyous, irreverent young men. "Our Special Correspondent in the Day after To-morrow reports," the journalist was saying—or rather shouting—when the Time Traveller came back. He was dressed in ordinary evening clothes, and nothing save his haggard look remained of the change that had startled me.

"I say," said the Editor hilariously, "these chaps here say you have been travelling into the middle of next week! Tell us all about little Rosebery, will you? What will you take for the lot?"

The Time Traveller came to the place reserved for him without a word. He smiled quietly, in his old way. "Where's my mutton?" he said. "What a treat it is to stick a fork into meat again!"

"Story!"cried the Editor.

"Story be damned!" said the Time Traveller. "I want something to eat. I won't say a word until I get some peptone into my arteries. Thanks. And the salt."

"One word," said I. "Have you been time travelling?"

"Yes," said the Time Traveller, with his mouth full, nodding his head.

"I'd give a shilling a line for a verbatim note," said the Editor. The Time Traveller pushed his glass towards the Silent Man and rang it with his finger nail; at which the Silent Man, who had been staring at his face, started convulsively, and poured him wine. The rest of the dinner was uncomfortable. For my own part, sudden questions kept on rising to my lips, and I dare say it was the same with the others. The journalist tried to relieve the tension by telling anecdotes of Hettie Potter. The Time Traveller devoted his attention to his dinner, and displayed the appetite of a tramp. The Medical Man smoked a cigarette, and watched the Time Traveller through his eyelashes. The Silent Man seemed even more clumsy than usual, and drank champagne with regularity and determination out of sheer nervousness. At last the Time Traveller pushed his plate away, and looked round us. "I suppose I must apologise," he said. "I was simply starving. I've had a most amazing time." He reached out his hand for a cigar, and cut the end. "But come into the smoking-room. It's too long a story to tell over greasy plates." And ringing the bell in passing, he led the way into the adjoining room.

"You have told Blank, and Dash, and Chose about the machine?" he said to me, leaning back in his easy chair and naming the three new guests.

"But the thing's a mere paradox," said the Editor.

"I can't argue to-night. I don't mind telling you the story, but I can't argue. I will," he went on, "tell you the story of what has happened to me, if you like, but you must refrain from interruptions. I want to tell it. Badly. Most of it will sound like lying. So be it! It's true—every word of it, all the same. I was in my laboratory at four o'clock, and since then … I've lived eight days … such days as no human being ever lived before! I'm nearly worn out, but I shan't sleep till I've told this thing over to you. Then I shall go to bed. But no interruptions! Is it agreed?"

"Agreed," said the Editor, and the rest of us echoed "Agreed." And with that the Time Traveller began his story as I have set it forth. He sat back in his chair at first, and spoke like a weary man. Afterwards he got more animated. In writing it down I feel with only too much keenness the inadequacy of pen and ink—and, above all, my own inadequacy—to express its quality. You read, I will suppose, attentively enough; but you cannot see the speaker's white, sincere face in the bright circle of the little lamp, nor hear the intonation of his voice. You cannot know how his expression followed the turns of his story! Most of us hearers were in shadow, for the candles in the smoking-room had not been lighted, and only the face of the journalist and the legs of the Silent Man from the knees downward were illuminated. At first we glanced now and again at each other. After a time we ceased to do that, and looked only at the Time Traveller's face.

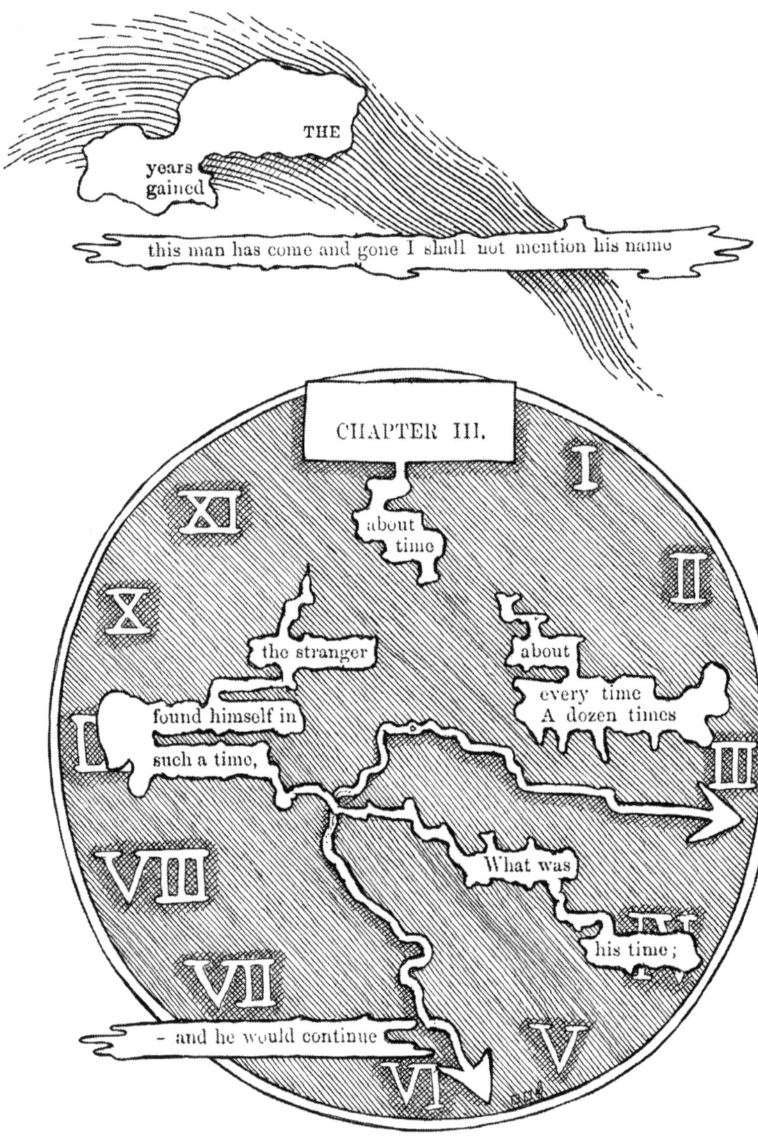

3

I TOLD some of you last Thursday of the principles of the Time Machine, and showed you the actual thing itself, incomplete in the workshop. There it is now, a little travel-worn, truly; and one of the ivory bars is cracked, and a brass rail bent but the rest of it's sound enough. I expected to finish it on Friday but on Friday, when the putting together was nearly done, I found that one of the nickel bars was exactly one inch too short, and this I had to get re-made; so that the thing was not complete until this morning. It was at ten o'clock to-day that the first of all Time Machines began its career. I gave it a last tap, tried all the screws again, put one more drop of oil on the quartz rod, and sat myself in the saddle. I suppose a suicide who holds a pistol to his skull feels much the same wonder at what will come next as I felt then. I took the starting lever in one hand and the stopping one in the other, pressed the first, and almost immediately the second. I seemed to reel; I felt a nightmare sensation of falling; and, looking round, I saw the laboratory exactly as before. Had anything happened? For a moment I suspected that my intellect had tricked me. Then I noted the clock. A moment before, as it seemed, it had stood at a minute or so past ten; now it was nearly half-past three!

"I drew a breath, set my teeth, gripped the starting lever with both hands, and went off with a thud. The laboratory got hazy and went dark. Mrs. Watchett came in, and walked, apparently without seeing me, towards the garden door. I suppose it took her a minute or so to traverse the place, but to me she seemed to shoot across the room like a rocket. I pressed the lever over to its extreme position. The night came like the turning out of a lamp, and in another moment came to-morrow. The laboratory grew faint and hazy, then fainter and ever fainter. To-morrow night came black, then day again, night again, day again, faster and faster still. An eddying murmur filled my ears, and a strange, dumb confusedness descended on my mind.

"I am afraid I cannot convey the peculiar sensations of time travelling. They are excessively unpleasant. There is a feeling exactly like that one has upon a switchback—of a helpless headlong motion! I felt the same horrible anticipation, too, of an imminent smash. As I put on pace, night followed day like the flapping of a black wing. The dim suggestion of the laboratory seemed presently to fall away from me, and I saw the sun hopping swiftly across the sky, leaping it every minute, and every minute marking a day. I supposed the laboratory had been destroyed, and I had come into the open air. I had a dim impression of scaffolding, but I was already going too fast to be conscious of any moving things. The slowest snail that ever crawled dashed by too fast for me. The twinkling succession of darkness and light was excessively painful to the eye. Then, in the intermittent darknesses, I saw the moon spinning swiftly through her quarters from new to full, and had a faint glimpse of the circling stars. Presently, as I went on, still gaining velocity, the palpitation of night and day merged into one continuous greyness; the sky took on a wonderful deepness of blue, a splendid luminous colour like that of early twilight; the jerking sun became a streak of fire, a brilliant arch, in space, the moon a fainter fluctuating band; and I could see nothing of the stars, save now and then a brighter circle flickering in the blue.

"The landscape was misty and vague. I was still on the hillside upon which this house now stands, and the shoulder rose above me grey and dim. I saw trees growing and changing like puffs of vapour, now brown, now green: they grew, spread, shivered, and passed away. I saw huge buildings rise up faint and fair, and pass like dreams. The whole surface of the earth seemed changed—melting and flowing under my eyes. The little hands upon the dials that registered my speed raced round faster and faster. Presently I noted that the sun-belt swayed up and down, from solstice to solstice, in a minute or less, and that, consequently, my pace was over a year a minute; and minute by minute the white snow flashed across the world, and vanished, and was followed by the bright, brief green of spring.

"The unpleasant sensations of the start were less poignant now. They merged at last into a kind of hysterical exhilaration. I remarked, indeed, a clumsy swaying of the machine, for which I was unable to account. But my mind was too confused to attend to it, so with a kind of madness growing upon me, I flung myself into futurity. At first I scarce thought of stopping, scarce thought of anything but these new sensations. But presently a fresh series of impressions grew up in my mind—a certain curiosity and therewith a certain dread—until at last they took complete possession of me. What strange developments of humanity, what wonderful advances upon our rudimentary civilisation, I thought, might not appear when I came to look nearly into the dim elusive world that raced and fluctuated before my eyes! I saw great and splendid architecture rising about me, more massive than any buildings of our own time, and yet, as it seemed, built of glimmer and mist. I saw a richer green flow up the hillside, and remain there without any wintry intermission. Even through the veil of my confusion the earth seemed very fair. And so my mind came round to the business of stopping.

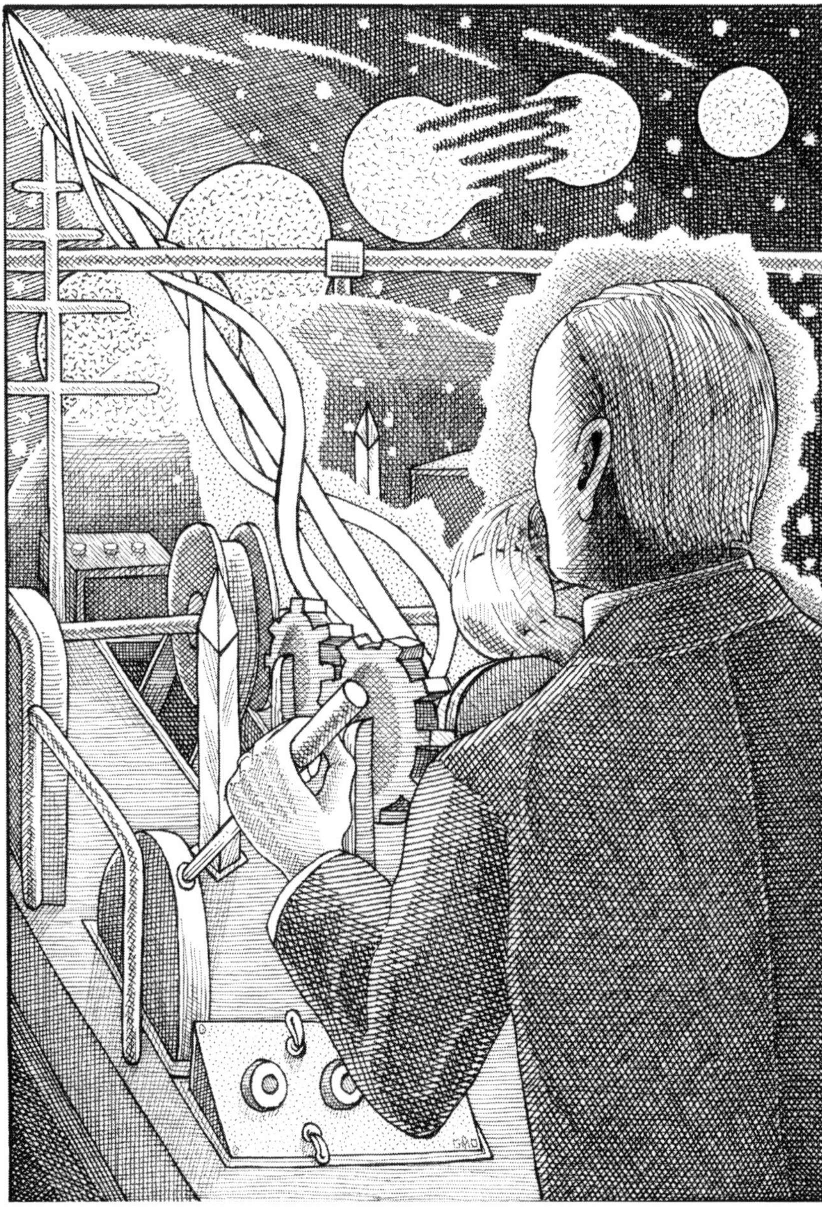

"The peculiar risk lay in the possibility of my finding some substance in the space which I, or the machine, occupied. So long as I travelled at a high velocity through time, this scarcely mattered: I was, so to speak, attenuated—was slipping like a vapour through the interstices of intervening substances! But to come to a stop involved the jamming of myself, molecule by molecule, into whatever lay in my way: meant bringing my atoms into such intimate contact with those of the obstacle that a profound chemical reaction—possibly a far-reaching explosion—would result, and blow myself and my apparatus out of all possible dimensions—into the Unknown. This possibility had occurred to me again and again while I was making the machine; but then I had cheerfully accepted it as an unavoidable risk—one of the risks a man has got to take! Now the risk was inevitable, I no longer saw it in the same cheerful light. The fact is that, insensibly, the absolute strangeness of everything, the sickly jarring and swaying of the machine, above all, the feeling of prolonged falling, had absolutely upset my nerve. I told myself that I could never stop, and with a gust of petulance I resolved to stop forthwith. Like an impatient fool, I lugged over the lever, and incontinently the thing went reeling over, and I was flung headlong through the air.

"There was the sound of a clap of thunder in my ears. I may have been stunned for a moment. A pitiless hail was hissing round me, and I was sitting on soft turf in front of the overset machine. Everything still seemed grey, but presently I remarked that the confusion in my ears was gone. I looked round me. I was on what seemed to be a little lawn in a garden, surrounded by rhododendron bushes, and I noticed that their mauve and purple blossoms were dropping in a shower under the beating of the hailstones. The rebounding, dancing hail hung in a cloud over the machine, and drove along the ground like smoke. In a moment I was wet to the skin. 'Fine hospitality,' said I, 'to a man who has travelled innumerable years to see you.'

"Presently I thought what a fool I was to get wet. I stood up and looked round me. A colossal figure, carved apparently in some white stone, loomed indistinctly beyond the rhododendrons through the hazy downpour. But all else of the world was invisible.

"My sensations would be hard to describe. As the columns of hail grew thinner, I saw the white figure more distinctly. It was very large, for a silver birch tree touched its shoulder. It was of white marble, in shape something like a winged sphinx, but the wings, instead of being carried vertically at the sides, were spread so that it seemed to hover. The pedestal, it appeared to me, was of bronze, and was thick with verdigris. It chanced that the face was towards me; the sightless eyes seemed to

watch me; there was the faint shadow of a smile on the lips. It was greatly weather-worn, and that imparted an unpleasant suggestion of disease. I stood looking at it for a little space—half a minute, perhaps, or half an hour. It seemed to advance and to recede as the hail drove before it denser or thinner. At last I tore my eyes from it for a moment, and saw that the hail curtain had worn threadbare, and that the sky was lightening with the promise of the sun.

"I looked up again at the crouching white shape, and the full temerity of my voyage came suddenly upon me. What might appear when that hazy curtain was altogether withdrawn? What might not have happened to men? What if cruelty had grown into a common passion? What if in this interval the race had lost its manliness, and had developed into something inhuman, unsympathetic, and overwhelmingly powerful? I might seem some old-world savage animal, only the more dreadful and disgusting for our common likeness—a foul creature to be incontinently slain.

"Already I saw other vast shapes—huge buildings with intricate parapets and tall columns, with a wooded hillside dimly creeping in upon me through the lessening storm. I was seized with a panic fear. I turned frantically to the Time Machine, and strove hard to readjust it. As I did so the shafts of the sun smote through the thunderstorm. The grey downpour was swept aside and vanished like the trailing garments of a ghost. Above me, in the intense blue of the summer sky, some faint brown shreds of cloud whirled into nothingness. The great buildings about me stood out clear and distinct, shining with the wet of the thunderstorm, and picked out in white by the unmelted hailstones piled along their courses. I felt naked in a strange world. I felt as perhaps a bird may feel in the clear air, knowing the hawk wings above and will swoop. My fear grew to frenzy. I took a breathing space, set my teeth, and again grappled fiercely, wrist and knee, with the machine. It gave under my desperate onset and turned over. It struck my chin violently. One hand on the saddle, the other on the lever, I stood panting heavily in attitude to mount again.

"But with this recovery of a prompt retreat my courage recovered. I looked more curiously and less fearfully at this world of the remote future. In a circular opening, high up in the wall of the nearer house, I saw a group of figures clad in rich soft robes. They had seen me, and their faces were directed towards me.

"Then I heard voices approaching me. Coming through the bushes by the White Sphinx were the heads and shoulders of men running. One of these emerged in a pathway leading straight to the little lawn upon which I stood with my machine. He was a slight creature—perhaps four feet high — clad in a purple tunic, girdled at the waist with a leather belt. Sandals or buskins — I could not clearly distinguish which — were on his feet; his legs were bare to the knees, and his head was bare. Noticing that, I noticed for the first time how warm the air was.

"He struck me as being a very beautiful and graceful creature, but indescribably frail. His flushed face reminded me of the more beautiful kind of consumptive — that hectic beauty of which we used to hear so much. At the sight of him I suddenly regained confidence. I took my hands from the machine."

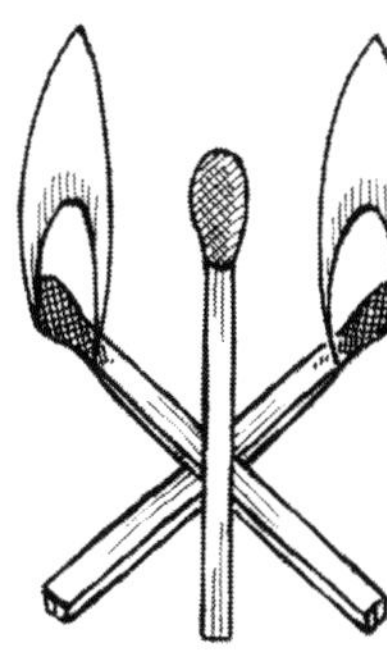

4

IN ANOTHER moment we were standing face to face, I and this fragile thing out of futurity. He came straight up to me and laughed into my eyes. The absence from his bearing of any sign of fear struck me at once. Then he turned to the two others who were following him and spoke to them in a strange and very sweet and liquid tongue.

"There were others coming, and presently a little group of perhaps eight or ten of these exquisite creatures were about me. One of them addressed me. It came into my head, oddly enough, that my voice was too harsh and deep for them. So I shook my head, and pointing to my ears, shook it again. He came a step forward, hesitated, and then touched my hand. Then I felt other soft little tentacles upon my back and shoulders. They wanted to make sure I was real. There was nothing in this at all alarming. Indeed, there was something in these pretty little people that inspired confidence—a graceful gentleness, a certain childlike ease. And besides, they looked so frail that I could fancy myself flinging the whole dozen of them about like nine-pins. But I made a sudden motion to warn them when I saw their little pink hands feeling at the Time Machine. Happily then, when it was not too late, I thought of a danger I had hitherto forgotten, and reaching over the bars of the machine, I unscrewed the little levers that would set it in motion, and put these in my pocket. Then I turned again to see what I could do in the way of communication.

"And then, looking more nearly into their features, I saw some further peculiarities in their Dresden china type of prettiness. Their hair, which was uniformly curly, came to a sharp end at the neck and cheek; there was not the faintest suggestion of it on the face, and their ears were singularly minute. The mouths were small, with bright red, rather thin lips, and the little chins ran to a point. The eyes were large and mild; and—this may seem egotism on my part—I fancied even then that there was a certain lack of the interest I might have expected in them.

"As they made no effort to communicate with me, but simply stood round me smiling and speaking in soft cooing notes to each other, I began the conversation. I pointed to the Time Machine and to myself. Then, hesitating for a moment how to express Time, I pointed to the sun. At once a quaintly pretty little figure in chequered purple and white followed my gesture, and then astonished me by imitating the sound of thunder.

"For a moment I was staggered, though the import of his gesture was plain enough. The question had come into my mind abruptly: were these creatures fools? You may hardly understand how it took me. You see I had always anticipated that the people of the year Eight Hundred and Two Thousand odd would be incredibly in front of us in knowledge, art, everything. Then one of them suddenly asked me a question that showed him to be on the intellectual level of one of our five-year-old children—asked me, in fact, if I had come from the sun in a thunderstorm! It let loose the judgment I had suspended upon their clothes, their frail light limbs and fragile features. A flow of disappointment rushed across my mind. For a moment I felt that I had built the Time Machine in vain.

"I nodded, pointed to the sun, and gave them such a vivid rendering of a thunderclap as startled them. They all withdrew a pace or so and bowed. Then came one laughing towards me, carrying a chain of beautiful flowers altogether new to me, and put it about my neck. The idea was received with melodious applause; and presently they were all running to and fro for flowers, and laughingly flinging them upon me until I was almost smothered with blossom. You who have never seen the like can scarcely imagine what delicate and wonderful flowers countless years of culture had created. Then someone suggested that their plaything should be exhibited in the nearest building, and so I was led past the sphinx of white marble, which had seemed to watch me all the while with a smile at my astonishment, towards a vast grey edifice of fretted stone. As I went with them the memory of my confident anticipations of a profoundly grave and intellectual posterity came, with irresistible merriment, to my mind.

"The building had a huge entry, and was altogether of colossal dimensions. I was naturally most occupied with the growing crowd of little people, and with the big open portals that yawned before me shadowy and mysterious. My general impression of the world I saw over their heads was of a tangled waste of beautiful bushes and flowers, a long neglected and yet weedless garden. I saw a number of tall spikes of strange white flowers, measuring a foot perhaps across the spread of the waxen petals. They grew scattered, as if wild, among the variegated shrubs, but, as I say, I did not examine them closely at this time. The Time Machine was left deserted on the turf among the rhododendrons.

"The arch of the doorway was richly carved, but naturally I did not observe the carving very narrowly, though I fancied I saw suggestions of old Phœnician decorations as I passed through, and it struck me that they were very badly broken and weather-worn. Several more brightly-clad people met me in the doorway, and so we entered, I, dressed in dingy nineteenth-century garments, looking grotesque enough, garlanded with flowers, and surrounded by an eddying mass of bright, soft-coloured robes and shining white limbs, in a melodious whirl of laughter and laughing speech.

"The big doorway opened into a proportionately great hall hung with brown. The roof was in shadow, and the windows, partially glazed with coloured glass and partially unglazed, admitted a tempered light. The floor was made up of huge blocks of some very hard white metal, not plates nor slabs,—blocks, and it was so much worn, as I judged by the going to and fro of past generations, as to be deeply channelled along the more frequented ways. Transverse to the length were innumerable tables made of slabs of polished stone, raised, perhaps, a foot from the floor, and upon these were heaps of fruits. Some I recognised as a kind of hypertrophied raspberry and orange, but for the most part they were strange.

"Between the tables was scattered a great number of cushions. Upon these my conductors seated themselves, signing for me to do likewise. With a pretty absence of ceremony they began to eat the fruit with their hands, flinging peel and stalks and so forth, into the round openings in the sides of the tables. I was not loth to follow their example, for I felt thirsty and hungry. As I did so I surveyed the hall at my leisure.

"And perhaps the thing that struck me most was its dilapidated look. The stained-glass windows, which displayed only a geometrical pattern, were broken in many places, and the curtains that hung across the lower end were thick with dust. And it caught my eye that the corner of the marble table near me was fractured. Nevertheless, the general effect was extremely rich and picturesque. There were, perhaps, a couple of hundred people dining in the hall, and most of them, seated as near to me as they could come, were watching me with interest, their little eyes shining over the fruit they were eating. All were clad in the same soft, and yet strong, silky material.

"Fruit, by the by, was all their diet. These people of the remote future were strict vegetarians, and while I was with them, in spite of some carnal cravings, I had to be frugivorous also. Indeed, I found afterwards that horses, cattle, sheep, dogs, had followed the Ichthyosaurus into extinction. But the fruits were very delightful; one, in particular, that seemed to be in season all the time I was there—a floury thing in a three-sided husk—was especially good, and I made it my staple. At first I was puzzled by all these strange fruits, and by the strange flowers I saw, but later I began to perceive their import.

"However, I am telling you of my fruit dinner in the distant future now. So soon as my appetite was a little checked, I determined to make a resolute attempt to learn the speech of these new men of mine. Clearly that was the next thing to do. The fruits seemed a convenient thing to begin upon, and holding one of these up I began a series of interrogative sounds and gestures. I had some considerable difficulty in conveying my meaning. At first my efforts met with a stare of surprise or inextinguishable laughter, but presently a fair-haired little creature seemed to grasp my intention and repeated a name. They had to chatter and explain the business at great length to each other, and my first attempts to make the exquisite little sounds of their language caused an immense amount of amusement. However, I felt like a schoolmaster amidst children, and persisted, and presently I had a score of noun substantives at least at my command; and then I got to demonstrative pronouns, and even the verb "to eat." But it was slow work, and the little people soon tired and wanted to get away from my interrogations, so I determined, rather of necessity, to let them give their lessons in little doses when they felt inclined. And very little doses I found they were before long, for I never met people more indolent or more easily fatigued.

"A queer thing I soon discovered about my little hosts, and that was their lack of interest. They would come to me with eager cries of astonishment, like children, but, like children, they would soon stop examining me, and wander away after some other toy. The dinner and my conversational beginnings, ended, I noted for the first time that almost all those who had surrounded me at first were gone. It is odd, too, how speedily I came to disregard these little people. I went out through the portal into the sunlit world again so soon as my hunger was satisfied. I was continually meeting more of these men of the future, who would follow me a little distance, chatter and laugh about me, and, having smiled and gesticulated in a friendly way, leave me again to my own devices.

"The calm of evening was upon the world as I merged from the great hall, and the scene was lit by the warm glow of the setting sun. At first things were very confusing. Everything was so entirely different from the world I had known—even the flowers. The big building I had left was situated on the slope of a broad river valley, but the Thames had shifted, perhaps, a mile from its present position. I resolved to mount to the summit of a crest, perhaps a mile and a half away, from which I could get a wider view of this our planet in the year Eight Hundred and Two Thousand Seven Hundred and One, A.D. For that, I should explain, was the date the little dials of my machine recorded.

"As I walked I was watchful for every impression that could possibly help to explain the condition of ruinous splendour in which I found the world—for ruinous it was. A little way up the hill, for instance, was a great heap of granite, bound together by masses of aluminium, a vast labyrinth of precipitous walls and crumbled heaps, amidst which were thick heaps of very beautiful pagoda-like plants—nettles possibly—but wonderfully tinted with brown about the leaves, and incapable of stinging. It was evidently the derelict remains of some vast structure, to what end built I could not determine. It was here that I was destined, at a later date, to have a very strange experience—the first intimation of a still stranger discovery—but of that I will speak in its proper place.

"Looking round, with a sudden thought, from a terrace on which I rested for a while, I realised that there were no small houses to be seen. Apparently, the single house, and possibly even the household, had vanished. Here and there among the greenery were palace-like buildings, but the house and the cottage, which form such characteristic features of our own English landscape, had disappeared.

"'Communism,' said I to myself.

"And on the heels of that came another thought. I looked at the half-dozen little figures that were following me. Then, in a flash, I perceived that all had the same form of costume, the same soft hairless visage, and the same girlish rotundity of limb. It may seem strange, perhaps, that I had not noticed this before. But everything was so strange. Now, I saw the fact plainly enough. In costume, and in all the differences of texture and bearing that now mark off the sexes from each other, these people of the future were alike. And the children seemed to my eyes to be but the miniatures of their parents. I judged then that the children of that time were extremely precocious, physically at least, and I found afterwards abundant verification of my opinion.

"Seeing the ease and security in which these people were living, I felt that this close resemblance of the sexes was after all what one would expect; for the strength of a man and the softness of a woman, the institution of the family, and the differentiation of occupations are mere militant necessities of an age of physical force. Where population is balanced and abundant, much childbearing becomes an evil rather than a blessing to the State: where violence comes but rarely and offspring are secure, there is less necessity—indeed there is no necessity—for an efficient family, and the specialisation of the sexes with reference to their children's needs disappears. We see some beginnings of this even in our own time, and in this future age it was complete. This, I must remind you, was my speculation at the time. Later, I was to appreciate how far it fell short of the reality.

"While I was musing upon these things, my attention was attracted by a pretty little structure, like a well under a cupola. I thought in a transitory way of the oddness of wells still existing, and then resumed the thread of my speculations. There were no large buildings towards the top of the hill, and as my walking powers were evidently miraculous, I was presently left alone for the first time. With a strange sense of freedom and adventure I pushed on up to the crest.

"There I found a seat of some yellow metal that I did not recognise, corroded in places with a kind of pinkish rust and half smothered in soft moss, the arm-rests cast and filed into the resemblance of griffins' heads. I sat down on it, and I surveyed the broad view of our old world under the sunset of that long day. It was as sweet and fair a view as I have ever seen. The sun had already gone below the horizon and the west was flaming gold, touched with some horizontal bars of purple and crimson. Below was the valley of the Thames, in which the river lay like a band of burnished steel. I have already spoken of the great palaces dotted about among the variegated greenery, some in ruins and some still occupied. Here and there rose a white or silvery figure in the waste garden of the earth, here and there came the sharp vertical line of some cupola or obelisk. There were no hedges, no signs of proprietary rights, no evidences of agriculture; the whole earth had become a garden.

"So watching, I began to put my interpretation upon the things I had seen, and as it shaped itself to me that evening, my interpretation was something in this way. (Afterwards I found I had got only a half-truth—or only a glimpse of one facet of the truth.)

"It seemed to me that I had happened upon humanity upon the wane. The ruddy sunset set me thinking of the sunset of mankind. For the first time I began to realise an odd consequence of the social effort in which we are at present engaged. And yet, come to think, it is a logical consequence enough. Strength is the outcome of need: security sets a premium on feebleness. The work of ameliorating the conditions of life—the true civilising process that makes life more and more secure—had gone steadily on to a climax. One triumph of a united humanity over Nature had followed another. Things that are now mere dreams had become projects deliberately put in hand and carried forward. And the harvest was what I saw!

"After all, the sanitation and the agriculture of to-day are still in the rudimentary stage. The science of our time has attacked but a little department of the field of human disease, but, even so, it spreads its operations very steadily and persistently. Our agriculture and horticulture destroy a weed just here and there and cultivate perhaps a score or so of wholesome plants, leaving the greater number to fight out a balance as they can. We improve our favourite plants and animals—and how few they are—gradually by selective breeding; now a new and better peach, now a seedless grape, now a sweeter and larger flower, now a more convenient breed of cattle. We improve them gradually, because our ideals are vague and tentative, and our knowledge is very limited; because Nature, too, is shy and slow in our clumsy hands. Some day all this will be better organised, and still better. That is the drift of the current in spite of the eddies. The whole world will be intelligent, educated, and co-operating; things will move faster and faster towards the subjugation of Nature. In the end, wisely and carefully we shall readjust the balance of animal and vegetable life to suit our human needs.

"This adjustment, I say, must have been done, and done well: done indeed for all time, in the space of Time across which my machine had leapt. The air was free from gnats, the earth from weeds or fungi; everywhere were fruits and sweet and delightful flowers; brilliant butterflies flew hither and thither. The ideal of preventive medicine was attained. Diseases had been stamped out. I saw no evidence of any contagious diseases during all my stay. And I shall have to tell you later that even the processes of putrefaction and decay had been profoundly affected by these changes.

"Social triumphs, too, had been effected. I saw mankind housed in splendid shelters, gloriously clothed, and as yet I had found them engaged in no toil. There were no signs of struggle, neither social nor economical struggle. The shop, the advertisement, traffic, all that commerce which constitutes the body of our world, was gone. It was natural on that golden evening that I should jump at the idea of a social paradise. The difficulty of increasing population had been met, I guessed, and population had ceased to increase.

But with this change in condition comes inevitably adaptations to the change. What, unless biological science is a mass of errors, is the cause of human intelligence and vigour? Hardship and freedom: conditions under which the active, strong, and subtle survive and the weaker go to the wall; conditions that put a premium upon the loyal alliance of capable men, upon self-restraint, patience, and decision. And the institution of the family, and the emotions that arise therein, the fierce jealousy, the tenderness for offspring, parental self-devotion, all found their justification and support in the imminent dangers of the young. *Now*, where are these imminent dangers? There is a sentiment arising, and it will grow, against connubial jealousy, against fierce maternity, against passion of all sorts; unnecessary things now, and things that make us uncomfortable, savage survivals, discords in a refined and pleasant life.

"I thought of the physical slightness of the people, their lack of intelligence and those big abundant ruins, and it strengthened my belief in a perfect conquest of Nature. For after the battle comes Quiet. Humanity had been strong, energetic, and intelligent, and had used all its abundant vitality to alter the conditions under which it lived. And now came the reaction of the altered conditions.

"Under the new conditions of perfect comfort and security, that restless energy, that with us is strength, would become weakness. Even in our own time certain tendencies and desires, once necessary to survival, are a constant source of failure. Physical courage and the love of battle, for instance, are no great help—may even be hindrances—to a civilised man. And in a state of physical balance and security, power, intellectual as well as physical, would be out of place. For countless years I judged there had been no danger of war or solitary violence, no danger from wild beasts, no wasting disease to require strength of constitution, no need of toil. For such a life, what we should call the weak are as well equipped as the strong, are indeed no longer weak. Better equipped indeed they are, for the strong would be fretted by an energy for which there was no outlet. No doubt the exquisite beauty of the buildings I saw was the outcome of the last surgings of the now purposeless energy of mankind before it settled down into perfect harmony with the conditions under which it lived—the flourish of that triumph which began the last great peace. This has ever been the fate of energy in security; it takes to art and to eroticism, and then come languor and decay.

"Even this artistic impetus would at last die away—had almost died in the Time I saw. To adorn themselves with flowers, to dance, to sing in the sunlight; so much was left of the artistic spirit, and no more. Even that would fade in the end into a contented inactivity. We are kept keen on the grindstone of pain and necessity, and, it seemed to me, that here was that hateful grindstone broken at last!

"As I stood there in the gathering dark I thought that in this simple explanation I had mastered the problem of the world—mastered the whole secret of these delicious people. Possibly the checks they had devised for the increase of population had succeeded too well, and their numbers had rather diminished than kept stationary. That would account for the abandoned ruins. Very simple was my explanation, and plausible enough—as most wrong theories are!"

5

AS I STOOD there musing over this too perfect triumph of man, the full moon, yellow and gibbous, came up out of an overflow of silver light in the north-east. The bright little figures ceased to move about below, a noiseless owl flitted by, and I shivered with the chill of the night. I determined to descend and find where I could sleep.

"I looked for the building I knew. Then my eye travelled, along to the figure of the White Sphinx upon the pedestal of bronze, growing distinct as the light of the rising moon grew brighter. I could see the silver birch against it. There was the tangle of rhododendron bushes, black in the pale light, and there was the little lawn. I looked at the lawn again. A queer doubt chilled my complacency. 'No,' said I stoutly to myself, 'that was not the lawn.'

"But it *was* the lawn. For the white leprous face of the sphinx was towards it. Can you imagine what I felt as this conviction came home to me? But you cannot. The Time Machine was gone!

"At once, like a lash across the face, came the possibility of losing my own age, of being left helpless in this strange new world. The bare thought of it was an actual physical sensation. I could feel it grip me at the throat and stop my breathing. In another moment I was in a passion of fear, and running with great leaping strides down the slope. Once I fell headlong and cut my face; I lost no time in stanching the blood, but jumped up and ran on, with a warm trickle down my cheek and chin. All the time I ran I was saying to myself, 'They have moved it a little, pushed it under the bushes out of the way.' Nevertheless, I ran with all my might. All the time, with the certainty that sometimes comes with excessive dread, I knew that such assurance was folly, knew instinctively that the machine was removed out of my reach. My breath came with pain. I suppose I covered the whole distance from the hill crest to the little lawn, two miles, perhaps, in ten minutes. And I am not a young man. I cursed aloud, as I ran, at my confident folly in leaving the machine, wasting good breath thereby. I cried aloud, and none answered. Not a creature seemed to be stirring in that moonlit world.

"When I reached the lawn my worst fears were realised. Not a trace of the thing was to be seen. I felt faint and cold when I faced the empty space, among the black tangle of bushes. I ran round it furiously, as if the thing might be hidden in a corner, and then stopped abruptly, with my hands clutching my hair. Above me towered the sphinx, upon the bronze pedestal, white, shining, leprous, in the light of the rising moon. It seemed to smile in mockery of my dismay.

"I might have consoled myself by imagining the little people had put the mechanism in some shelter for me, had I not felt assured of their physical and intellectual inadequacy. That is what dismayed me: the sense of some hitherto unsuspected power, through whose intervention my invention had vanished. Yet, of one thing I felt assured: unless some other age had produced its exact duplicate, the machine could not have moved in time. The attachment of the levers—I will show you the method later—prevented any one from tampering with it in that way when they were removed. It had moved, and was hid, only in space. But then, where could it be?

"I think I must have had a kind of frenzy. I remember running violently in and out among the moonlit bushes all round the sphinx, and startling some white animal that, in the dim light, I took for a small deer. I remember, too, late that night, beating the bushes with my clenched fists until my knuckles were gashed and bleeding from the broken twigs. Then, sobbing and raving in my anguish of mind, I went down to the great building of stone. The big hall was dark, silent, and deserted. I slipped on the uneven floor, and fell over one of the malachite tables, almost breaking my shin. I lit a match and went on past the dusty curtains, of which I have told you.

"There I found a second great hall covered with cushions, upon which, perhaps, a score or so of the little people were sleeping. I have no doubt they found my second appearance strange enough, coming suddenly out of the quiet darkness with inarticulate noises and the splutter and flare of a match. For they had forgotten about matches. 'Where is my Time Machine?' I began, bawling like an angry child, laying hands upon them and shaking them up together. It must have been very queer to them. Some laughed, most of them looked sorely frightened. When I saw them standing round me, it came into my head that I was doing as foolish a thing as it was possible for me to do under the circumstances, in trying to revive the sensation of fear. For, reasoning from their daylight behaviour, I thought that fear must be forgotten.

"Abruptly, I dashed down the match, and knocking one of the people over in my course, went blundering across the big dining-hall again, out under the moonlight. I heard cries of terror and their little feet running and stumbling this way and that. I do not remember all I did as the moon crept up the sky. I suppose it was the unexpected nature of my loss that maddened me. I felt hopelessly cut off from my own kind—a strange animal in an unknown world. I must have raved to and fro, screaming and crying upon God and Fate. I have a memory of horrible fatigue, as the long night of despair wore away; of looking in this impossible place and that; of groping among moonlit ruins and touching strange creatures in the black shadows; at last, of lying on the ground near the sphinx, and weeping with absolute wretchedness. I had nothing left but misery. Then I slept, and when I woke again it was full day, and a couple of sparrows were hopping round me on the turf within reach of my arm.

"I sat up in the freshness of the morning, trying to remember how I had got there, and why I had such a profound sense of desertion and despair. Then things came clear in my mind. With the plain, reasonable daylight, I could look my circumstances fairly in the face. I saw the wild folly of my frenzy overnight, and I could reason with myself. 'Suppose the worst?' I said. 'Suppose the machine altogether lost—perhaps destroyed? It behoves me to be calm and patient, to learn the way of the people, to get a clear idea of the method of my loss, and the means of getting materials and tools; so that in the end, perhaps, I may make another.' That would be my only hope, a poor hope, perhaps, but better than despair. And, after all, it was a beautiful and curious world.

"But probably the machine had only been taken away. Still, I must be calm and patient, find its hiding-place, and recover it by force or cunning. And with that I scrambled to my feet and looked about me, wondering where I could bathe. I felt weary, stiff, and travel-soiled. The freshness of the morning made me desire an equal freshness. I had exhausted my emotion. Indeed, as I went about my business, I found myself wondering at my intense excitement overnight. I made a careful examination of the ground about the little lawn. I wasted some time in futile questionings, conveyed, as well as I was able, to such of the little people as came by. They all failed to understand my gestures: some were simply stolid; some thought it was a jest, and laughed at me. I had the hardest task in the world to keep my hands off their pretty laughing faces. It was a foolish impulse, but the devil begotten of fear and blind anger was ill curbed, and still eager to take advantage of my perplexity. The turf gave better counsel. I found a groove ripped in it, about midway between the pedestal of the sphinx and he marks of my feet where, on arrival, I had struggled with the overturned machine. There were other signs of removal about, with queer narrow footprints like those I could imagine made by a sloth. This directed my closer attention to the pedestal. It was, as I think I have said, of bronze. It was not a mere block, but highly decorated with deep framed panels on either side. I went and rapped at these. The pedestal was hollow. Examining the panels with care I found them discontinuous with the frames. There were no handles or keyholes, but possibly the panels, if they were doors, as I supposed, opened from within. One thing was clear enough to my mind. It took no very great mental effort to infer that my Time Machine was inside that pedestal. But how it got there was a different problem.

"I saw the heads of two orange-clad people coming through the bushes and under some blossom-covered apple-trees towards me. I turned smiling to them, and beckoned them to me. They came, and then, pointing to the bronze pedestal, I tried to intimate my wish to open it. But at my first gesture towards this they behaved very oddly. I don't know how to convey their expression to you. Suppose you were to use a grossly improper gesture to a delicate-minded woman—it is how she would look. They went off as if they had received the last possible insult. I tried a sweet-looking little chap in white next, with exactly the same result. Somehow, his manner made me feel ashamed of myself. But, as you know, I wanted the Time Machine, and I tried him once more. As he turned off, like the others, my temper got the better of me. In three strides I was after him, had him by the loose part of his robe round the neck, and began dragging him towards the sphinx. Then I saw the horror and repugnance of his face, and all of a sudden I let him go.

"But I was not beaten yet. I banged with my fist at the bronze panels. I thought I heard something stir inside—to be explicit, I thought I heard a sound like a chuckle—but I must have been mistaken. Then I got a big pebble from the river, and came and hammered till I had flattened a coil in the decorations, and the verdigris came off in powdery flakes. The delicate little people must have heard me hammering in gusty outbreaks a mile away on either hand, but nothing came of it. I saw a crowd of them upon the slopes, looking furtively at me. At last, hot and tired, I sat down to watch the place. But I was too restless to watch long; I am too Occidental for a long vigil. I could work at a problem for years, but to wait inactive for twenty-four hours, that is another matter.

"I got up after a time, and began walking aimlessly through the bushes towards the hill again. 'Patience,' said I to myself. 'If you want your machine again you must leave that sphinx alone. If they mean to take your machine away, it's little good your wrecking their bronze panels, and if they don't, you will get it back as soon as you can ask for it. To sit among all those unknown things before a puzzle like that is hopeless. That way lies monomania. Face this world. Learn its ways, watch it, be careful of too hasty guesses at its meaning. In the end you will find clues to it all.' Then suddenly the humour of the situation came into my mind: the thought of the years I had spent in study and toil to get into the future age, and now my passion of anxiety to get out of it. I had made myself the most complicated and the most hopeless trap that ever a man devised. Although it was at my own expense, I could not help myself. I laughed aloud.

"Going through the big palace, it seemed to me that the little people avoided me. It may have been my fancy, or it may have had something to do with my hammering at the gates of bronze. Yet I felt tolerably sure of the avoidance. I was careful, however, to show no concern, and to abstain from any pursuit of them, and in the course of a day or two things got back to the old footing. I made what progress I could in the language, and, in addition, I pushed my explorations here and there. Either I missed some subtle point, or their language was excessively simple—almost exclusively composed of concrete substantives and verbs. There seemed to be few, if any, abstract terms, or little use of figurative language. Their sentences were usually simple and of two words, and I failed to convey or understand any but the simplest propositions. I determined to put the thought of my Time Machine, and the mystery of the bronze doors under the sphinx, as much as possible in a corner of memory, until my growing knowledge would lead me back to them in a natural way. Yet a certain feeling, you may understand, tethered me in a circle of a few miles round the point of my arrival.

"So far as I could see, all the world displayed the same exuberant richness as the Thames valley. From every hill I climbed I saw the same abundance of splendid buildings, endlessly varied in material and style; the sane clustering thickets of evergreens, the same blossom-laden trees and tree ferns. Here and there water shone like silver, and beyond, the land rose into blue undulating hills, and so faded into the serenity of the sky. A peculiar feature, which presently attracted my attention, was the presence of certain circular wells, several, as it seemed to me, of a very great depth. One lay by the path up the hill, which I had followed during my first walk. Like the others it was rimmed with bronze, curiously wrought, and protected by a little cupola from the rain. Sitting by the side of these wells, and peering down into the shafted darkness, I could see no gleam of water, nor could I start any reflection with a lighted match.

But in all of them I heard a certain sound: a thud—thud—thud, like the beating of some big engine; and I discovered, from the flaring of my matches, that a steady current of air set down the shafts. Further, I threw a scrap of paper into the throat of one; and, instead of fluttering slowly down, it was at once sucked swiftly out of sight.

"After a time, too, I came to connect these wells with tall towers standing here and there upon the slopes; for above them there was often just such a flicker in the air as one sees on a hot day above a sun-scorched beach. Putting things together, I reached a strong suggestion of an extensive system of subterranean ventilation, whose true import it was difficult to imagine. I was at first inclined to associate it with the sanitary apparatus of these people. It was an obvious conclusion, but it was absolutely wrong.

"And here I must admit that I learned very little of drains and bells and modes of conveyance, and the like conveniences, during my time in this real future. In some of these visions of Utopias and coming times which I have read, there is a vast amount of detail about building, and social arrangements, and so forth. But while such details are easy enough to obtain when the whole world is contained in one's imagination, they are altogether inaccessible to a real traveller amid such realities as I found here. Conceive the tale of London which a negro, fresh from Central Africa, would take back to his tribe! What would he know of railway companies, of social movements, of telephone and telegraph wires, of the Parcels Delivery Company, and postal orders and the like? Yet we, at least, should be willing enough to explain these things to him! And even of what he knew, how much could he make his untravelled friend either apprehend or believe? Then, think how narrow the gap between a negro and a white man of our own times, and how wide the interval between myself and these of the Golden Age! I was sensible of much which was unseen, and which contributed to my comfort; but, save for a general impression of automatic organisation, I fear I can convey very little of the difference to your mind.

"In the matter of sepulture, for instance, I could see no signs of crematoria nor anything suggestive of tombs. But it occurred to me that, possibly, there might be cemeteries (or crematoria) somewhere beyond the range of my explorings. This, again, was a question I deliberately put to myself, and my curiosity was at first entirely defeated upon the point. The thing puzzled me, and I was led to make a further remark, which puzzled me still more: that aged and infirm among this people there were none.

"I must confess that my satisfaction with my first theories of an automatic civilisation and a decadent humanity did not long endure. Yet

I could think of no other. Let me put my difficulties. The several big palaces I had explored were mere living places, great dining-halls and sleeping apartments. I could find no machinery, no appliances of any kind. Yet these people were clothed in pleasant fabrics that must at times need renewal, and their sandals, though undecorated, were fairly complex specimens of metal-work. Somehow such things must be made. And the little people displayed no vestige of a creative tendency. There were no shops, no workshops, no sign of importations among them. They spent all their time in playing gently, in bathing in the river, in making love in a half-playful fashion, in eating fruit and sleeping. I could not see how things were kept going.

"Then, again, about the Time Machine: something, I knew not what, had taken it into the hollow pedestal of the White Sphinx. *Why?* For the life of me I could not imagine. Those waterless wells, too, those flickering pillars. I felt I lacked a clue. I felt—how shall I put it? Suppose you found an inscription, with sentences here and there in excellent plain English, and, interpolated therewith, others made up of words, of letters even, absolutely unknown to you? Well, on the third day of my visit, that was how the world of Eight Hundred and Two Thousand Seven Hundred and One presented itself to me!

"That day, too, I made a friend—of a sort. It happened that, as I was watching some of the little people bathing in a shallow, one of them was seized with cramp, and began drifting downstream. The main current ran rather swiftly, but not too strongly for even a moderate swimmer. It will give you an idea, therefore, of the strange deficiency in these creatures, when I tell you that none made the slightest attempt to rescue the weakly-crying little thing which was drowning before their eyes. When I realised this, I hurriedly slipped off my clothes, and, wading in at a point lower down, I caught the poor mite, and drew her safe to land. A little rubbing of the limbs soon brought her round, and I had the satisfaction of seeing she was all right before I left her. I had got to such a low estimate of her kind that I did not expect any gratitude from her. In that, however, I was wrong.

"This happened in the morning. In the afternoon I met my little woman, as I believe it was, as I was returning towards my centre from an exploration: and she received me with cries of delight, and presented me with a big garland of flowers—evidently made for me and me alone. The thing took my imagination. Very possibly I had been feeling desolate. At any rate I did my best to display my appreciation of the gift. We were soon seated together in a little stone arbour, engaged in conversation, chiefly of smiles. The creature's friendliness affected me exactly as a

child's might have done. We passed each other flowers, and she kissed my hands. I did the same to hers. Then I tried talk, and found that her name was Weena, which, though I don't know what it meant, somehow seemed appropriate enough. That was the beginning of a queer friendship which lasted a week, and ended—as I will tell you!

"She was exactly like a child. She wanted to be with me always. She tried to follow me everywhere, and on my next journey out and about it went to my heart to tire her down, and leave her at last, exhausted and calling after me rather plaintively. But the problems of the world had to be mastered. I had not, I said to myself, come into the future to carry on a miniature flirtation. Yet her distress when I left her was very great, her expostulations at the parting were sometimes frantic, and I think, altogether, I had as much trouble as comfort from her devotion. Nevertheless she was, somehow, a very great comfort. I thought it was mere childish affection that made her cling to me. Until it was too late, I did not clearly know what I had inflicted upon her when I left her. Nor until it was too late did I clearly understand what she was to me. For, by merely seeming fond of me, and showing in her weak futile way that she cared for me, the little doll of a creature presently gave my return to the neighbourhood of the White Sphinx almost the feeling of coming home; and I would watch for her tiny figure of white and gold so soon as I came over the hill.

"It was from her, too, that I learned that fear had not yet left the world. She was fearless enough in the daylight and she had the oddest confidence in me; for once, in a foolish moment, I made threatening grimaces at her, and she simply laughed at them. But she dreaded the dark, dreaded shadows, dreaded black things. Darkness to her was the one thing dreadful. It was a singularly passionate emotion, and it set me thinking and observing. I discovered then, among other things, that these little people gathered into the great houses after dark, and slept in droves. To enter upon them without a light was to put them into a tumult of apprehension. I never found one out of doors, or one sleeping alone within doors, after dark. Yet I was still such a blockhead that I missed the lesson of that fear, and, in spite of Weena's distress, I insisted upon sleeping away from these slumbering multitudes.

"It troubled her greatly, but in the end her odd affection for me triumphed, and for five of the nights of our acquaintance, including the last night of all, she slept with her head pillowed on my arm. But my story slips away from me as I speak of her. It must have been the night before her rescue that I was awakened about dawn. I had been restless, dreaming most disagreeably that I was drowned, and that sea-anemones were feeling over my face with their soft pales. I woke with a start, and with an odd fancy that some greyish animal had just rushed out of the chamber. I tried to get to sleep again, but I felt restless and uncomfortable. It was that dim grey hour when things are just creeping out of darkness, when everything is colourless and clear cut, and yet unreal. I got up, and went down into the great hall, and so out upon the flagstones in front of the palace. I thought I would make a virtue of necessity, and see the sunrise.

"The moon was setting, and the dying moonlight and the first pallor of dawn were mingled in a ghastly half-light. The bushes were inky black, the ground a sombre grey, the sky colourless and cheerless. And up the hill I thought I could see ghosts. There several times, as I scanned the slope, I saw white figures. Twice I fancied I saw a solitary white, ape-like creature running rather quickly up the hill, and once near the ruins I saw a leash of them carrying some dark body. They moved hastily. I did not see what became of them. It seemed that they vanished among the bushes. The dawn was still indistinct, you must understand. I was feeling that chill, uncertain, early-morning feeling you may have known. I doubted my eyes.

"As the eastern sky grew brighter, and the light of the day came on and its vivid colouring returned upon the world once more, I scanned the view keenly. But I saw no vestige of my white figures. They were mere creatures of the half-light. 'They must have been ghosts,' I said; 'I wonder whence they dated.' For a queer notion of Grant Allen's came into my head, and amused me. If each generation die and leave ghosts, he argued, the world at last will get overcrowded with them. On that theory they would have grown innumerable some Eight Hundred Thousand Years hence, and it was no great wonder to see four at once. But the jest was unsatisfying, and I was thinking of these figures all the morning, until Weena's rescue drove them out of my head. I associated them in some indefinite way with the white animal I had startled in my first passionate search for the Time Machine. But Weena was a pleasant substitute. Yet all the same, they were soon destined to take far deadlier possession of my mind.

"I think I have said how much hotter than our own was the weather of this Golden Age. I cannot account for it. It may be that the sun was hotter, or the earth nearer the sun. It is usual to assume that the sun will go on cooling steadily in the future. But people, unfamiliar with such speculations as those of the younger Darwin, forget that the planets must ultimately fall back one by one into the parent body. As these catastrophes occur, the sun will blaze with renewed energy; and it may be that some inner planet had suffered this fate. Whatever the reason, the fact remains that the sun was very much hotter than we know it.

"Well, one very hot morning—my fourth, I think—as I was seeking shelter from the heat and glare in a colossal ruin near the great house where I slept and fed, there happened this strange thing. Clambering among these heaps of masonry, I found a narrow gallery whose end and side windows were blocked by fallen masses of stone. By contrast with the brilliancy outside, it seemed at first impenetrably dark to me. I entered it groping, for the change from light to blackness made spots of colour swim before me. Suddenly I halted spellbound. A pair of eyes, luminous by reflection against the daylight without, was watching me out of the darkness.

"The old instinctive dread of wild beasts came upon me. I clenched my hands and steadfastly looked into the glaring eyeballs. I was afraid to turn. Then the thought of the absolute security in which humanity appeared to be living came to my mind. And then I remembered that strange terror of the dark. Overcoming my fear to some extent, I advanced a step and spoke. I will admit that my voice was harsh and ill-controlled. I put out my hand and touched something soft. At once the eyes darted sideways, and something white ran past me. I turned with my heart in my mouth, and saw a queer little ape-like figure, its head held down in a peculiar manner, running across the sunlit space behind me. It blundered against a block of granite, staggered aside, and in a moment was hidden in a black shadow beneath another pile of ruined masonry.

"My impression of it is, of course, imperfect; but I know it was a dull white, and had strange large greyish-red eyes; also that there was flaxen hair on its head and down its back. But, as I say, it went too fast for me to see distinctly. I cannot even say whether it ran on all fours, or only with its forearms held very low. After an instant's pause I followed it into the second heap of ruins. I could not find it at first; but, after a time in the profound obscurity, I came upon one of those round well-like openings of which I have told you, half closed by a fallen pillar. A sudden thought came to me. Could this Thing have vanished down the shaft? I lit a match, and, looking down, I saw a small, white, moving creature, with large bright eyes which regarded me steadfastly as it retreated. It made me shudder. It was so like a human spider! It was clambering down the wall, and now I saw for the first time a number of metal foot and hand rests forming a kind of ladder down the shaft. Then the light burned my fingers and fell out of my hand, going out as it dropped, and when I had lit another the little monster had disappeared.

"I do not know how long I sat peering down that well. It was not for some time that I could succeed in persuading myself that the thing I had seen was human. But, gradually, the truth dawned on me: that Man had not remained one species, but had differentiated into two distinct animals: that my graceful children of the Upper World were not the sole descendants of our generation, but that this bleached, obscene, nocturnal Thing, which had flashed before me, was also heir to all the ages.

"I thought of the flickering pillars and of my theory of an underground ventilation. I began to suspect their true import. And what, I wondered, was this Lemur doing in my scheme of a perfectly balanced organisation? How was it related to the indolent serenity of the beautiful Upper-worlders? And what was hidden down there, at the foot of that shaft? I sat upon the edge of the well telling myself that, at any rate, there was nothing to fear, and that there I must descend for the solution of my difficulties. And withal I was absolutely afraid to go! As I hesitated, two of the beautiful Upper-world people came running in their amorous sport across the daylight into the shadow. The male pursued the female, flinging flowers at her as he ran.

"They seemed distressed to find me, my arm against the overturned pillar, peering down the well. Apparently it was considered bad form to remark these apertures; for when I pointed to this one, and tried to frame a question about it in their tongue, they were still more visibly distressed and turned away. But they were interested by my matches, and I struck some to amuse them. I tried them again about the well, and again I failed. So presently I left them, meaning to go back to Weena, and see what I could get from her. But my mind was already in revolution; my guesses and impressions were slipping and sliding to a new adjustment. I had now a clue to the import of these wells, to the ventilating towers, to the mystery of the ghosts: to say nothing of a hint at the meaning of the bronze gates and the fate of the Time Machine! And very vaguely there came a suggestion towards the solution of the economic problem that had puzzled me.

"Here was the new view. Plainly, this second species of Man was subterranean. There were three circumstances in particular which made me think that its rare emergence above ground was the outcome of a long-continued underground habit. In the first place, there was the bleached look common in most animals that live largely in the dark—the white fish of the Kentucky caves, for instance. Then, those large eyes, with that capacity for reflecting light, are common features of nocturnal things—witness the owl and the cat. And last of all, that evident confusion in the sunshine, that hasty yet fumbling and awkward flight towards dark shadow, and that peculiar carriage of the head while in the light—all reinforced the theory of an extreme sensitiveness of the retina.

"Beneath my feet then the earth must be tunnelled enormously, and these tunnellings were the habitat of the new race. The presence of ventilating-shafts and wells along the hill slopes—everywhere, in fact, except along the river valley—showed how universal were its ramifications. What so natural, then, as to assume that it was in this artificial underworld that such work as was necessary to the comfort of the daylight race was done? The notion was so plausible that I at once accepted it, and went on to assume the how of this splitting of the human species. I dare say you will anticipate the shape of my theory, though, for myself, I very soon felt that it fell far short of the truth.

"At first, proceeding from the problems of our own age, it seemed clear as daylight to me that the gradual widening of the present merely temporary and social difference between the Capitalist and the Labourer, was the key to the whole position. No doubt it will seem grotesque enough to you—and wildly incredible!—and yet even now there are existing circumstances to point that way. There is a tendency to utilise underground space for the less ornamental purposes of civilisation; there is the Metropolitan Railway in London, for instance, there are new electric railways, there are subways, there are underground workrooms and restaurants, and they increase and multiply. Evidently, I thought, this tendency had increased till Industry had gradually lost its birthright in the sky. I mean that it had gone deeper and deeper into larger and ever larger underground factories, spending a still-increasing amount of its time therein, till, in the end—! Even now, does not an East-end worker live in such artificial conditions as practically to be cut off from the natural surface of the earth?

"Again, the exclusive tendency of richer people—due, no doubt, to the increasing refinement of their education, and the widening gulf between them and the rude violence of the poor—is already leading to the closing, in their interest, of considerable portions of the surface of the land. About London, for instance, perhaps half the prettier country is shut in against intrusion. And this same widening gulf—which is due to the length and expense of the higher educational process and the increased facilities for and temptations towards refined habits on the part of the rich—will make that exchange between class and class, that promotion by inter-marriage which at present retards the splitting of our species along lines of social stratification, less and less frequent. So, in the end, above ground you must have the Haves, pursuing pleasure and comfort and beauty, and below ground the Have-nots; the Workers getting continually adapted to the conditions of their labour. Once they were there they would, no doubt, have to pay rent, and not a little of it, for the ventilation of their caverns; and if they refused, they would starve or be suffocated for arrears. Such of them as were so constituted as to be miserable and rebellious would die; and, in the end, the balance being permanent, the survivors would become as well adapted to the conditions of underground life, and as happy in their way, as the Upper-world people were to theirs. As it seemed to me, the refined beauty and the etiolated pallor followed naturally enough.

"The great triumph of Humanity I had dreamed of took a different shape in my mind. It had been no such triumph of moral education and general co-operation as I had imagined. Instead, I saw a real aristocracy, armed with a perfected science and working to a logical conclusion the industrial system of today. Its triumph had not been simply a triumph over nature, but a triumph over nature and the fellow-man. This, I must warn you, was my theory at the time. I had no convenient cicerone in the pattern of the Utopian books. My explanation may be absolutely wrong. I still think it is the most plausible one. But even on this supposition the balanced civilisation that was at last attained must have long since passed its zenith, and was now far fallen into decay. The too-perfect security of the Upper-worlders had led them to a slow movement of degeneration, to a general dwindling in size, strength, and intelligence. That I could see clearly enough already. What had happened to the Undergrounders I did not yet suspect; but, from what I had seen of the Morlocks — that, by the by, was the name by which these creatures were called — I could imagine that the modification of the human type was even far more profound than among the 'Eloi,' the beautiful race that I already knew.

"Then came troublesome doubts. Why had the Morlocks taken my Time Machine? For I felt sure it was they who had taken it. Why, too, if the Eloi were masters, could they not restore the machine to me? And why were they so terribly afraid of the dark? I proceeded, as I have said, to question Weena about this Underworld, but here again I was disappointed. At first she would not understand my questions, and presently she refused to answer them. She shivered as though the topic was unendurable. And when I pressed her, perhaps a little harshly, she burst into tears. They were the only tears, except my own, I ever saw in that Golden Age. When I saw them I ceased abruptly to trouble about the Morlocks, and was only concerned in banishing these signs of the human inheritance from Weena's eyes. And very soon she was smiling and clapping her hands, while I solemnly burnt a match."

6

IT MAY seem odd to you, but it was two days before I could follow up the new-found clue in what was manifestly the proper way. I felt a peculiar shrinking from those pallid bodies. They were just the half-bleached colour of the worms and things one sees preserved in spirit in a zoological museum. And they were filthily cold to the touch. Probably my shrinking was largely due to the sympathetic influence of the Eloi, whose disgust of the Morlocks I now began to appreciate.

"The next night I did not sleep well. Probably my health was a little disordered. I was oppressed with perplexity and doubt. Once or twice I had a feeling of intense fear for which I could perceive no definite reason. I remember creeping noiselessly into the great hall where the little people were sleeping in the moonlight—that night Weena was among them—and feeling reassured by their presence. It occurred to me, even then, that in the course of a few days the moon must pass through its last quarter, and the nights grow dark, when the appearances of these unpleasant creatures from below, these whitened Lemurs, this new vermin that had replaced the old, might be more abundant. And on both these days I had the restless feeling of one who shirks an inevitable duty. I felt assured that the Time Machine was only to be recovered by boldly penetrating these underground mysteries. Yet I could not face the mystery. If only I had had a companion it would have been different. But I was so horribly alone, and even to clamber down into the darkness of the well appalled me. I don't know if you will understand my feeling, but I never felt quite safe at my back.

"It was this restlessness, this insecurity, perhaps, that drove me further and further afield in my exploring expeditions. Going to the south-westward towards the rising country that is now called Combe Wood, I observed far off, in the direction of nineteenth-century Banstead, a vast green structure, different in character from any I had hitherto seen. It was larger than the largest of the palaces or ruins I knew, and the façade had an Oriental look: the face of it having the lustre, as well as the pale-green tint, a kind of bluish-green, of a certain type of Chinese porcelain. This difference in aspect suggested a difference in use, and I was minded to push on and explore. But the day was growing late, and I had come upon the sight of the place after a long and tiring circuit; so I resolved to hold over the adventure for the following day, and I returned to the welcome and the caresses of little Weena. But next morning I perceived clearly enough that my curiosity regarding the Palace of Green Porcelain was a piece of self-deception, to enable me to shirk, by another day, an experience I dreaded. I resolved I would make the descent without further waste of time, and started out in the early morning towards a well near the ruins of granite and aluminium.

"Little Weena ran with me. She danced beside me to the well, but when she saw me lean over the mouth and look downward, she seemed strangely disconcerted. 'Good-bye, little Weena,' I said, kissing her; and then, putting her down, I began to feel over the parapet for the climbing hooks. Rather hastily, I may as well confess, for I feared my courage might leak away! At first she watched me in amazement. Then she gave a most piteous cry, and, running to me, began to pull at me with her little hands. I think her opposition nerved me rather to proceed. I shook her off, perhaps a little roughly, and in another moment I was in the throat of the well. I saw her agonised face over the parapet, and smiled to reassure her. Then I had to look down at the unstable hooks to which I clung.

"I had to clamber down a shaft of perhaps two hundred yards. The descent was effected by means of metallic bars projecting from the sides of the well, and these being adapted to the needs of a creature much smaller and lighter than myself, I was speedily cramped and fatigued by the descent. And not simply fatigued! One of the bars bent suddenly under my weight, and almost swung me off into the blackness beneath. For a moment I hung by one hand, and after that experience I did not dare to rest again. Though my arms and back were presently acutely painful, I went on clambering down the sheer descent with as quick a motion as possible. Glancing upward, I saw the aperture, a small blue disk, in which a star was visible, while little Weena's head showed as a round black projection. The thudding sound of a machine below grew louder and more oppressive. Everything save that little disk above was profoundly dark, and when I looked up again Weena had disappeared.

"I was in an agony of discomfort. I had some thought of trying to go up the shaft again, and leave the Underworld alone. But even while I turned this over in my mind I continued to descend. At last, with intense relief, I saw dimly coming up, a foot to the right of me, a slender loophole in the wall. Swinging myself in, I found it was the aperture of a narrow horizontal tunnel in which I could lie down and rest. It was not too soon. My arms ached, my back was cramped, and I was trembling with the prolonged terror of a fall. Besides this, the unbroken darkness had had a distressing effect upon my eyes. The air was full of the throb and hum of machinery pumping air down the shaft.

"I do not know how long I lay. I was roused by a soft hand touching my face. Starting up in the darkness I snatched at my matches and, hastily striking one, I saw three stooping white creatures similar to the one I had seen above ground in the ruin, hastily retreating before the light. Living, as they did, in what appeared to me impenetrable darkness, their eyes were abnormally large and sensitive, just as are the pupils of the abysmal fishes, and they reflected the light in the same way. I have no doubt they could see me in that rayless obscurity, and they did not seem to have any fear of me apart from the light. But, so soon as I struck a match in order to see them, they fled incontinently, vanishing into dark gutters and tunnels, from which their eyes glared at me in the strangest fashion.

"I tried to call to them, but the language they had was apparently different from that of the Upper-world people; so that I was needs left to my own unaided efforts, and the thought of flight before exploration was even then in my mind. But I said to myself, 'You are in for it now,' and, feeling my way along the tunnel, I found the noise of machinery grow louder. Presently the walls fell away from me, and I came to a large open space, and, striking another match, saw that I had entered a vast arched cavern, which stretched into utter darkness beyond the range of my light. The view I had of it was as much as one could see in the burning of a match.

"Necessarily my memory is vague. Great shapes like big machines rose out of the dimness, and cast grotesque black shadows, in which dim spectral Morlocks sheltered from the glare. The place, by the by, was very stuffy and oppressive, and the faint halitus of freshly-shed blood was in the air. Some way down the central vista was a little table of white metal, laid with what seemed a meal. The Morlocks at any rate were carnivorous! Even at the time, I remember wondering what large animal could have survived to furnish the red joint I saw. It was all very indistinct: the heavy smell, the big unmeaning shapes, the obscene figures lurking in the shadows, and only waiting for the darkness to come at me again! Then the match burned down, and stung my fingers, and fell, a wriggling red spot in the blackness.

"I have thought since how particularly ill-equipped I was for such an experience. When I had started with the Time Machine, I had started with the absurd assumption that the men of the Future would certainly be infinitely ahead of ourselves in all their appliances. I had come without arms, without medicine, without anything to smoke—at times I missed tobacco frightfully!—even without enough matches. If only I had thought of a Kodak! I could have flashed that glimpse of the Underworld in a

second, and examined it at leisure. But, as it was, I stood there with only the weapons and the powers that Nature had endowed me with—hands, feet, and teeth; these, and four safety matches that still remained to me.

"I was afraid to push my way in among all this machinery in the dark, and it was only with my last glimpse of light I discovered that my store of matches had run low. It had never occurred to me until that moment that there was any need to economise them, and I had wasted almost half the box in astonishing the Upperworlders, to whom fire was a novelty. Now, as I say, I had four left, and while I stood in the dark, a hand touched mine, lank fingers came feeling over my face, and I was sensible of a peculiar unpleasant odour. I fancied I heard the breathing of a crowd of those dreadful little beings about me. I felt the box of matches in my hand being gently disengaged, and other hands behind me plucking at my clothing. The sense of these unseen creatures examining me was indescribably unpleasant. The sudden realisation of my ignorance of their ways of thinking and doing came home to me very vividly in the darkness. I shouted at them as loudly as I could. They started away, and then I could feel them approaching me again. They clutched at me more boldly, whispering odd sounds to each other. I shivered violently, and shouted again—rather discordantly. This time they were not so seriously alarmed, and they made a queer laughing noise as they came back at me. I will confess I was horribly frightened. I determined to strike another match and escape under the protection of its glare. I did so, and eking out the flicker with a scrap of paper from my pocket, I made good my retreat to the narrow tunnel. But I had scarce entered this when my light was blown out, and in the blackness I could hear the Morlocks rustling like wind among leaves, and pattering like the rain, as they hurried after me.

"In a moment I was clutched by several hands, and there was no mistaking that they were trying to haul me back. I struck another light, and waved it in their dazzled faces. You can scarce imagine how nauseatingly inhuman they looked—those pale, chinless faces and great, lidless, pinkish-grey eyes!—as they stared in their blindness and bewilderment. But I did not stay to look, I promise you: I retreated again, and when my second match had ended, I struck my third. It had almost burned through when I reached the opening into the shaft. I lay down on the edge, for the throb of the great pump below made me giddy. Then I felt sideways for the projecting hooks, and, as I did so, my feet were grasped from behind, and I was violently tugged backward. I lit my last match … and it incontinently went out. But I had my hand on the climbing bars now, and, kicking violently, I disengaged myself from the clutches of the Morlocks, and was speedily clambering up the shaft, while they stayed peering and blinking up at me: all but one little wretch who followed me for some way, and well-nigh secured my boot as a trophy.

"That climb seemed interminable to me. With the last twenty or thirty feet of it a deadly nausea came upon me. I had the greatest difficulty in keeping my hold. The last few yards was a frightful struggle against this faintness. Several times my head swam, and I felt all the sensations of falling. At last, however, I got over the well-mouth somehow, and staggered out of the ruin into the blinding sunlight. I fell upon my face. Even the soil smelt sweet and clean. Then I remember Weena kissing my hands and ears, and the voices of others among the Eloi. Then, for a time, I was insensible."

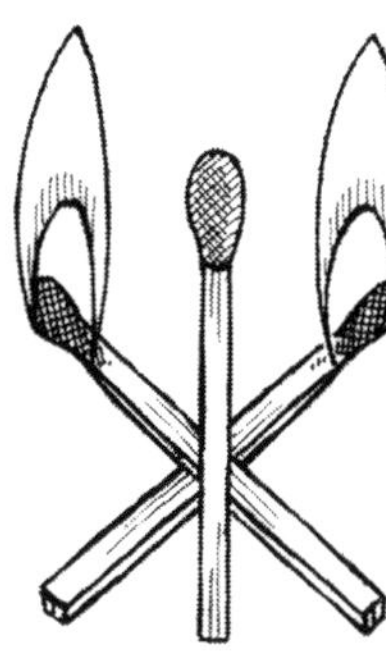

7

NOW, INDEED, I seemed in a worse case than before. Hitherto, except during my night's anguish at the loss of the Time Machine, I had felt a sustaining hope of ultimate escape, but that hope was staggered by these new discoveries. Hitherto I had merely thought myself impeded by the childish simplicity of the little people, and by some unknown forces which I had only to understand to overcome; but there was an altogether new element in the sickening quality of the Morlocks—a something inhuman and malign. Instinctively I loathed them. Before, I had felt as a man might feel who had fallen into a pit; my concern was with the pit and how to get out of it. Now I felt like a beast in a trap, whose enemy would come upon him soon.

"The enemy I dreaded may surprise you. It was the darkness of the new moon. Weena had put this into my head by some at first incomprehensible remarks about the Dark Nights. It was not now such a very difficult problem to guess what the coming Dark Nights might mean. The moon was on the wane: each night there was a longer interval of darkness. And I now understood to some slight degree at least the reason of the fear of the little Upper-world people for the dark. I wondered vaguely what foul villainy it might be that the Morlocks did under the new moon. I felt pretty sure now that my second hypothesis was all wrong. The Upper-world people might once have been the favoured aristocracy, and the Morlocks their mechanical servants; but that had long since passed away. The two species that had resulted from the evolution of man were sliding down towards, or had already arrived at, an altogether new relationship, The Eloi, like the Carlovingian kings, had decayed to a mere beautiful futility. They still possessed the earth on sufferance: since the Morlocks, subterranean for innumerable generations, had come at last to find the daylit surface intolerable. And the Morlocks made their garments, I inferred, and maintained them in their habitual needs, perhaps through the survival of an old habit of service. They did it as a standing horse paws with his foot, or as a man enjoys killing animals in sport: because ancient and departed necessities had impressed it on the organism. But, clearly, the old order was already in part reversed. The Nemesis of the delicate ones was creeping on apace. Ages ago, thousands of generations ago, man had thrust his brother man out of the ease and the sunshine. And now that brother was coming back—changed! Already the Eloi had begun to learn one old lesson anew. They were becoming re-acquainted with Fear. And suddenly there came into my head the memory of the meat I had seen in the Underworld. It seemed odd how it floated into my mind: not stirred up as it were by the current of my meditations, but coming in almost like a question from outside. I tried to recall the form of it. I had a vague sense of something familiar, but I could not tell what it was at the time.

"Still, however helpless the little people in the presence of their mysterious Fear, I was differently constituted. I came out of this age of ours, this ripe prime of the human race, when Fear does not paralyse and mystery has lost its terrors. I at least would defend myself. Without further delay I determined to make myself arms and a fastness where I might sleep. With that refuge as a base, I could face this strange world with some of that confidence I had lost in realising to what creatures night by night I lay exposed. I felt I could never sleep again until my bed was secure from them. I shuddered with horror to think how they must already have examined me.

"I wandered during the afternoon along the valley of the Thames, but found nothing that commended itself to my mind as inaccessible. All the buildings and trees seemed easily practicable to such dexterous climbers as the Morlocks, to judge by their wells, must be. Then the tall pinnacles of the Palace of Green Porcelain and the polished gleam of its walls came back to my memory; and in the evening, taking Weena like a child upon my shoulder, I went up the hills towards the south-west. The distance, I had reckoned, was seven or eight miles, but it must have been nearer eighteen. I had first seen the place on a moist afternoon when distances are deceptively diminished. In addition, the heel of one of my shoes was loose, and a nail was working through the sole—they were comfortable old shoes I wore about indoors—so that I was lame. And it was already long past sunset when I came in sight of the palace, silhouetted black against the pale yellow of the sky.

"Weena had been hugely delighted when I began to carry her, but after a time she desired me to let her down, and ran along by the side of me, occasionally darting off on either hand to pick flowers to stick in my pockets. My pockets had always puzzled Weena, but at the last she had concluded that they were an eccentric kind of vase for floral decoration. At least she utilised them for that purpose. And that reminds me! In changing my jacket I found ..."

The Time Traveller paused, put his hand into his pocket, and silently placed two withered flowers, not unlike very large white mallows, upon the little table. Then he resumed his narrative.

"As the hush of evening crept over the world and we proceeded over the hill crest towards Wimbledon, Weena grew tired and wanted to return to the house of grey stone. But I pointed out the distant pinnacles of the Palace of Green Porcelain to her, and contrived to make her understand that we were seeking a refuge there from her Fear. You know that great pause that comes upon things before the dusk? Even the breeze stops in the trees. To me there is always an air of expectation about that evening stillness. The sky was clear, remote, and empty save for a few horizontal bars far down in the sunset. Well, that night the expectation took the colour of my fears. In that darkling calm my senses seemed preternaturally sharpened. I fancied I could even feel the hollowness of the ground beneath my feet: could, indeed, almost see through it the Morlocks on their ant-hill going hither and thither and waiting for the dark. In my excitement I fancied that they would receive my invasion of their burrows as a declaration of war. And why had they taken my Time Machine?

"So we went on in the quiet, and the twilight deepened into night. The clear blue of the distance faded, and one star after another came out. The ground grew dim and the trees black. Weena's fears and her fatigue grew upon her. I took her in my arms and talked to her and caressed her. Then, as the darkness grew deeper, she put her arms round my neck, and, closing her eyes, tightly pressed her face against my shoulder. So we went down a long slope into a valley, and there in the dimness I almost walked into a little river. This I waded, and went up the opposite side of the valley, past a number of sleeping houses, and by a statue—a Faun, or some such figure, *minus* the head. Here, too, were acacias. So far I had seen nothing of the Morlocks, but it was yet early in the night, and the darker hours before the old moon rose were still to come.

"From the brow of the next hill I saw a thick wood spreading wide and black before me. I hesitated at this. I could see no end to it, either to the right or the left. Feeling tired—my feet in particular, were very sore—I carefully lowered Weena from my shoulder as I halted, and sat down upon the turf. I could no longer see the Palace of Green Porcelain, and I was in doubt of my direction. I looked into the thickness of the wood and thought of what it might hide. Under that dense tangle of branches one would be out of sight of the stars. Even were there no other lurking danger—a danger I did not care to let my imagination loose upon—there would still be all the roots to stumble over and the tree boles to strike against. I was very tired, too, after the excitements of the day; so I decided that I would not face it, but would pass the night upon the open hill.

"Weena, I was glad to find, was fast asleep. I carefully wrapped her in my jacket, and sat down beside her to wait for the moonrise. The hillside was quiet and deserted, but from the black of the wood there came now and then a stir of living things. Above me shone the stars, for the night was very clear. I felt a certain sense of friendly comfort in their twinkling. All the old constellations had gone from the sky, however: that slow movement which is imperceptible in a hundred human lifetimes, had long since re-arranged them in unfamiliar groupings. But the Milky Way, it seemed to me, was still the same tattered streamer of star-dust as of yore. Southward (as I judged it) was a very bright red star that was new to me: it was even more splendid than our own green Sirius. And amid all these scintillating points of light one bright planet shone kindly and steadily like the face of an old friend.

"Looking at these stars suddenly dwarfed my own troubles and all the gravities of terrestrial life. I thought of their unfathomable distance, and the slow inevitable drift of their movements out of the unknown past into the unknown future. I thought of the great precessional cycle that the pole of the earth describes. Only forty times had that silent revolution occurred during all the years that I had traversed. And during these few revolutions all the activity, all the traditions, the complex organisations, the nations, languages, literatures, aspirations, even the mere memory of Man as I knew him, had been swept out of existence. Instead were these frail creatures who had forgotten their high ancestry, and the white Things of which I went in terror. Then I thought of the Great Fear that was between the two species, and for the first time, with a sudden shiver, came the clear knowledge of what the meat I had seen might be. Yet it was too horrible! I looked at little Weena sleeping beside me, her face white and starlike under the stars, and forthwith dismissed the thought.

"Through that long night I held my mind off the Morlocks as well as I could, and whiled away the time by trying to fancy I could find signs of the old constellations in the new confusion. The sky kept very clear, except for a hazy cloud or so. No doubt I dozed at times. Then, as my vigil wore on, came a faintness in the eastward sky, like the reflection of some colourless fire, and the old moon rose, thin and peaked and white. And close behind, and overtaking it, and overflowing it, the dawn came, pale at first, and then growing pink and warm. No Morlocks had approached us. Indeed, I had seen none upon the hill that night. And in the confidence of renewed day it almost seemed to me that my fear had been unreasonable. I stood up and found my foot with the loose heel swollen at the ankle and painful under the heel; so I sat down again, took off my shoes, and flung them away.

"I awakened Weena, and we went down into the wood, now green and pleasant instead of black and forbidding. We found some fruit wherewith to break our fast. We soon met others of the dainty ones, laughing and dancing in the sunlight as though there was no such thing in nature as the night. And then I thought once more of the meat that I had seen. I felt assured now of what it was, and from the bottom of my heart I pitied this last feeble rill from the great flood of humanity. Clearly, at some time in the Long-Ago of human decay the Morlocks' food had run short. Possibly they had lived on rats and suchlike vermin. Even now man is far less discriminating and exclusive in his food than he was—far less than any monkey. His prejudice against human flesh is no deep-seated instinct. And so these inhuman sons of men—! I tried to look at the thing in a scientific spirit. After all, they were less human and more remote than our cannibal ancestors of three or four thousand years ago. And the intelligence that would have made this state of things a torment had gone. Why should I trouble myself? These Eloi were mere fatted cattle, which the ant-like Morlocks preserved and preyed upon—probably saw to the breeding of. And there was Weena dancing at my side!

"Then I tried to preserve myself from the horror that was coming upon me, by regarding it as a rigorous punishment of human selfishness. Man had been content to live in ease and delight upon the labours of his fellow-man, had taken Necessity as his watchword and excuse, and in the fulness of time Necessity had come home to him. I even tried a Carlyle-like scorn of this wretched aristocracy in decay. But this attitude of mind was impossible. However great their intellectual degradation, the Eloi had kept too much of the human form not to claim my sympathy, and to make me perforce a sharer in their degradation and their Fear.

"I had at that time very vague ideas as to the course I should pursue. My first was to secure some safe place of refuge, and to make myself such arms of metal or stone as I could contrive. That necessity was immediate. In the next place, I hoped to procure some means of fire, so that I should have the weapon of a torch at hand, for nothing, I knew, would be more efficient against these Morlocks. Then I wanted to arrange some contrivance to break open the doors of bronze under the White Sphinx. I had in mind a battering-ram. I had a persuasion that if I could enter these doors and carry a blaze of light before me I should discover the Time Machine and escape. I could not imagine the Morlocks were strong enough to move it far away. Weena I had resolved to bring with me to our own time. And turning such schemes over in my mind I pursued our way towards the building which my fancy had chosen as our dwelling."

8

I FOUND the Palace of Green Porcelain, when we approached it about noon, deserted and falling into ruin. Only ragged vestiges of glass remained in its windows, and great sheets of the green facing had fallen away from the corroded metallic framework. It lay very high upon a turfy down, and looking north-eastward before I entered it, I was surprised to see a large estuary, or even creek, where I judged Wandsworth and Battersea must once have been. I thought then—though I never followed up the thought—of what might have happened, or might be happening, to the living things in the sea.

"The material of the Palace proved on examination to be indeed porcelain, and along the face of it I saw an inscription in some unknown character. I thought, rather foolishly, that Weena might help me to interpret this, buy I only learned that the bare idea of writing had never entered her head. She always seemed to me, I fancy, more human than she was, perhaps because her affection was so human.

"Within the big valves of the door—which were open and broken—we found, instead of the customary hall, a long gallery lit by many side windows. At the first glance I was reminded of a museum. The tiled floor was thick with dust, and a remarkable array of miscellaneous objects was shrouded in the same grey covering. Then I perceived, standing strange and gaunt in the centre of the hall, what was clearly the lower part of a huge skeleton. I recognised by the oblique feet that it was some extinct creature after the fashion of the Megatherium. The skull and the upper bones lay beside it in the thick dust, and in one place, where rain-water had dropped through a leak in the roof, the thing itself had been worn away. Further in the gallery was the huge skeleton barrel of a Brontosaurus. My museum hypothesis was confirmed. Going towards the side I found what appeared to be sloping shelves, and, clearing away the thick dust, I found the old familiar glass cases of our own time. But they must have been air-tight, to judge from the fair preservation of some of their contents.

"Clearly we stood among the ruins of some latter-day South Kensington! Here, apparently, was the Palæontological Section, and a very splendid array of fossils it must have been, though the inevitable process of decay that had been staved off for a time, and had, through the extinction of bacteria and fungi, lost ninety-nine hundredths of its force, was, nevertheless, with extreme sureness if with extreme slowness at work again upon all its treasures. Here and there I found traces of the

little people in the shape of rare fossils broken to pieces or threaded in strings upon reeds. And the cases had in some instances been bodily removed—by the Morlocks as I judged. The place was very silent. The thick dust deadened our footsteps. Weena, who had been rolling a sea-urchin down the sloping glass of a case, presently came, as I stared about me, and very quietly took my hand and stood beside me.

"And at first I was so much surprised by this ancient monument of an intellectual age, that I gave no thought to the possibilities it presented. Even my preoccupation about the Time Machine receded a little from my mind.

"To judge from the size of the place, this Palace of Green Porcelain had a great deal more in it than a Gallery of Palæontology; possibly historical galleries; it might be, even a library! To me, at least in my present circumstances, these would be vastly more interesting than this spectacle of old-time geology in decay. Exploring, I found another short gallery running transversely to the first. This appeared to be devoted to minerals, and the sight of a block of sulphur set my mind running on gun-powder. But I could find no saltpetre; indeed, no nitrates of any kind. Doubtless they had deliquesced ages ago. Yet the sulphur hung in my mind, and set up a train of thinking. As for the rest of the contents of that gallery, though on the whole they were the best preserved of all I saw, I had little interest. I am no specialist in mineralogy, and I went on down a very ruinous aisle running parallel to the first hall I had entered. Apparently this section had been devoted to natural history, but everything had long since passed out of recognition. A few shrivelled and blackened vestiges of what had once been stuffed animals, desiccated mummies in jars that had once held spirit, a brown dust of departed plants; that was all! I was sorry for that, because I should have been glad to trace the patient re-adjustments by which the conquest of animated nature had been attained. Then we came to a gallery of simply colossal proportions, but singularly ill-lit, the floor of it running downward at a slight angle from the end at which I entered. At intervals white globes hung from the ceiling—many of them cracked and smashed—which suggested that originally the place had been artificially lit. Here I was more in my element, for rising on either side of me were the huge bulks of big machines, all greatly corroded and many broken down, but some still fairly complete. You know I have a certain weakness for mechanism, and I was inclined to linger among these: the more so as for the most part they had the interest of puzzles, and I could make only the vaguest guesses at what they were for. I fancied that if I could solve their puzzles I should find myself in possession of powers that might be of use against the Morlocks.

"Suddenly Weena came very close to my side. So suddenly that she startled me. Had it not been for her I do not think I should have noticed that the floor of the gallery sloped at all.[1] The end I had come in at was quite above ground, and was lit by rare slit-like windows. As you went down the length, the ground came up against these windows, until at last there was a pit like the 'area' of a London house before each, and only a narrow line of daylight at the top. I went slowly along, puzzling about the machines, and had been too intent upon them to notice the gradual diminution of the light, until Weena's increasing apprehensions drew my attention. Then I saw that the gallery ran down at last into a thick darkness. I hesitated, and then, as I looked round me, I saw that the dust was less abundant and its surface less even. Further away towards the dimness, it appeared to be broken by a number of small narrow footprints. My sense of the immediate presence of the Morlocks revived at that. I felt that I was wasting my time in this academic examination of machinery. I called to mind that it was already far advanced in the afternoon, and that I had still no weapon, no refuge, and no means of making a fire. And then down in the remote blackness of the gallery I heard a peculiar pattering, and the same odd noises I had heard down the well.

"I took Weena's hand. Then, struck with a sudden idea, I left her and turned to a machine from which projected a lever not unlike those in a signal-box. Clambering upon the stand, and grasping this lever in my hands, I put all my weight upon it sideways. Suddenly Weena, deserted in the central aisle, began to whimper. I had judged the strength of the lever pretty correctly, for it snapped after a minute's strain, and I rejoined her with a mace in my hand more than sufficient, I judged, for any Morlock skull I might encounter. And I longed very much to kill a Morlock or so. Very inhuman, you may think, to want to go killing one's own descendants! But it was impossible, somehow, to feel any humanity in the things. Only my disinclination to leave Weena, and a persuasion that if I began to slake my thirst for murder my Time Machine might suffer, restrained me from going straight down the gallery and killing the brutes I heard.

"Well, mace in one hand and Weena in the other, I went out of that gallery and into another and still larger one, which at the first glance reminded me of a military chapel hung with tattered flags. The brown and charred rags that hung from the sides of it, I presently recognised as the decaying vestiges of books. They had long since dropped to pieces, and

---

1. It may be, of course, that the floor did not slope; but that the museum was built into the side of a hill.—Ed.

every semblance of print had left them. But here and there were warped boards and cracked metallic clasps that told the tale well enough. Had I been a literary man I might, perhaps, have moralised upon the futility of all ambition. But as it was, the thing that struck me with keenest force was the enormous waste of labour to which this sombre wilderness of rotting paper testified. At the time I will confess that I thought chiefly of the *Philosophical Transactions* and my own seventeen papers upon physical optics.

"Then, going up a broad staircase, we came to what may once have been a gallery of technical chemistry. And here I had not a little hope of useful discoveries. Except at one end where the roof had collapsed, this gallery was well preserved. I went eagerly to every unbroken case. And at last, in one of the really air-tight cases, I found a box of matches. Very eagerly I tried them. They were perfectly good. They were not even damp. I turned to Weena. 'Dance,' I cried to her in her own tongue. For now I had a weapon indeed against the horrible creatures we feared. And so, in that derelict museum, upon the thick soft carpeting of dust, to Weena's huge delight, I solemnly performed a kind of composite dance, whistling *The Land of the Leal* as cheerfully as I could. In part it was a modest *cancan*, in part a step dance, in part a skirt dance (so far as my tail-coat permitted), and in part original. For I am naturally inventive, as you know.

"Now, I still think that for this box of matches to have escaped the wear of time for immemorial years was a most strange, as for me it was a most fortunate, thing. Yet, oddly enough, I found a far unlikelier substance, and that was camphor. I found it in a sealed jar, that by chance, I suppose, had been really hermetically sealed. I fancied at first that it was paraffin wax, and smashed the glass accordingly. But the odour of camphor was unmistakable. In the universal decay this volatile substance had chanced to survive, perhaps through many thousands of centuries. It reminded me of a sepia painting I had once seen done from the ink of a fossil Belemnite that must have perished and become fossilised millions of years ago. I was about to throw it away, but I remembered that it was inflammable and burned with a good bright flame—was, in fact, an excellent candle—and I put it in my pocket. I found no explosives, however, nor any means of breaking down the bronze doors. As yet my iron crowbar was the most helpful thing I had chanced upon. Nevertheless I left that gallery greatly elated.

"I cannot tell you all the story of that long afternoon. It would require a great effort of memory to recall my explorations in at all the proper order. I remember a long gallery of rusting stands of arms, and how I hesitated between my crowbar and a hatchet or a sword. I could not carry both, however, and my bar of iron promised best against the bronze gates. There were numbers of guns, pistols, and rifles. The most were masses of rust, but many were of some new metal, and still fairly sound. But any cartridges or powder there may once have been had rotted into dust. One corner I saw was charred and shattered: perhaps, I thought, by an explosion among the specimens. In another place was a vast array of idols—Polynesian, Mexican, Grecian, Phœnician, every country on earth I should think. And here, yielding to an irresistible impulse, I wrote my name upon the nose of a steatite monster from South America that particularly took my fancy.

"As the evening drew on, my interest waned. I went through gallery after gallery, dusty, silent, often ruinous, the exhibit's sometimes mere heaps of rust and lignite, sometimes fresher. In one place I suddenly found myself near the model of a tin-mine, and then by the merest accident I discovered, in an air-tight case, two dynamite cartridges! I shouted 'Eureka,' and smashed the case with joy. Then came a doubt. I hesitated. Then, selecting a little side gallery, I made my essay. I never felt such a disappointment as I did in waiting five, ten, fifteen minutes for an explosion that never came. Of course the things were dummies, as I might have guessed from their presence. I really believe that, had they not been so, I should have rushed off incontinently and blown Sphinx, bronze doors, and (as it proved) my chances of finding the Time Machine, all together into non-existence.

"It was after that, I think, that we came to a little open court within the palace. It was turfed, and had three fruit-trees. So we rested and refreshed ourselves. Towards sunset I began to consider our position. Night was creeping upon us, and my inaccessible hiding-place had still to be found. But that troubled me very little now. I had in my possession a thing that was, perhaps, the best of all defences against the Morlocks—I had matches! I had the camphor in my pocket, too, if a blaze were needed. It seemed to me that the best thing we could do would be to pass the night in the open, protected by a fire. In the morning there was the getting of the Time Machine. Towards that, as yet, I had only my iron mace. But now, with my growing knowledge, I felt very differently towards those bronze doors. Up to this, I had refrained from forcing them, largely because of the mystery on the other side. They had never impressed me as being very strong, and I hoped to find my bar of iron not altogether inadequate for the work."

9

WE EMERGED from the palace while the sun was still in part above the horizon. I was determined to reach the White Sphinx early the next morning, and ere the dusk I purposed pushing through the woods that had stopped me on the previous journey. My plan was to go as far as possible that night, and then, building a fire, to sleep in the protection of its glare. Accordingly, as we went along I gathered any sticks or dried grass I saw, and presently had my arms full of such litter. Thus loaded, our progress was slower than I had anticipated, and besides Weena was tired. And I began to suffer from sleepiness too; so that it was full night before we reached the wood. Upon the shrubby hill of its edge Weena would have stopped, fearing the darkness before us; but a singular sense of impending calamity, that should indeed have served me as a warning, drove me onward. I had been without sleep for a night and two days, and I was feverish and irritable. I felt sleep coming upon me, and the Morlocks with it.

"While we hesitated, among the black bushes behind us, and dim against their blackness, I saw three crouching figures. There was scrub and long grass all about us, and I did not feel safe from their insidious approach. The forest, I calculated, was rather less than a mile across. If we could get through it to the bare hill-side, there, as it seemed to me, was an altogether safer resting-place: I thought that with my matches and my camphor I could contrive to keep my path illuminated through the woods. Yet it was evident that if I was to flourish matches with my hands I should have to abandon my firewood; so, rather reluctantly, I put it down. And then it came into my head that I would amaze our friends behind by lighting it. I was to discover the atrocious folly of this proceeding, but it came to my mind as an ingenious move for covering our retreat.

"I don't know if you have ever thought what a rare thing flame must be in the absence of man and in a temperate climate. The sun's heat is rarely strong enough to burn, even when it is focussed by dew-drops, as is sometimes the case in more tropical districts. Lightning may blast and blacken, but it rarely gives rise to widespread fire. Decaying vegetation may occasionally smoulder with the heat of its fermentation, but this rarely results in flame. In this decadence, too, the art of fire-making had been forgotten on the earth. The red tongues that went licking up my heap of wood were an altogether new and strange thing to Weena.

"She wanted to run to it and play with it. I believe she would have cast herself into it had I not restrained her. But I caught her up, and, in spite of her struggles, plunged boldly before me into the wood. For a little way the glare of my fire lit the path. Looking back presently, I could see, through the crowded stems, that from my heap of sticks the blaze had spread to some bushes adjacent, and a curved line of fire was creeping up the grass of the hill. I laughed at that, and turned again to the dark trees before me. It was very black, and Weena clung to me convulsively, but there was still, as my eyes grew accustomed to the darkness, sufficient light for me to avoid the stems. Overhead it was simply black, except where a gap of remote blue sky shone down upon us here and there. I struck none of my matches because I had no hands free. Upon my left arm I carried my little one, in my right hand I had my iron bar.

"For some way I heard nothing but the crackling twigs under my feet, the faint rustle of the breeze above, and my own breathing and the throb of the blood-vessels in my ears. Then I seemed to know of a pattering about me. I pushed on grimly. The pattering grew more distinct, and then I caught the same queer sounds and voices I had heard in the Underworld. There were evidently several of the Morlocks, and they were closing in upon me. Indeed, in another minute I felt a tug at my coat, then something at my arm. And Weena shivered violently, and became quite still.

"It was time for a match. But to get one I must put her down. I did so, and, as I fumbled with my pocket, a struggle began in the darkness about my knees, perfectly silent on her part and with the same peculiar cooing sounds from the Morlocks. Soft little hands, too, were creeping over my coat and back, touching even my neck. Then the match scratched and fizzed. I held it flaring, and saw the white backs of the Morlocks in flight amid the trees. I hastily took a lump of camphor from my pocket, and prepared to light it as soon as the match should wane. Then I looked at Weena. She was lying clutching my feet and quite motionless, with her face to the ground. With a sudden fright I stooped to her. She seemed scarcely to breathe. I lit the block of camphor and flung it to the ground, and as it split and flared up and drove back the Morlocks and the shadows, I knelt down and lifted her. The wood behind seemed full of the stir and murmur of a great company!

"She seemed to have fainted. I put her carefully upon my shoulder and rose to push on, and then there came a horrible realisation. In manœuvring with my matches and Weena, I had turned myself about several times, and now I had not the faintest idea in what direction lay my path. For all I knew, I might be facing back towards the Palace of Green Porcelain. I found myself in a cold sweat. I had to think rapidly what to do. I determined to build a fire and encamp where we were. I put Weena, still motionless, down upon a turfy bole, and very hastily, as my first lump of camphor waned, I began collecting sticks and leaves. Here and there out of the darkness round me the Morlocks' eyes shone like carbuncles.

"The camphor flickered and went out. I lit a match, and as I did so, two white forms that had been approaching Weena dashed hastily away. One was so blinded by the light that he came straight for me and I felt his bones grind under the blow of my fist. He gave a whoop of dismay, staggered a little way, and fell down. I lit another piece of camphor, and went on gathering my bonfire. Presently I noticed how dry was some of the foliage above me, for since my arrival on the Time Machine, a matter of a week, no rain had fallen. So, instead of casting about among the trees for fallen twigs, I began leaping up and dragging down branches. Very soon I had a choking smoky fire of green wood and dry sticks, and could economise my camphor. Then I turned to where Weena lay beside my iron mace. I tried what I could to revive her, but she lay like one dead. I could not even satisfy myself whether or not she breathed.

"Now, the smoke of the fire beat over towards me, and it must have made me heavy of a sudden. Moreover, the vapour of camphor was in the air. My fire would not need replenishing for an hour or so. I felt very weary after my exertion, and sat down. The wood, too, was full of a slumbrous murmur that I did not understand. I seemed just to nod and open my eyes. But all was dark, and the Morlocks had their hands upon me. Flinging off their clinging fingers I hastily felt in any pocket for the match-box, and—it had gone! Then they gripped and closed with me again. In a moment I knew what had happened. I had slept, and my fire had gone out, and the bitterness of death came over my soul. The forest seemed full of the smell of burning wood. I was caught by the neck, by the hair, by the arms, and pulled down. It was indescribably horrible in the darkness to feel all these soft creatures heaped upon me. I felt as if I was in a monstrous spider's web. I was overpowered, and went down. I felt little teeth nipping at my neck. I rolled over, and as I did so my hand came against my iron lever. It gave me strength. I struggled up, shaking the human rats from me, and, holding the bar short, I thrust where I judged their faces might be. I could feel the succulent giving of flesh and bone under my blows, and for a moment I was free.

"The strange exultation that so often seems to accompany hard fighting came upon me. I knew that both I and Weena were lost, but I determined to make the Morlocks pay for their meat. I stood with my back to a tree, swinging the iron bar before me. The whole wood was full of the stir and cries of them. A minute passed. Their voices seemed to rise to a higher pitch of excitement, and their movements grew faster. Yet none came within reach. I stood glaring at the blackness. Then suddenly came hope. What if the Morlocks were afraid? And close on the heels of that came a strange thing. The darkness seemed to grow luminous. Very dimly I began to see the Morlocks about me—three battered at my feet—and then I recognised, with incredulous surprise, that the others were running, in an incessant stream, as it seemed, from behind me, and away through the wood in front. And their backs seemed no longer white, but reddish. As I stood agape, I saw a little red spark go drifting across a gap of starlight between the branches, and vanish. And at that I understood the smell of burning wood, the slumbrous murmur that was growing now into a gusty roar, the red glow, and the Morlocks' flight.

"Stepping out from behind my tree and looking back, I saw, through the black pillars of the nearer trees, the flames of the burning forest. It was my first fire coming after me. With that I looked for Weena, but she was gone. The hissing and crackling behind me, the explosive thud as each fresh tree burst into flame, left little time for reflection. My iron bar still gripped, I followed in the Morlocks' path. It was a close race. Once the flames crept forward so swiftly on my right as I ran, that I was outflanked, and had to strike off to the left. But at last I emerged upon a small open space, and as I did so, a Morlock came blundering towards me, and past me, and went on straight into the fire!

"And now I was to see the most weird and horrible thing, I think, of all that I beheld in that future age. This whole space was as bright as day with the reflection of the fire. In the centre was a hillock or tumulus, surmounted by a scorched hawthorn. Beyond this was another arm of the burning forest, with yellow tongues already writhing from it, completely encircling the space with a fence of fire. Upon the hill-side were some thirty or forty Morlocks, dazzled by the light and heat, and blundering hither and thither against each other in their bewilderment. At first I did not realise their blindness, and struck furiously at them with my bar, in a frenzy of fear, as they approached me, killing one and crippling several more. But when I had watched the gestures of one of them groping under the hawthorn against the red sky, and heard their moans, I was assured of their absolute helplessness and misery in the glare, and I struck no more of them.

"Yet every now and then one would come straight towards me, setting loose a quivering horror that made me quick to elude him. At one time the flames died down somewhat, and I feared the foul creatures would presently be able to see me. I was even thinking of beginning the fight by killing some of them before this should happen; but the fire burst out again brightly, and I stayed my hand. I walked about the hill among them and avoided them, looking for some trace of Weena. But Weena was gone.

"At last I sat down on the sun-unit of the hillock, and watched this strange incredible company of blind things groping to and fro, and making uncanny noises to each other, as the glare of the fire beat on them. The coiling uprush of smoke streamed across the sky, and through the rare tatters of that red canopy, remote as though they belonged to another universe, shone the little stars. Two or three Morlocks came blundering into me, and I drove them off with blows of my fists, trembling as I did so.

"For the most part of that night I was persuaded it was a nightmare. I bit myself and screamed in a passionate desire to awake. I beat the ground with my hands, and got up and sat down again, and wandered here and there, and again sat down. Then I would fall to rubbing my eyes and calling upon God to let me awake. Thrice I saw Morlocks put their heads down in a kind of agony and rush into the flames. But, at last, above the subsiding red of the fire, above the streaming masses of black smoke and the whitening and blackening tree stumps, and the diminishing numbers of these dim creatures, came the white light of the day.

"I searched again for traces of Weena, but there were none. It was plain that they had left her poor little body in the forest. I cannot describe how it relieved me to think that it had escaped the awful fate to which it seemed destined. As I thought of that, I was almost moved to begin a massacre of the helpless abominations about me, but I contained myself. The hillock, as I have said, was a kind of island in the forest. From its summit I could now make out through a haze of smoke the Palace of Green Porcelain, and from that I could get my bearings for the White Sphinx. And so, leaving the remnant of these damned souls still going hither and thither and moaning, as the day grew clearer, I tied some grass about my feet and limped on across smoking ashes and among black stems that still pulsated internally with fire, towards the hiding place of the Time Machine. I walked slowly, for I was almost exhausted, as well as lame, and I felt the intensest wretchedness for the horrible death of little Weena. It seemed an overwhelming calamity. Now, in this old familiar room, it is more like the sorrow of a dream than an actual loss. But that morning it left me absolutely lonely again—terribly alone. I began to think of this house of mine, of this fireside, of some of you, and with such thoughts came a longing that was pain.

"But, as I walked over the smoking ashes under the bright morning sky, I made a discovery. In my trouser pocket were still some loose matches. The box must have leaked before it was lost."

10

ABOUT eight or nine in the morning I came to the same seat of yellow metal from which I had viewed the world upon the evening of my arrival. I thought of my hasty conclusions upon that evening, and could not refrain from laughing bitterly at my confidence. Here was the same beautiful scene, the same abundant foliage, the same splendid palaces and magnificent ruins, the same silver river running between its fertile banks. The gay robes of the beautiful people moved hither and thither among the trees. Some were bathing in exactly the place where I had saved Weena, and that suddenly gave me a keen stab of pain. And like blots upon the landscape rose the cupolas above the ways to the under-world. I understood now what all the beauty of the over-world people covered. Very pleasant was their day, as pleasant as the day of the cattle in the field. Like the cattle, they knew of no enemies, and provided against no needs. And their end was the same.

"I grieved to think how brief the dream of the human intellect had been. It had committed suicide. It had set itself steadfastly towards comfort and ease, a balanced society with security and permanency as its watchword, it had attained its hopes— to come to this at last. Once, life and property must have reached almost absolute safety. The rich had been assured of his wealth and comfort, the toiler assured of his life and work. No doubt in that perfect world there had been no unemployed problem, no social question left unsolved. And a great quiet had followed.

"It is a law of nature we overlook, that intellectual versatility is the compensation for change, danger, and trouble. An animal perfectly in harmony with its environment is a perfect mechanism. Nature never appeals to intelligence until habit and instinct are useless. There is no intelligence where there is no change and no need of change. Only those animals partake of intelligence that have to meet a huge variety of needs and dangers.

"So, as I see it, the Upper-world man had drifted towards his feeble prettiness, and the Under-world to mere mechanical industry. But that perfect state had lacked one thing even for mechanical perfection—absolute permanency. Apparently, as time went on, the feeding of the Under-world, however it was effected, had become disjointed. Mother Necessity, who had been staved off for a few thousand years, came back again, and she began below. The Under-world being in contact with machinery, which, however perfect, still needs some little thought outside

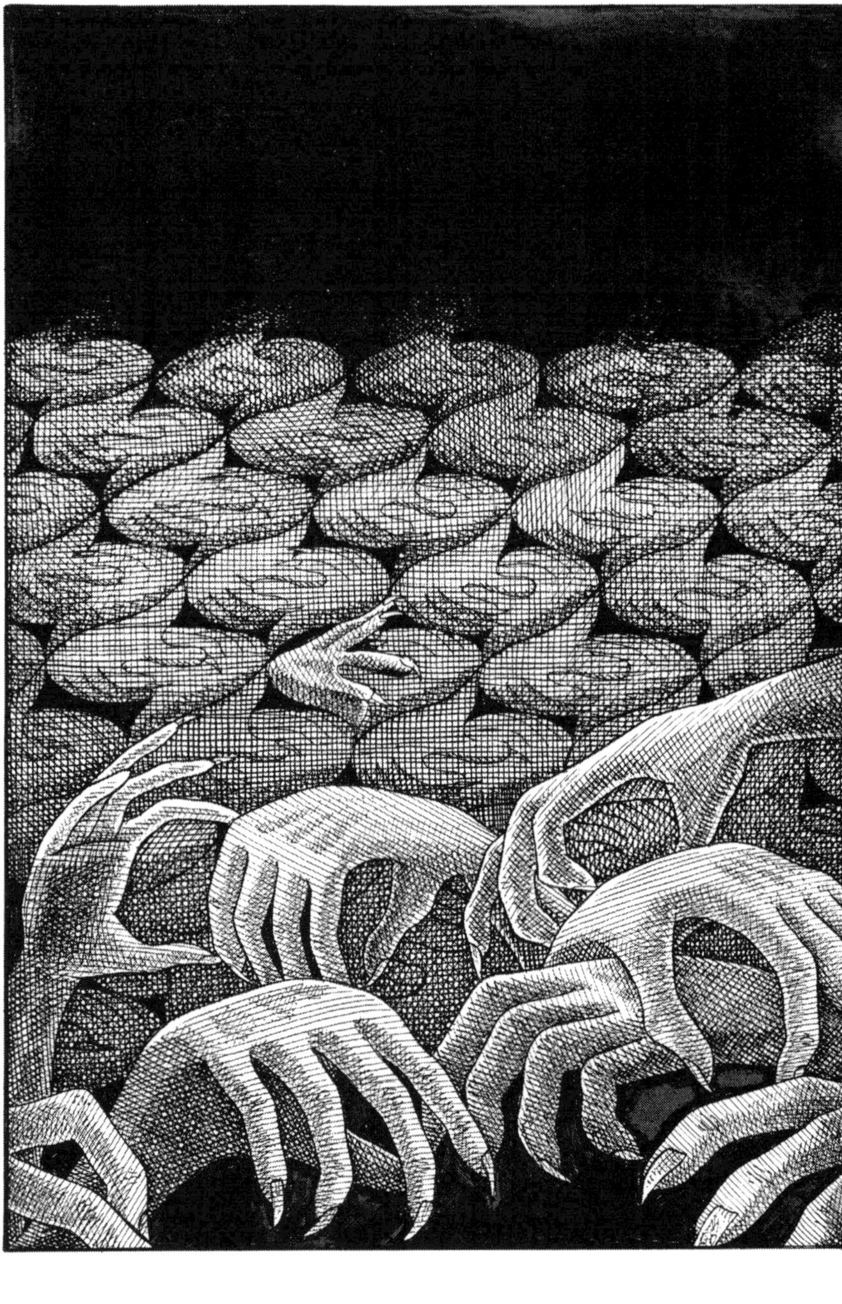

habit, had probably retained perforce rather more initiative, if less of every other human character, than the upper. And when other meat failed them, they turned to what old habit had hitherto forbidden. So I say I saw it in my last view of the world of Eight Hundred and Two Thousand Seven Hundred and One. It may be as wrong an explanation as mortal wit could invent. It is how the thing shaped itself to me, and as that I give it to you.

"After the fatigues, excitements, and terrors of the past days, and in spite of my grief, this seat and the tranquil view and the warm sunlight were very pleasant. I was very tired and sleepy, and soon my theorising passed into dozing. Catching myself at that, I took my own hint, and spreading myself out upon the turf I had a long and refreshing sleep.

"I awoke a little before sunsetting. I now felt safe against being caught napping by the Morlocks, and, stretching myself, I came on down the hill towards the White Sphinx. I had my crowbar in one hand, and the other hand played with the matches in my pocket.

"And now came a most unexpected thing. As I approached the pedestal of the sphinx I found the bronze valves were open. They had slid down into grooves.

"At that I stopped short before them, hesitating to enter.

"Within was a small apartment, and on a raised place in the corner of this was the Time Machine. I had the small levers in my pocket. So here, after all my elaborate preparations for the siege of the White Sphinx, was a meek surrender. I threw my iron bar away, almost sorry not to use it.

"A sudden thought came into my head as I stooped towards the portal. For once, at least, I grasped the mental operations of the Morlocks. Suppressing a strong inclination to laugh, I stepped through the bronze frame and up to the Time Machine. I was surprised to find it had been carefully oiled and cleaned. I have suspected since that the Morlocks had even partially taken it to pieces while trying in their dim way to grasp its purpose.

"Now as I stood and examined it, finding a pleasure in the mere touch of the contrivance, the thing I had expected happened. The bronze panels suddenly slid up and struck the frame with a clang. I was in the dark—trapped. So the Morlocks thought. At that I chuckled gleefully.

"I could already hear their murmuring laughter as they came towards me. Very calmly I tried to strike the match. I had only to fix on the levers and depart then like a ghost. But I had overlooked one little thing. The matches were of that abominable kind that light only on the box.

"You may imagine how all my calm vanished. The little brutes were close upon me. One touched me. I made a sweeping blow in the dark at them with the levers, and began to scramble into the saddle of the machine. Then came one hand upon me and then another. Then I had simply to fight against their persistent fingers for my levers, and at the same time feel for the studs over which these fitted. One, indeed, they almost got away from me. As it slipped from my hand, I had to butt in the dark with my head—I could hear the Morlock's skull ring—to recover it. It was a nearer thing than the fight in the forest, I think, this last scramble.

"But at last the lever was fixed and pulled over. The clinging hands slipped from me. The darkness presently fell from my eyes. I found myself in the same grey light and tumult I have already described."

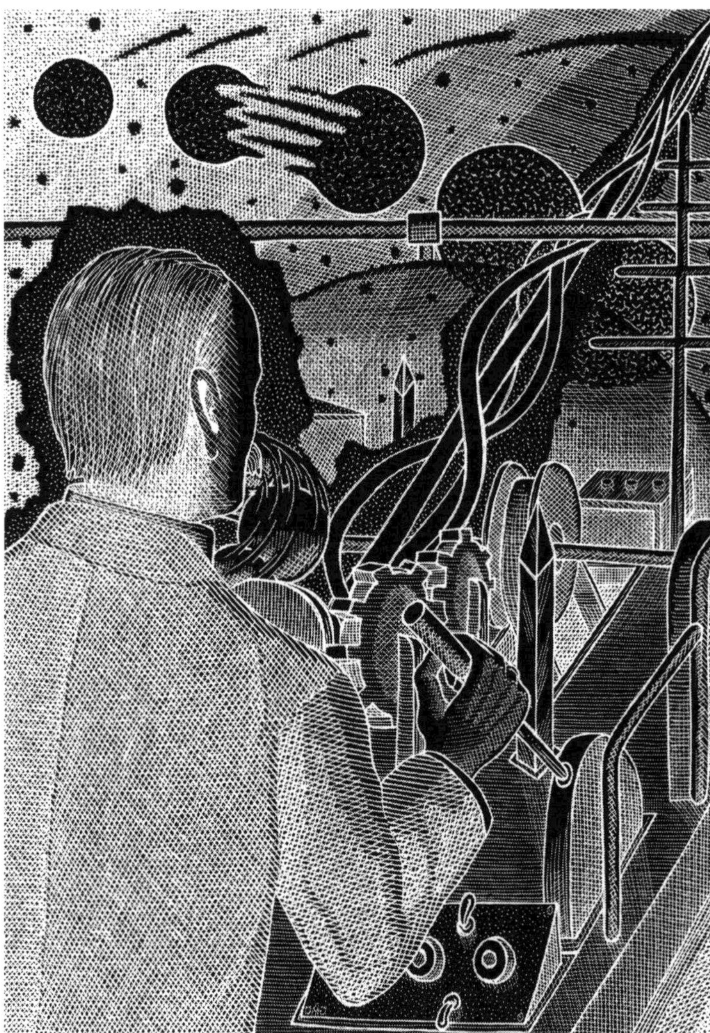

11

I HAVE already told you of the sickness and confusion that comes with time travelling. And this time I was not seated properly in the saddle, but sideways and in an unstable fashion. For an indefinite time I clung to the machine as it swayed and vibrated, quite unheeding how I went, and when I brought myself to look at the dials again I was amazed to find where I had arrived. One dial records days, another thousands of days, another millions of days, and another thousands of millions. Now, instead of reversing the levers I had pulled them over so as to go forward with them, and when I came to look at these indicators I found that the thousands hand was sweeping round as fast as the seconds hand of a watch—into futurity.

"As I drove on, a peculiar change crept over the appearance of things. The palpitating greyness grew darker; then—though I was still travelling with prodigious velocity—the blinking succession of day and night, which was usually indicative of a slower pace, returned, and grew more and more marked. This puzzled me very much at first. The alternations of night and day grew slower and slower, and so did the passage of the sun across the sky, until they seemed to stretch through centuries. At last a steady twilight brooded over the earth, a twilight only broken now and then when a comet glared across the darkling sky. The band of light that had indicated the sun had long since disappeared; for the sun had ceased to set—it simply rose and fell in the west, and grew ever broader and more red. All trace of the moon had vanished. The circling of the stars, growing slower and slower, had given place to creeping points of light. At last, some time before I stopped, the sun, red and very large, halted motionless upon the horizon, a vast dome glowing with a dull heat, and now and then suffering a momentary extinction. At one time it had for a little while glowed more brilliantly again, but it speedily reverted to its sullen red-heat. I perceived by this slowing down of its rising and setting that the work of the tidal drag was done. The earth had come to rest with one face to the sun, even as in our own time the moon faces the earth. Very cautiously, for I remembered my former headlong fall, I began to reverse my motion. Slower and slower went the circling hands until the thousands one seemed motionless, and the daily one was no longer a mere mist upon its scale. Still slower, until the dire outlines of a desolate beach grew visible.

"I stopped very gently and sat upon the Time Machine, looking round. The sky was no longer blue. North-eastward it was inky black, and out of the blackness shone brightly and steadily the pale white stars. Overhead it was a deep Indian red and starless, and south-eastward it grew brighter to a glowing scarlet where, cut by the horizon, lay the huge hull of the sun, red and motionless. The rocks about me were of a harsh reddish colour, and all the trace of life that I could see at first was the intensely green vegetation that covered every projecting point on their south-eastern face. It was the same rich green that one sees on forest moss or on the lichen in caves: plants which like these grow in a perpetual twilight.

"The machine was standing on a sloping beach. The sea stretched away to the south-west, to rise into a sharp bright horizon against the wan sky. There were no breakers and no waves, for not a breath of wind was stirring. Only a slight oily swell rose and fell like a gentle breathing, and showed that the eternal sea was still moving and living. And along the margin where the water sometimes broke was a thick incrustation of salt—pink under the lurid sky. There was a sense of oppression in my head, and I noticed that I was breathing very fast. The sensation reminded me of my only experience of mountaineering, and from that I judged the air to be more rarefied than it is now.

"Far away up the desolate slope I heard a harsh scream, and saw a thing like a huge white butterfly go slanting and fluttering up into the sky and, circling, disappear over some low hillocks beyond. The sound

of its voice was so dismal that I shivered and seated myself more firmly upon the machine. Looking round me again, I saw that, quite near, what I had taken to be a reddish mass of rock was moving slowly towards me. Then I saw the thing was really a monstrous crab-like creature. Can you imagine a crab as large as yonder table, with its many legs moving slowly and uncertainly, its big claws swaying, its long antennæ, like carters' whips, waving and feeling, and its stalked eyes gleaming at you on either side of its metallic front? Its back was corrugated and ornamented with ungainly bosses, and a greenish incrustation blotched it here and there. I could see the many palps of its complicated mouth flickering and feeling as it moved.

"As I stared at this sinister apparition crawling towards me, I felt a tickling on my cheek as though a fly had lighted there. I tried to brush it away with my hand, but in a moment it returned, and almost immediately came another by my ear. I struck at this, and caught something threadlike. It was drawn swiftly out of my hand. With a frightful qualm, I turned, and saw that I had grasped the antenna of another monster crab that stood

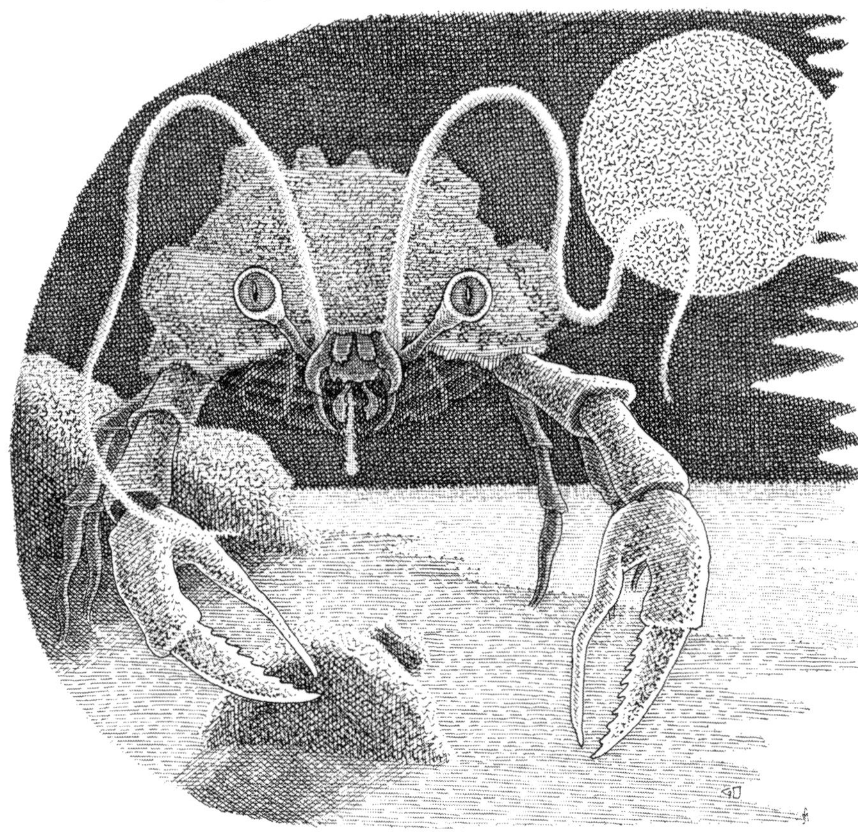

just behind me. Its evil eyes were wriggling on their stalks, its mouth was all alive with appetite, and its vast ungainly claws, smeared with an algal slime, were descending upon me. In a moment my hand was on the lever, and I had placed a month between myself and these monsters. But I was still on the same beach, and I saw them distinctly now as soon as I stopped. Dozens of them seemed to be crawling here and there, in the sombre light, among the foliated sheets of intense green.

"I cannot convey the sense of abominable desolation that hung over the world. The red eastern sky, the northward blackness, the salt Dead Sea, the stony beach crawling with these foul, slow-stirring monsters, the uniform poisonous-looking green of the lichenous plants, the thin air that hurt one's lungs; all contributed to an appalling effect. I moved on a hundred years, and there was the same red sun—a little larger, a little duller—the same dying sea, the same chill air, and the same crowd of earthly crustacea creeping in and out among the green weed and the red rocks. And in the westward sky I saw a curved pale line like a vast new moon.

"So I travelled, stopping ever and again, in great strides of a thousand years or more, drawn on by the mystery of the earth's fate, watching with a strange fascination the sun grow larger and duller in the westward sky, and the life of the old earth ebb away. At last, more than thirty million years hence, the huge red-hot dome of the sun had come to obscure nearly a tenth part of the darkling heavens. Then I stopped once more, for the crawling multitude of crabs had disappeared, and the red beach, save for its livid green liverworts and lichens, seemed lifeless. And now it was flecked with white. A bitter cold assailed me. Rare white flakes ever and again came eddying down. To the north-eastward, the glare of snow lay under the starlight of the sable sky, and I could see an undulating crest of hillocks pinkish-white. There were fringes of ice along the sea margin, with drifting masses further out; but the main expanse of that salt ocean, all bloody under the eternal sunset, was still unfrozen.

"I looked about me to see if any traces of animal-life remained. A certain indefinable apprehension still kept me in the saddle of the machine. But I saw nothing moving, in earth or sky or sea. The green slime on the rocks alone testified that life was not extinct. A shallow sandbank had appeared in the sea and the water had receded from the beach. I fancied I saw some black object flopping about upon this bank, but it became motionless as I looked at it, and I judged that my eye had been deceived, and that the black object was merely a rock. The stars in the sky were intensely bright and seemed to me to twinkle very little.

"Suddenly I noticed that the circular westward outline of the sun had changed; that a concavity, a bay, had appeared in the curve. I saw this grow larger. For a minute perhaps I stared aghast at this blackness that was creeping over the day, and then I realised that an eclipse was beginning. Either the moon or the planet Mercury was passing across the sun's disk. Naturally, at first I took it to be the moon, but there is much to incline me to believe that what I really saw was the transit of an inner planet passing very near to the earth.

"The darkness grew apace; a cold wind began to blow in freshening gusts from the east, and the showering white flakes in the air increased in number. From the edge of the sea came a ripple and whisper. Beyond these lifeless sounds the world was silent. Silent? It would be hard to convey the stillness of it. All the sounds of man, the bleating of sheep, the cries of birds, the hum of insects, the stir that makes the background of our lives—all that was over. As the darkness thickened, the eddying flakes grew more abundant, dancing before my eyes; and the cold of the air more intense. At last, one by one, swiftly, one after the other, the white peaks of the distant hills vanished into blackness. The breeze rose to a moaning wind. I saw the black central shadow of the eclipse sweeping towards me. In another moment the pale stars alone were visible. All else was rayless obscurity. The sky was absolutely black.

"A horror of this great darkness came on me. The cold, that smote to my marrow, and the pain I felt in breathing overcame me. I shivered, and a deadly nausea seized me. Then like a red-hot bow in the sky appeared the edge of the sun. I got off the machine to recover myself. I felt giddy and incapable of facing the return journey. As I stood sick and confused I saw again the moving thing upon the shoal—there was no mistake now that it was a moving thing—against the red water of the sea. It was a round thing, the size of a football perhaps, or, it may be, bigger, and tentacles trailed down from it; it seemed black against the weltering blood-red water, and it was hopping fitfully about. Then I felt I was fainting. But a terrible dread of lying helpless in that remote and awful twilight sustained me while I clambered upon the saddle."

12

SO I CAME back. For a long time I must have been insensible upon the machine. The blinking succession of the days and nights was resumed, the sun got golden again, the sky blue. I breathed with greater freedom. The fluctuating contours of the land ebbed and flowed. The hands spun backward upon the dials. At last I saw again the dim shadows of houses, the evidences of decadent humanity. These, too, changed and passed, and others came. Presently, when the million dial was at zero, I slackened speed. I began to recognise our own petty and familiar architecture, the thousands hand ran back to the starting-point, the night and day flapped slower and slower. Then the old walls of the laboratory came round me. Very gently, now, I slowed the mechanism down.

"I saw one little thing that seemed odd to me. I think I have told you that when I set out, before my velocity became very high, Mrs. Watchett had walked across the room, travelling, as it seemed to me, like a rocket. As I returned, I passed again across that minute when she traversed the laboratory. But now her every motion appeared to be the exact inversion of her previous ones. The door at the lower end opened, and she glided quietly up the laboratory, back foremost, and disappeared behind the door by which she had previously entered. Just before that I seemed to see Hillyer for a moment; but he passed like a flash.

"Then I stopped the machine, and saw about me again the old familiar laboratory, my tools, my appliances just as I had left them. I got off the thing very shakily, and sat down upon my bench. For several minutes I trembled violently. Then I became calmer. Around me was my old workshop again, exactly as it had been. I might have slept there, and the whole thing have been a dream.

"And yet, not exactly! The thing had started from the south-east corner of the laboratory. It had come to rest again in the north-west, against the wall where you saw it. That gives you the exact distance from my little lawn to the pedestal of the White Sphinx, into which the Morlocks had carried my machine.

"For a time my brain went stagnant. Presently I got up and came through the passage here, limping, because my heel was still painful, and feeling sorely begrimed. I saw the *Pall Mall Gazette* on the table by the door. I found the date was indeed to-day, and looking at the timepiece, saw the hour was almost eight o'clock. I heard your voices and the clatter of plates. I hesitated—I felt so sick and weak. Then I sniffed good wholesome meat, and opened the door on you. You know the rest. I washed, and dined, and now I am telling you the story.

"I know," he said, after a pause, "that all this will be absolutely incredible to you, but to me the one incredible thing is that I am here to-night in this old familiar room, looking into your friendly faces, and telling you these strange adventures." He looked at the Medical Man. "No. I cannot expect you to believe it. Take it as a lie—or a prophecy. Say I dreamed it in the workshop. Consider I have been speculating upon the destinies of our race until I have hatched this fiction. Treat my assertion of its truth as a mere stroke of art to enhance its interest. And, taking it as a story, what do you think of it?"

He took up his pipe, and began, in his old accustomed manner, to tap with it nervously upon the bars of the grate. There was a momentary stillness. Then chairs began to creak and shoes to scrape upon the carpet. I took my eyes off the Time Traveller's face, and looked round at his audience. They were in the dark, and little spots of colour swam before them. The Medical Man seemed absorbed in the contemplation of our host. The Editor was looking hard at the end of his cigar—the sixth. The Journalist fumbled for his watch. The others, as far as I remember, were motionless.

The Editor stood up with a sigh. "What a pity it is you're not a writer of stories!" he said, putting his hand on the Time Traveller's shoulder.

"You don't believe it?"

"Well—"

"I thought not."

The Time Traveller turned to us. "Where are the matches?" he said. He lit one and spoke over his pipe, puffing. "To tell you the truth … I hardly believe it myself… . And yet … "

His eye fell with a mute inquiry upon the withered white flowers upon the little table. Then he turned over the hand holding his pipe, and I saw he was looking at some half-healed scars on his knuckles.

The Medical Man rose, came to the lamp, and examined the flowers. "The gynæceum's odd," he said. The Psychologist leant forward to see, holding out his hand for a specimen.

"I'm hanged if it isn't a quarter to one," said the Journalist. "How shall we get home?"

"Plenty of cabs at the station," said the Psychologist.

"It's a curious thing," said the Medical Man; "but I certainly don't know the natural order of these flowers. May I have them?"

The Time Traveller hesitated. Then suddenly: "Certainly not."

"Where did you really get them?" said the Medical Man.

The Time Traveller put his hand to his head. He spoke like one who was trying to keep hold of an idea that eluded him.

"They were put into my pocket by Weena, when I travelled into Time." He stared round the room. "I'm damned if it isn't all going. This room and you and the atmosphere of every day is too much for my memory. Did I ever make a Time Machine, or a model of a Time Machine? Or is it all only a dream? They say life is a dream, a precious poor dream at times—but I can't stand another that won't fit. It's madness. And where did the dream come from? ... I must look at that machine. If there *is* one!"

He caught up the lamp swiftly, and carried it, flaring red, through the door into the corridor. We followed him. There in the flickering light of the lamp was the machine sure enough, squat, ugly, and askew, a thing of brass, ebony, ivory, and translucent glimmering quartz. Solid to the touch—for I put out my hand and felt the rail of it—and with brown spots and smears upon the ivory, and bits of grass and moss upon the lower parts, and one rail bent awry.

The Time Traveller put the lamp down on the bench, and ran his hand along the damaged rail. "It's all right now," he said. "The story I told you was true. I'm sorry to have brought you out here in the cold." He took up the lamp, and, in an absolute silence, we returned to the smoking-room.

He came into the hall with us, and helped the Editor on with his coat. The Medical Man looked into his face and, with a certain hesitation, told him he was suffering from overwork, at which he laughed hugely. I remember him standing in the open doorway, bawling good-night.

I shared a cab with the Editor. He thought the tale a "gaudy lie." For my own part I was unable to come to a conclusion. The story was so fantastic and incredible, the telling so credible and sober. I lay awake most of the night thinking about it. I determined to go next day and see the Time Traveller again. I was told he was in the laboratory, and, being on easy terms in the house, I went up to him. The laboratory however was empty. I stared for a minute at the Time Machine and put out my hand and touched the lever. At that the squat substantial-looking mass swayed like a bough shaken by the wind. Its instability startled me extremely, and I had a queer reminiscence of the childish days when I used to be forbidden to meddle. I came back through the corridor. The Time Traveller met me in the smoking-room. He was coming from the house. He had a small camera under one arm and a knapsack under the other. He laughed when he saw me, and gave me an elbow to shake. "I'm frightfully busy," said he, "with that thing in there."

"But is it not some hoax? "I said. "Do you really travel through Time?"

"Really and truly I do." And he looked frankly into my eyes.

He hesitated. His eye wandered about the room. "I only want half an hour," he said. "I know why you came, and it's awfully good of you. There's some magazines here. If you'll stop to lunch I'll prove you this time travelling up to the hilt, specimens and all. If you'll forgive my leaving you now?"

I consented, hardly comprehending then the full import of his words, and he nodded and went on down the corridor. I heard the door of the laboratory slam, seated myself in a chair, and took up a daily paper. What was he going to do before lunch-time? Then suddenly I was reminded by an advertisement that I had promised to meet Richardson, the publisher, at two. I looked at my watch, and saw that I could barely save that engagement. I got up and went down the passage to tell the Time Traveller.

As I took hold of the handle of the door I heard an exclamation, oddly truncated at the end, and a click and a thud. A gust of air whirled round me as I opened the door, and from within came the sound of broken glass falling on the floor. The Time Traveller was not there. I seemed to see a ghostly, indistinct figure sitting in a whirling mass of black and brass for a moment—a figure so transparent that the bench behind with its sheets of drawings was absolutely distinct; but this phantasm vanished as I rubbed my eyes. The Time Machine had gone. Save for a subsiding stir of dust, the further end of the laboratory was empty. A pane of the skylight had, apparently, just been blown in.

I felt an unreasonable amazement. I knew that something strange had happened, and for the moment could not distinguish what the strange thing might be. As I stood staring, the door into the garden opened, and the man-servant appeared.

We looked at each other. Then ideas began to come. "Has Mr.—gone out that way?" said I.

"No, sir. No one has come out this way. I was expecting to find him here."

At that I understood. At the risk of disappointing Richardson I stayed on waiting for the Time Traveller: waiting for the second, perhaps still stranger story, and the specimens and photographs he would bring with him. But I am beginning now to fear that I must wait a lifetime. The Time Traveller vanished three years ago. And, as everybody knows now, he has never returned.

EPILOGUE

ONE CANNOT choose but wonder. Will he ever return? It may be that he swept back into the past, and fell among the blood-drinking, hairy savages of the Age of Unpolished Stone; into the abysses of the Cretaceous Sea; or among the grotesque saurians, the huge reptilian brutes of the Jurassic times. He may even now—if I may use the phrase—be wandering on some plesiosaurus-haunted Oolitic coral reef or beside the lonely saline lakes of the Triassic Age. Or did he go forward, into one of the nearer ages, in which men are still men, but with the riddles of our own time answered and its wearisome problems solved? Into the manhood of the race: for I, for my own part, cannot think that these latter days of weak experiment, fragmentary theory, and mutual discord are indeed man's culminating time! I say, for my own part. He, I know—for the question had been discussed among us long before the Time Machine was made—thought but cheerlessly of the Advancement of Mankind, and saw in the growing pile of civilisation only a foolish heaping that must inevitably fall back upon and destroy its makers in the end. If that is so, it remains for us to live as though it were not so. But to me the future is still black and blank—is a vast ignorance, lit at a few casual places by the memory of his story. And I have by me, for my comfort, two strange white flowers—shrivelled now, and brown and flat and brittle—to witness that even when mind and strength had gone, gratitude and a mutual tenderness still lived on in the heart of man.

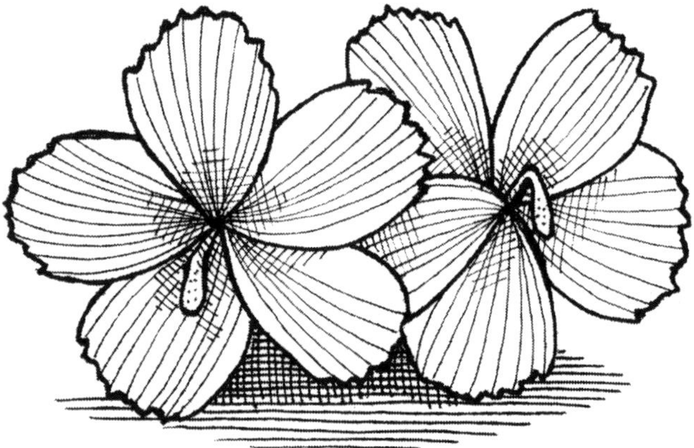

Nebogipfel at the End of Time

THE FIRST of them to appear came from the sky. There was a flash like ball lightning, there was a clap of thunder, there was the rush and flutter of great heavy wings, and he was there—a gleaming, godlike figure with streaming golden hair, perfect features, a torso all sinew and strength.

With his wings he pressed himself upward through the thick weary air, surveying the water and its gray, ragged rocks, the black graveled beach, and dun mossy dunes. A few horrid creatures slid through the dark, oily waters, their sharp senses tuned, their quick brains devoted to the endless quest of nourishment gained ultimately at one another's expense.

The gleaming newcomer tilted his pinions, banked, swept lower over the face of the water. Behind him, sunk perpetually half below the horizon, a fat misty sun glared redly across dim, dispirited ripples. Greedy tentacles whipped upward from beneath the surface of the sea. The tentacles were as thin as wires, as agile as wolf eels, as powerful as woven steel. The great winged man eluded them with casual ease, rose a short distance above the dark, coarse beach, and dropped softly onto the cinder-like gravel. At once a spider crab the size of the man's doubled hands sprang from its lair and shot at his softest parts, black pebbles clattering back against the beach. The man seemed not to notice the predator. Carelessly, he turned to stare in moody silence across the dull dunes, his shadow long and black before him outlined by the dim red glare of the dying sun. The man's turning, easy and nonchalant, seemed somehow to disconcert the leaping predator. The man's hand caught it an almost accidental blow and sent it skittering back onto the gravelish beach, where it landed with a clatter on its back and began at once to struggle frantically. Even so the crab had not righted itself before a dozen rival predators had attacked it from all sides, tearing away its waving claws and then boring through the exposed openings in its carapace to find the soft nourishment inside.

A hundred strides down the beach, there was a sudden pop as a globe like a shimmering great soap bubble appeared just over the black cinders, hovered and shook briefly, then exploded softly. From within it a couple set foot upon the strand. They stood, gazing tentatively for a short while at the winged man, then began carefully on quivering pipestem legs to make their way toward him.

The winged man advanced to meet the newcomers, his great muscular strides devouring the distance that their tiny thin legs could barely nibble at. The couple seemed to be man and woman, but each showed only vestigal characteristics of gender—or of their animal nature at all. Their heads were huge and domelike, with only the lightest suggestion of down above the ears. Their ears were huge and moved as if of their own will, their eyes were tiny and deep sunken, but still they blinked and squinted in the dire red sunlight.

Above there was a screaming roar as a great black ellipsoid half-appeared, circling over the beach, growing alternately more and less solid in appearance. The noise that the object made faded and grew in concert with its growing and lessening solidity. Great aerial screws held the thing above the beach, and multi-faceted gemlike surfaces glowed and dimmed as it moved this way and that through the heavy air.

Slowly the machine seemed to stabilize in the air, then to lower itself carefully until it had come to rest on the strand. One of the jewels in its skin revolved slowly, then rolled away from the ellipsoid and lay against the black, dull surface of the machine. A small party of people slowly emerged from the machine. They wore dark, form-fitting garments marked with red hexagonal insignia. Their outfits included black, pointed hoods that largely concealed their faces; what could be seen of these showed them to be as black and dull as the clothing and the ship in which they had arrived.

For what seemed like hour upon hour they arrived. Some by strange, grotesque vehicles. Some by spectacularly announced projection. Some by chronian gas, or drugs, or spiritual exercise, or by sheer mental power. Some involuntarily. Some unknowingly. At one point not far inland from the beach, across the first row of dim, ugly dunes, there suddenly appeared an entire city. Its towers were of white marble and shining glass, its gates were of yellow horn and blackened teak. Its people had pale skin and wore robes of indigo and gold.

When it appeared inland of the beach, the city's ruler climbed to the highest point of its highest tower and gazed into the center of the glowing, half-hidden sun, and sent his chief advisor to have himself let out through the yellow horn and teakwood gates, and make his way to join the others on the beach, and confer with them.

We are here, the man from the city of towers said as he approached the others standing on the beach. It seemed a pointless comment; he did not himself know what he meant.

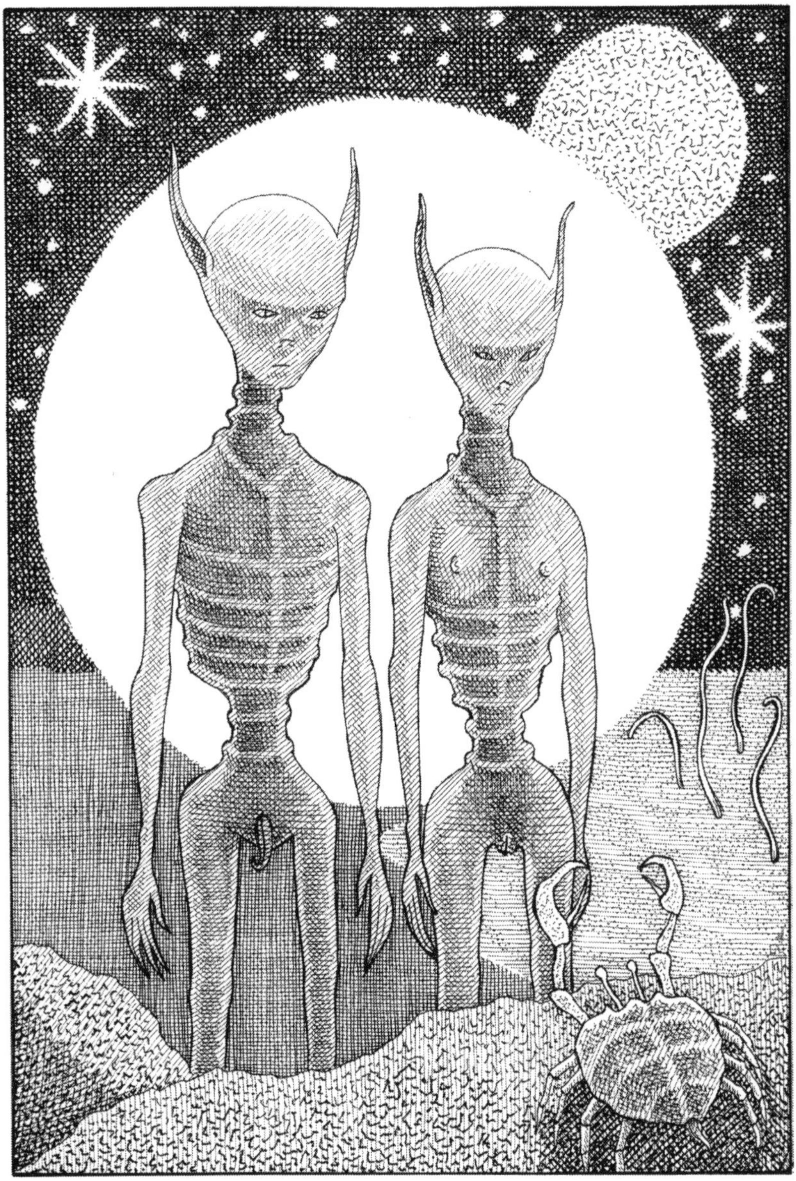

The nearest to him, a woman of the black ellipsoid, turned her black-hooded face toward him. She nodded. All, we are all here. Your master and your people will not leave their city?

The other shook his head in the universal sign, his indigo robes rustling.

It is time that he arrive, another voice said. The two turned to see whose it was. The speaker was one of the wizened couple. It is time, the speaker's companion added. Time, the first said. They nodded.

He is coming, a voice asserted. There was a rustling all up and down the beach. He is coming, is coming, is coming, voices echoed, whispered, shivered back to silence.

It is time, the golden, winged man said. He raised a muscled arm, pointed across the oily sea. Where half the sun's blood-red disk stood in changless demi-sunset, a black circle had rolled along the horizon and now stood in the center of the sun like a black hole punctured in a red bull's-eye target.

A chorus of intaken breaths were drawn.

The travelers on the beach—there were scores now—drew themselves into a great half-ring. The tiny, spindly-legged couple from the shimmering bubble stationed themselves facing each other, forty paces apart at the edge of the sea. Tiny wavelets lapped at the edges of their soft-shod feet, leaving a residue of pinkish foam on the pliant, leathery slippers that they wore.

Between them, strung in a gentle curve, were all the others. The black-clad, hooded figures from the gem-colored ellipsoid, the men and the women who had arrived by time-gas and by time-drug, by time-quake and by time-slip, those who had arrived by machine, those who had arrived by mind, one who had risen naked and weeping from a great glass coffin of cushions and of blossoms, and one who had struggled wild-eyed and screaming from a barrow beneath the black cindery beach itself, the indigo-robed seer from the city of towers, and the winged godling from the sky above the water.

There was a hush as they all stared at the black disk upon the red disk, the stripes of color reflecting from them across the face of the oily sea to the edge of the black cindery beach. Then a voice broke the silence. How will we know him, the voice asked.

By his face, one replied. By his haggard face, his bruised face, his face of despair.

By his clothing another said. By his quaint clothing, his rough cloth trousers and oddly buttoned jacket and the strange cloth cap he wears on his head and the stranger cloth streamer that he ties about his throat.

By his machine, a third claimed. By his strange, squat, ugly machine that looks all askew with its ivory bars and its brass railings, its shining rod of quartz and its odd ugly saddle.

And how will he know us, the seer from the city of towers asked to know.

We will call him by name. We will call him Nebogipfel.

Nebogipfel.

It was as if the name had summoned the man from out of time's grasp. In the center of their half-circle he appeared. The time traveler and the time machine. The machine was truly squat and ugly and askew. The traveler bore his face of despair.

He rose from the saddle of his machine, slid the starting lever carefully into a notched position and locked it there. He stepped onto the crunching gravel, stared at the black disk that stood before the sun's blood-red demicircle for a little while, then wheeled slowly, gazing at the face of each of the many who had waited to greet him.

He shook his head sadly.

Is this—? He gestured with both hands, holding them as far apart as his feet were spread on the black cinders. The palms were turned toward each other.

Is this—all? Is this—the end? The end of it all?

He pointed at the red, dying sun with the round black blemish now rolling slowly past its center, toward the edge where the dim glare faded into the blackness of the sky. He moved his hand so that the eye that followed was led across the oily surface of the sea, where only the occasional furious eruption of predator and prey broke the red-trimmed mourning field.

All striving, all dreaming, all thought and suffering brings us to—this?

He gave a shrug of hopelessness. A rictus tugged his face into a momentary hideous grin.

But we had greatness, one of the others challenged. In my time—in my time men built cities that towered above the tallest trees, filled their halls with philosophers and actors, musicians and tumblers, and living, naked tableaux. Our glories were recorded on parchment and canvas, in marble and in granite. The world beheld us and—Trembled? Nebogipfel supplied.

No, the other shook his head. No one trembled before us. The world smiled in joy, traded its goods for our art, sang the praises of our creators. We were beloved of the whole world. This was our greatness.

And now? Nebogipfel asked. And now? What is there now of your greatness?

The other was silent.

In my day, a different voice spoke; in my day, we marched! The voice was harsh, strong, confident. All who stood before us, we slew! The rest we made slaves! In my day none could resist! We were the bravest, we were the strongest, we were the hardest! We were never beaten! Never! Never! Never! Never!

Well, said Nebogipfel. I bow to your splendor. I am dazzled by your might! Your empire stretches before me and I cringe in awe.

He swept an arm, encompassing black cinders, blood-red waters, black sky.

In my day, another claimed, we saw these limits. Yes, we had our time on the earth. We dug and we learned and we saw that we had not been the first, and we knew that we would not be the last, either, unless we burned the world and left behind only a dead stone. So we built. Not cities! No! Not fortresses! We built argosies to other worlds, ships to sail to other stars, bolts to carry our seed from the loins of this world to the wombs of a million waiting mothers scattered across God's whole realm! Down into the dust for us, down into the dust, but our children live! Yes, they live yet on a million stars in every direction!

And yet we just begin! A million stars? What did your age know of the universe, Nebogipfel? How many worlds did you visage? Seven? Seventy? Seventy thousand?

A billion worlds, Nebogipfel, a billion worlds in one cinder!

The speaker bent and lifted a blackened pebble from beneath his feet. What are a billion of these, Nebogipfel?

He hurled the cinder at the tweed-suited time traveler in the center of the ring. The cinder struck Nebogipfel on the cheek, split the skin above the bone and fell, clattering, onto the beach. A narrow trickle of blood dribbled down the time traveler's face and soaked into his soft shirt collar.

The time traveler smiled.

A billion suns? Nebogipfel asked. What are ten billion billion suns? How long will they burn? Ten billion years? And then—what?

He threw out an arm, gesturing across the sea.

This?

The black disk had transited the half-set redness; a little warmth returned to the tired, musty air.

And after this? In another hundred thousand years, or another hundred million, even this ends.

He pulled his soft cloth cap from his head. Straw-colored hair stuck up in all directions. The time traveler drew the cap across his face so the smooth silken lining covered his eyes. He bowed his head, face still covered, shoulders slumped, the image of a mourner to his own inevitable end. But our children! the other exclaimed.

Nebogipfel did not move.

The other stared, stricken, at the dying sun. Around him the ranks of the assembled time travelers stood silent and motionless.

Then our grandchildren! Our great-grandchildren!

Nebogipfel did not move.

The travelers remained in silence.

One of the two pipestem-legged travelers advanced across the black cinders, unsteady limbs quavering with every step. The figure halted, facing Nebogipfel, staring up at Nebogipfel, who stood twice the height of the other.

The taller figure lowered the cap from before his eyes and stood, holding it in his hand, looking downward into the great, solemn, squinting-eyed countenance. An involuntary grin worked its way across Nebogipfel's features.

Yes?

We knew you were coming here today, Nebogipfel. Why do you think this assemblage awaited you? Do you think this is all a coincidence? Do you think that these travelers from so many eras, so many races, so many civilizations, all happened to arrive here on this beach, today, by chance? The tiny mouth drew back in a wry expression.

Nebogipfel tugged his cloth cap back onto his straw-colored head. I suppose there was a plan of some sort, then, he said. He drew himself up to his full height so he towered more than ever over the tiny figure. This is the end of my journey, Nebogipfel said. I miss the London of my era. I lost my Weena. I hate the world of A.D. 802,701, and every later age I ever visited only made me more laden with gloom, more burdened with hopelessness.

All I want is to go back to my home. Here—

He slapped a hand on the saddle of his time machine, setting the whole thing to quivering and tipping as if it were about to tumble into the black cinders or the blood-red water.

That is precisely what you must not do, the tiny figure piped.

I shall board again with Mrs. Watchett, Nebogipfel said. I shall contribute another seventeen papers on physical optics to the *Philosophical Review*. I shall become the most ordinary of men among ordinary men. No more shall I see the white sphinx.

There you are wrong! the little being piped. Officiously, he gestured and men and women moved forward from the semicircle that stood surrounding Nebogipfel. Strong arms seized the original time traveler. Cords appeared and he was bound and placed on the saddle of his machine.

We are all time travelers, Nebogipfel, the little being, said. But you are the prototype, you are the ideal of whom we are all faint reflections. You say that you despair of the ultimate end of life. What would you call it? Some would say, the ultimate entropy. Some would say the heat death of the universe. Some would say, the cosmic nirvana.

But your own philosophy says, there is no forever. There is nothing that endures unending. When the universe reaches its end, Nebogipfel, what lies beyond the end? What lies beyond the end?

Again the little being gestured. A hand moved an ivory bar on Nebogipfel's time machine. Another turned the glittering quartz rod. Nebogipfel shouted, No! Send me back! Send me back!

But the other said, Yes! You must go on, Nebogipfel! Once you have tasted of futurity, there is no returning! You must go onward, not back! What lies beyond the end, Nebogipfel? What lies beyond the end?

A tiny hand gestured. A powerful hand reached, unlocked the starting lever of Nebogipfel's time machine. The lever was thrown. Nebogipfel shouted. The machine and its rider flickered, faded, disappeared from the beach.

The tiny figure returned to its place at the edge of the pink foaming sea. None of us will know, one of the people standing there said. Nebogipfel knows, another said.

The Grey Man

I HAVE already told you of the sickness and confusion that comes with time travelling. And this time I was not seated properly in the saddle, but sideways and in an unstable fashion. For an indefinite time I clung to the machine as it swayed and vibrated, quite unheeding how I went, and when I brought myself to look at the dials again I was amazed to find where I had arrived. One dial records days, another thousands of days, another millions of days, and another thousands of millions. Now, instead of reversing the levers I had pulled them over so as to go forward with them, and when I came to look at these indicators I found that the thousands hand was sweeping round as fast as the seconds hand of a watch—into futurity. Very cautiously, for I remembered my former headlong fall, I began to reverse my motion. Slower and slower went the circling hands until the thousands one seemed motionless and the daily one was no longer a mere mist upon its scale. Still slower, until the grey haze around me became distincter and dim outlines of an undulating waste grew visible.

"I stopped. I was on a bleak moorland, covered with a sparse vegetation, and grey with a thin hoarfrost. The time was midday, the orange sun, shorn of its effulgence, brooding near the meridian in a sky of drabby grey. Only a few black bushes broke the monotony of the scene. The great buildings of the decadent men among whom, it seemed to me, I had been so recently, had vanished and left no trace, not a mound even marked their position. Hill and valley, sea and river—all, under the wear and work of the rain and frost, had melted into new forms. No doubt, too, the rain and snow had long since washed out the Morlock tunnels. A nipping breeze stung my hands and face. So far as I could see there were neither hills, nor trees, nor rivers: only an uneven stretch of cheerless plateau.

"Then suddenly a dark bulk rose out of the moor, something that gleamed like a serrated row of iron plates, and vanished almost immediately in a depression. And then I became aware of a number of faint-grey things, coloured to almost the exact tint of the frost-bitten soil, which were browsing here and there upon its scanty grass, and running to and fro. I saw one jump with a sudden start, and then my eye detected perhaps a score of them. At first I thought they were rabbits, or some small breed of kangaroo. Then, as one came hopping near me, I perceived that it belonged to neither of these groups. It was plantigrade, its hind legs rather the longer; it was tailless, and covered with a straight greyish hair that thickened about the head into a Skye terrier's mane. As I had understood that in the Golden Age man had killed out almost all the other animals, sparing only a few of the more ornamental, I was naturally curious about the creatures. They did not seem afraid of me, but browsed on, much as rabbits would do in a place unfrequented by men; and it occurred to me that I might perhaps secure a specimen.

"I got off the machine, and picked up a big stone. I had scarcely done so when one of the little creatures came within easy range. I was so lucky as to hit it on the head, and it rolled over at once and lay motionless. I ran to it at once. It remained still, almost as if it were killed. I was surprised to see that the things had five feeble digits to both its fore and hind feet—the fore feet, indeed, were almost as human as the fore feet of a frog. It had, moreover, a roundish head, with a projecting forehead and forward-looking eyes, obscured by its lank hair. A disagreeable apprehension flashed across my mind. As I knelt down and seized my capture, intending to examine its teeth and other anatomical points which might show human characteristics, the metallic-looking object, to which I have already alluded, reappeared above a ridge in the moor, coming towards me and making a strange clattering sound as it came. Forthwith the grey animals about me began to answer with a short, weak yelping—as if of terror—and bolted off in a direction opposite to that from which this new creature approached. They must have hidden in burrows or behind bushes and tussocks, for in a moment not one of them was visible.

"I rose to my feet, and stared at this grotesque monster. I can only describe it by comparing it to a centipede. It stood about three feet high, and had a long segmented body, perhaps thirty feet long, with curiously overlapping greenish-black plates. It seemed to crawl upon a multitude of feet, looping its body as it advanced. Its blunt round head with a polygonal arrangement of black eye spots, carried two flexible, writhing, horn-like antennae. It was coming along, I should judge, at a pace of about eight or ten miles an hour, and it left me little time for thinking. Leaving my grey animal, or grey man, whichever it was, on the ground, I set off for the machine. Halfway I paused, regretting that abandonment, but a glance over my shoulder destroyed any such regret. When I gained the machine the monster was scarce fifty yards away. It was certainly not a vertebrated animal. It had no snout, and its mouth was fringed with jointed dark-coloured plates. But I did not care for a nearer view.

"I traversed one day and stopped again, hoping to find colossus gone and some vestige of my victim; but, I should judge, the giant centipede did not trouble itself about bones. At any rate both had vanished. The faintly human touch of these little creatures perplexed me greatly. If you come to think, there is no reason why a degenerate humanity should not come at last to differentiate into as many species as the descendants of the mud fish who fathered all the land vertebrates. I saw no more of any insect colossus, as to my thinking the segmented creature must have been. Evidently the physiological difficulty that at present keeps all the insects small had been surmounted at last, and this division of the

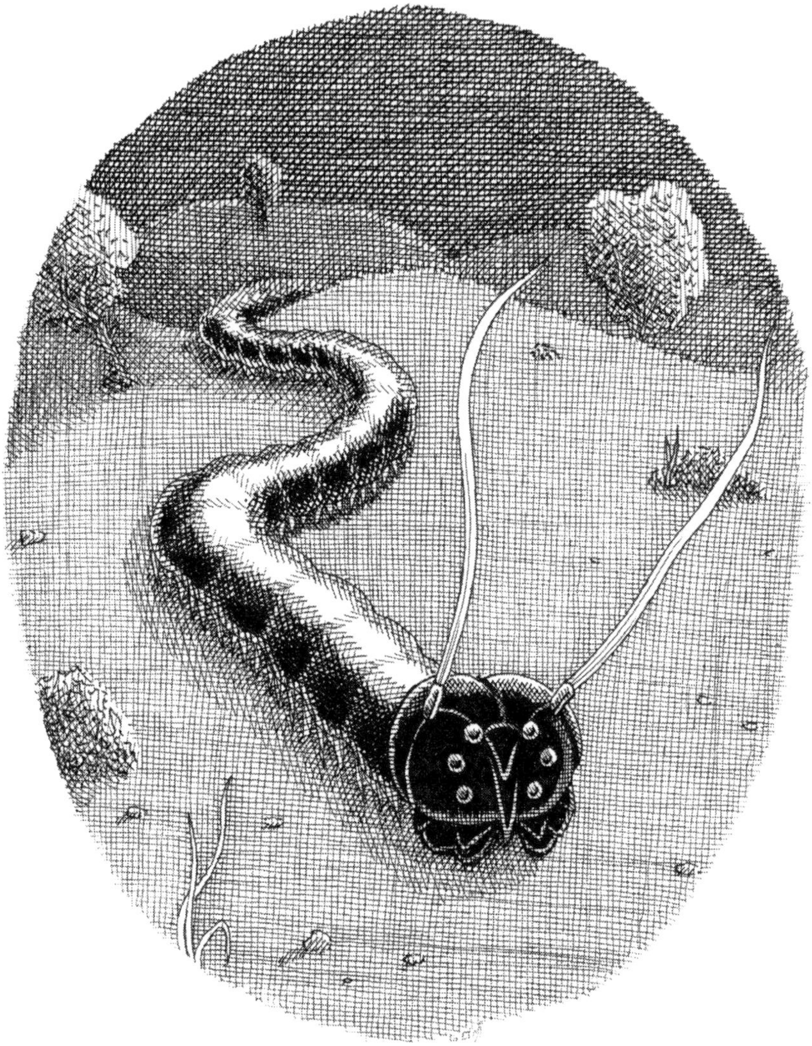

animal kingdom had arrived at the long awaited supremacy which its enormous energy and vitality deserve. I made several attempts to kill or capture another of the greyish vermin, but none of my missiles were so successful as my first; and, after perhaps a dozen disappointing throws, that left my arm aching, I felt a gust of irritation at my folly in coming so far into futurity without weapons or equipment. I resolved to run on for one glimpse of the still remoter future—one peep into the deeper abysm of time—and then to return to you and my own epoch. Once more I remounted the machine, and once more the world grew hazy and grey.

"As I drove on, a peculiar change crept over the appearance of things. The unwonted greyness grew lighter; then—though I was travelling with prodigious velocity—the blinking succession of day and night, which was usually indicative of a slower pace, returned, and grew more and more marked. This puzzled me very much at first. The alternations of night and day grew slower and slower, and so did the passage of the sun across the sky, until they seemed to stretch through centuries. At last a steady twilight brooded over the earth, a twilight only broken now and then when a comet glared across the darkling sky. The band of light that had indicated the sun had long since disappeared; for the sun had ceased to set—it simply rose and fell in the west, and grew ever broader and more red. All trace of the moon had vanished. The circling of the stars, growing slower and slower, had given place to creeping points of light. At last, some time before I stopped, the sun, red and very large, halted motionless upon the horizon, a vast dome glowing with a dull heat, and now and then suffering a momentary extinction. At one time it had for a little while glowed more brilliantly again, but it speedily reverted to its sullen red-heat. I perceived by this slowing down of its rising and setting that the work of the tidal drag was done. The earth had come to rest with one face to the sun, even as in our own time the moon faces the earth.

"I stopped very gently and sat upon the Time Machine, looking round."

The Chronic Argonauts

Chapter 1

Being the Account of Dr. Nebogipfel's Sojourn in Llyddwdd

ABOUT half-a-mile outside the village of Llyddwdd by the road that goes up over the eastern flank of the mountain called Pen-y-pwll to Rwstog is a large farm-building known as the Manse. It derives this title from the fact that it was at one time the residence of the minister of the Calvinistic Methodists. It is a quaint, low, irregular erection, lying back some hundred yards from the railway, and now fast passing into a ruinous state.

Since its construction in the latter half of the last century this house has undergone many changes of fortune, having been abandoned long since by the farmer of the surrounding acres for less pretentious and more commodious headquarters. Among others Miss Carnot, "the Gallic Sappho" at one time made it her home, and later on an old man named Williams became its occupier. The foul murder of this tenant by his two sons was the cause of its remaining for some considerable period uninhabited; with the inevitable consequence of its undergoing very extensive dilapidation.

The house had got a bad name, and adolescent man and Nature combined to bring swift desolation upon it. The fear of the Williamses which kept the Llyddwdd lads from gratifying their propensity to invade its deserted interior, manifested itself in unusually destructive resentment against its external breakables. The missiles with which they at once confessed and defied their spiritual dread, left scarcely a splinter of glass, and only battered relics of the old-fashioned leaden frames, in its narrow windows, while numberless shattered tiles about the house, and four or five black apertures yawning behind the naked rafters in the roof, also witnessed vividly to the energy of their rejection. Rain and wind thus had free way to enter the empty rooms and work their will there, old Time aiding and abetting. Alternately soaked and desiccated, the planks of flooring and wainscot warped apart strangely, split here and there, and tore themselves away in paroxysms of rheumatic pain from the rust devoured nails that had once held them firm. The plaster of walls and ceiling, growing green-black with a rain-fed crust of lowly life, parted slowly from the fermenting laths; and large fragments thereof falling down inexplicably in tranquil hours, with loud concussion and clatter, gave strength to the popular superstition that old Williams and his sons were fated to re-enact their fearful tragedy until the final judgment. White roses and daedal creepers, that Miss Carnot had first adorned the walls with, spread now luxuriantly over the lichen-filmed tiles of the roof, and in slender graceful sprays timidly invaded the ghostly cobweb-draped apartments. Fungi, sickly pale, began to displace and uplift the bricks in the cellar floor; while on the rotting wood everywhere they clustered, in all the glory of the purple and mottled crimson, yellow-brown and hepatite. Woodlice and ants, beetles and moths, winged and creeping things innumerable, found each day a more congenial home among the ruins; and after them in ever-increasing multitudes swarmed the blotchy toads. Swallows and martins built every year more thickly in the silent, airy, upper chambers. Bats and owls struggled for the crepuscular corners of the lower rooms. Thus, in the Spring of the year eighteen hundred and eighty-seven, was Nature taking over, gradually but certainly, the tenancy of the old Manse. "The house was falling into decay," as men who do not appreciate the application of human derelicts to other beings' use would say, "surely and swiftly." But it was destined nevertheless to shelter another human tenant before its final dissolution.

There was no intelligence of the advent of a new inhabitant in quiet Llyddwdd. He came without a solitary premonition out of the vast unknown into the sphere of minute village observation and gossip. He fell into the Llyddwdd world, as it were, like a thunderbolt falling in the daytime. Suddenly, out of nothingness, he was. Rumour, indeed, vaguely averred that he was seen to arrive by a certain train from London, and to walk straight without hesitation to the old Manse, giving neither explanatory word nor sign to mortal as to his purpose there: but then the same fertile source of information also hinted that he was first beheld skimming down the slopes of steep Pen-y-pwll with exceeding swiftness, riding, as it appeared to the intelligent observer, upon an instrument not unlike a sieve and that he entered the house by the chimney. Of these conflicting reports, the former was the first to be generally circulated, but the latter, in view of the bizarre presence and eccentric ways of the newest inhabitant, obtained wider credence. By whatever means he arrived, there can be no doubt that he was in, and in possession of the Manse, on the first of May; because on the morning of that day he was inspected by Mrs. Morgan ap Lloyd Jones, and subsequently by the numerous persons her report brought up the mountain slope, engaged in the curious occupation of nailing sheet-tin across the void window sockets of his new domicile—"blinding his house," as Mrs. Morgan ap Lloyd Jones not inaptly termed it.

He was a small-bodied, sallow faced little man, clad in a close-fitting garment of some stiff, dark material, which Mr. Parry Davies the Llyddwdd shoemaker, opined was leather. His aquiline nose, thin lips, high cheek-ridges, and pointed chin, were all small and mutually well proportioned; but the bones and muscles of his face were rendered excessively prominent and distinct by his extreme leanness. The same cause contributed to the sunken appearance of the large eager-looking grey eyes, that gazed forth from under his phenomenally wide and high forehead. It was this latter feature that most powerfully attracted the attention of an observer. It seemed to be great beyond all preconceived ratio to the rest of his countenance. Dimensions, corrugations, wrinkles, venation, were alike abnormally exaggerated. Below it his eyes glowed like lights in some cave at a cliff's foot. It so over-powered and suppressed the rest of his face as to give an unhuman appearance almost, to what would otherwise have been an unquestionably handsome profile. The lank black hair that hung unkempt before his eyes served to increase rather than conceal this effect, by adding to unnatural altitude a suggestion of hydrocephalic projection: and the idea of something ultra human was furthermore accentuated by the temporal arteries that pulsated visibly through his transparent yellow skin. No wonder, in view even of these things, that among the highly and over-poetical Cymric of Llyddwdd the sieve theory of arrival found considerable favour.

It was his bearing and actions, however, much more than his personality, that won over believers to the warlock notion of matters. In almost every circumstance of life the observant villagers soon found his ways were not only not their ways, but altogether inexplicable upon any theory of motives they could conceive. Thus, in a small matter at the beginning, when Arthur Price Williams, eminent and famous in every tavern in Caernarvonshire for his social gifts, endeavoured, in choicest Welsh and even choicer English, to inveigle the stranger into conversation over the sheet-tin performance, he failed utterly. Inquisitional supposition, straightforward enquiry, offer of assistance, suggestion of method, sarcasm, irony, abuse, and at last, gage of battle, though shouted with much effort from the road hedge, went unanswered and apparently unheard. Missile weapons, Arthur Price Williams found, were equally unavailing for the purpose of introduction, and the gathered crowd dispersed with unappeased curiosity and suspicion. Later in the day, the swarth apparition was seen striding down the mountain road towards the village, hatless, and with such swift width of step and set resolution of countenance, that Arthur Price Williams, beholding him from afar from the Pig and Whistle doorway was seized with dire consternation, and hid behind the Dutch oven in the kitchen till he was past. Wild panic also smote the school-house as the children were coming out, and drove them indoors like leaves before a gale. He was merely seeking the provision shop, however, and erupted thencefrom after a prolonged stay, loaded with a various armful of blue parcels, a loaf, herrings, pigs' trotters, salt pork, and a black bottle, with which he returned in the same swift projectile gait to the Manse. His way of shopping was to name, and to name simply, without solitary other word of explanation, civility or request, the article he required.

The shopkeeper's crude meteorological superstitions and inquisitive commonplaces, he seemed not to hear, and he might have been esteemed deaf if he had not evinced the promptest attention to the faintest relevant remark. Consequently it was speedily rumoured that he was determined to avoid all but the most necessary human intercourse. He lived altogether mysteriously, in the decaying manse, without mortal service or companionship, presumably sleeping on planks or litter, and either preparing his own food or eating it raw. This, coupled with the popular conception of the haunting patricides, did much to strengthen the popular supposition of some vast gulf between the newcomer and common humanity. The only thing that was inharmonious with this idea of severance from mankind was a constant flux of crates filled with grotesquely contorted glassware, cases of brazen and steel instruments, huge coils of wire, vast iron and fire-clay implements, of inconceivable purpose, jars and phials labelled in black and scarlet—POISON, huge packages of books, and gargantuan rolls of cartridge paper, which set in towards his Llyddwdd quarters from the outer world. The apparently hieroglyphic inscriptions on these various consignments revealed at the profound scrutiny of Pugh Jones that the style and title of the new inhabitant was Dr. Moses Nebogipfel, Ph.D., F.R.S., N.W.R., PAID: at which discovery much edification was felt, especially among the purely Welsh-speaking community. Further than this, these arrivals, by their evident unfitness for any allowable mortal use, and inferential diabolicalness, filled the neighbourhood with a vague horror and lively curiosity, which were greatly augmented by the extraordinary phenomena, and still more extraordinary accounts thereof, that followed their reception in the Manse.

The first of these was on Wednesday, the fifteenth of May, when the Calvinistic Methodists of Llyddwdd had their annual commemoration festival; on which occasion, in accordance with custom, dwellers in the surrounding parishes of Rwstog, Pen-y-garn, Caergyllwdd, Llanrdd, and even distant Llanrwst flocked into the village. Popular thanks to Providence were materialised in the usual way, by means of plum-bread and butter, mixed tea, terza, consecrated flirtations, kiss-in-the-ring, rough-and-tumble football, and vituperative political speechmaking. About half-past eight the fun began to tarnish, and the assembly to break up; and by nine numerous couples and occasional groups were wending their way in the darkling along the hilly Llyddwdd and Rwstog road. It was a calm warm night; one of those nights when lamps, gas and heavy sleep seem stupid ingratitude to the Creator. The zenith sky was an ineffable deep lucent blue, and the evening star hung golden in the liquid darkness of the west. In the north-north-west, a faint phosphorescence marked the sunken day. The moon was just rising, pallid and gibbous over the huge haze-dimmed shoulder of Pen-y-pwll. Against the wan eastern sky, from the vague outline of the mountain slope, the Manse stood out black, clear and solitary. The stillness of the twilight had hushed the myriad murmurs of the day. Only the sounds of footsteps and voices and laughter, that came fitfully rising and falling from the roadway, and an intermittent hammering in the darkened dwelling, broke the silence. Suddenly a strange whizzing, buzzing whirr filled the night air, and a bright flicker glanced across the dim path of the wayfarers. All eyes were turned in astonishment to the old Manse. The house no longer loomed a black featureless block but was filled to overflowing with light. From the gaping holes in the roof, from chinks and fissures amid tiles and brickwork, from every gap which Nature or man had pierced in the crumbling old shell, a blinding blue-white glare was streaming, beside which the rising moon seemed a disc of opaque sulphur. The thin mist of the dewy night had caught the violet glow and hung, unearthly smoke, over the colourless blaze. A strange turmoil and outcrying in the old Manse now began, and grew ever more audible to the clustering spectators, and therewith came clanging loud impacts against the window-guarding tin. Then from the gleaming roof-gaps of the house suddenly vomited forth a wonderous swarm of heteromerous living things—swallows, sparrows, martins, owls, bats, insects in visible multitudes, to hang for many minutes a noisy, gyring, spreading cloud over the black gables and chimneys... and then slowly to thin out and vanish away in the night.

As this tumult died away the throbbing humming that had first arrested attention grew once more in the listener's hearing, until at last it was the only sound in the long stillness. Presently, however, the road gradually awoke again to the beating and shuffling of feet, as the knots of Rwstog people, one by one, turned their blinking eyes from the dazzling whiteness and, pondering deeply, continued their homeward way.

The cultivated reader will have already discerned that this phenomenon, which sowed a whole crop of uncanny thoughts in the minds of these worthy folk, was simply the installation of the electric light in the Manse. Truly, this last vicissitude of the old house was its strangest one. Its revival to mortal life was like the raising of Lazarus. From that hour forth, by night and day, behind the tin-blinded windows, the tamed lightning illuminated every corner of its quickly changing interior. The almost frenzied energy of the lank-haired, leather-clad little doctor swept away into obscure holes and corners and common destruction, creeper sprays, toadstools, rose leaves, birds' nests, birds' eggs, cobwebs, and all the coatings and lovingly fanciful trimmings with which that maternal old dotard, Dame Nature, had tricked out the decaying house for its lying in state. The magneto-electric apparatus whirred incessantly amid the vestiges of the wainscoted dining-room, where once the eighteenth-century tenant had piously read morning prayer and eaten his Sunday dinner; and in the place of his sacred symbolical sideboard was a nasty heap of coke. The oven of the bakehouse supplied substratum and material for a forge, whose snorting, panting bellows, and intermittent, ruddy spark-laden blast made the benighted, but Bible-lit Welsh women murmur in liquid Cymric, as they hurried by: "Whose breath kindleth coals, and out of his mouth is a flame of fire." For the idea these good people formed of it was that a tame, but occasionally restive, leviathan had been added to the terrors of the haunted house. The constantly increasing accumulation of pieces of machinery, big brass castings, block tin, casks, crates, and packages of innumerable articles, by their demands for space, necessitated the sacrifice of most of the slighter partitions of the house, and the beams and flooring of the upper chambers were also mercilessly sawn away by the tireless scientist in such a way as to convert them into mere shelves and corner brackets of the atrial space between cellars and rafters. Some of the sounder planking was utilised in the making of a rude broad table, upon which files and heaps of geometrical diagrams speedily accumulated. The production of these latter seemed to be the object upon which the mind of Dr. Nebogipfel was so inflexibly set. All other circumstances of his life were made entirely subsidiary to this one occupation. Strangely complicated traceries of lines they were—plans, elevations, sections by surfaces and solids, that, with the help of logarithmic mechanical apparatus and involved curvigraphical machines, spread swiftly under his expert hands over yard after yard of paper. Some of these symbolised shapes he despatched to London, and they presently returned, realised, in forms of brass and ivory, and nickel and mahogany. Some of them he himself translated into solid models of metal and wood; occasionally casting the metallic ones in moulds of sand, but often laboriously hewing them out of the block for greater precision of dimension. In this second process, among other appliances, he employed a steel circular saw set with diamond powder and made to rotate with extraordinary swiftness, by means of steam and multiplying gear. It was this latter thing, more than all else, that filled Llyddwdd with a sickly loathing of the Doctor as a man of blood and darkness. Often in the silence of midnight—for the newest inhabitant heeded the sun but little in his incessant research—the awakened dwellers around Pen-ypwll would hear, what was at first a complaining murmur, like the groaning of a wounded man, "gurr-urrurr-URR," rising by slow gradations in pitch and intensity to the likeness of a voice in despairing passionate protest, and at last ending abruptly in a sharp piercing shriek that rang in the ears for hours afterwards and begot numberless gruesome dreams.

The mystery of all these unearthly noises and inexplicable phenomena, the Doctor's inhumanly brusque bearing and evident uneasiness when away from his absorbing occupation, his entire and jealous seclusion, and his terrifying behaviour to certain officious intruders, roused popular resentment and curiously to the highest, and a plot was already on foot to make some sort of popular inquisition (probably accompanied by an experimental ducking) into his proceedings, when the sudden death of the hunchback Hughes in a fit, brought matters to an unexpected crisis. It happened in broad daylight, in the roadway just opposite the Manse. Half a dozen people witnessed it. The unfortunate creature was seen to fall suddenly and roll about on the pathway, struggling violently, as it appeared to the spectators, with some invisible assailant. When assistance reached him he was purple in the face and his blue lips were covered with a glairy foam. He died almost as soon as they laid hands on him.

Owen Thomas, the general practitioner, vainly assured the excited crowd which speedily gathered outside the Pig and Whistle, whither the body had been carried, that death was unquestionably natural. A horrible zymotic suspicion had gone forth that the deceased was the victim of Dr. Nebogipfel's imputed aerial powers. The contagion was with the news that passed like a flash through the village and set all Llyddwdd seething with a fierce desire for action against the worker of this iniquity. Downright superstition, which had previously walked somewhat modestly about the village, in the fear of ridicule and the Doctor, now appeared boldly before the sight of all men, clad in the terrible majesty of truth. People who had hitherto kept entire silence as to their fears of the imp-like philosopher suddenly discovered a fearsome pleasure in whispering dread possibilities to kindred souls, and from whispers of possibilities their sympathy-fostered utterances soon developed into unhesitating asserverations in laud and even high-pitched tones. The fancy of a captive leviathan, already alluded to, which had up to now been the horrid but secret joy of a certain conclave of ignorant old women, was published to all the world as indisputable fact; it being stated, on her own authority, that the animal had, on one occasion, chased Mrs. Morgan ap Lloyd Jones almost into Rwstog. The story that Nebogipfel had been heard within the Manse chanting, in conjunction with the Williamses, horrible blasphemy, and that a "black flapping thing, of the size of a young calf," had thereupon entered the gap in the roof, was universally believed in. A grisly anecdote, that owed its origination to a stumble in the churchyard, was circulated, to the effect that the Doctor had been caught ghoulishly tearing with his long white fingers at a new-made grave. The numerously attested declaration that Nebogipfel and the murdered Williams had been seen hanging the sons on a ghostly gibbet, at the back of the house, was due to the electric illumination of a fitfully wind-shaken tree. A hundred like stories hurtled thickly about the village and darkened the moral atmosphere. The Reverend Elijah Ulysses Cook, hearing of the tumult, sallied forth to allay it, and narrowly escaped drawing on himself the gathering lightning.

By eight o'clock (it was Monday the twenty-second of July) a grand demonstration had organised itself against the "necromancer." A number of bolder hearts among the men formed the nucleus of the gathering, and at nightfall Arthur Price Williams, John Peters, and others brought torches and raised their spark-raining flames aloft with curt ominous suggestions. The less adventurous village manhood came straggling late to the rendezvous, and with them the married women came in groups of four or five, greatly increasing the excitement of the assembly with their shrill hysterical talk and active imaginations. After these the children and young girls, overcome by undefinable dread, crept quietly out of the too silent and shadowy houses into the yellow glare of the pine knots, and the tumultuary noise of the thickening people. By nine, nearly half the Llyddwdd population was massed before the Pig and Whistle. There was a confused murmur of many tongues, but above all the stir and chatter of the growing crowd could be heard the coarse, cracked voice of the blood-thirsty old fanatic, Pritchard, drawing a congenial lesson from the fate of the four hundred and fifty idolators of Carmel.

Just as the church clock was beating out the hour, an occultly originated movement up hill began, and soon the whole assembly, men, women, and children, was moving in a fear-compacted mass, towards the ill-fated doctor's abode. As they left the brightly-lit public house behind them, a quavering female voice began singing one of those grim-sounding canticles that so satisfy the Calvinistic ear. In a wonderfully short time, the tune had been caught up, first by two or three, and then by the whole procession, and the manifold shuffling of heavy shoon grew swiftly into rhythm with the beats of the hymn. When, however, their goal rose, like a blazing star, over the undulation of the road, the volume of the chanting suddenly died away, leaving only the voices of the ringleaders, shouting indeed now somewhat out of tune, but, if anything, more vigorously than before. Their persistence and example nevertheless failed to prevent a perceptible breaking and slackening of the pace, as the Manse was neared, and when the gate was reached, the whole crowd came to a dead halt. Vague fear for the future had begotten the courage that had brought the villagers thus far: fear for the present now smothered its kindred birth. The intense blaze from the gaps in the death-like silent pile lit up rows of livid, hesitating faces: and a smothered, frightened sobbing broke out among the children. "Well," said Arthur Price Williams, addressing Jack Peters, with an expert assumption of the modest discipleship, "what do we do now, Jack?" But Peters was regarding the Manse with manifest dubiety, and ignored the question. The Llyddwdd witch-find seemed to be suddenly aborting.

At this juncture old Pritchard suddenly pushed his way forward, gesticulating weirdly with his bony hands and long arms. "What!" he shouted, in broken notes, "fear ye to smite when the Lord hateth? Burn the warlock!" And seizing a flambeau from Peters, he flung open the rickety gate and strode on down the drive, his torch leaving a coiling trail of scintillant sparks on the night wind. "Burn the warlock," screamed a shrill voice from the wavering crowd, and in a moment the gregarious human instinct had prevailed. With an outburst of incoherent, threatening voice, the mob poured after the fanatic.

Woe betide the Philosopher now! They expected barricaded doors; but with a groan of a conscious insufficiency, the hinge-rusted portals swung at the push of Pritchard. Blinded by the light, he hesitated for a second on the threshold, while his followers came crowding up behind him.

Those who were there say that they saw Dr. Nebogipfel, standing in the toneless electric glare, on a peculiar erection of brass and ebony and ivory; and that he seemed to be smiling at them, half pityingly and half scornfully, as it is said martyrs are wont to smile. Some assert, moreover, that by his side was sitting a tall man, clad in ravenswing, and some even aver that this second man—whom others deny—bore on his face the likeness of the Reverend Elijah Ulysses Cook, while others declare that he resembled the description of the murdered Williams. Be that as it may, it must now go unproven for ever, for suddenly a wonderous thing smote the crowd as it swarmed in through the entrance. Pritchard pitched headlong on the floor senseless. While shouts and shrieks of anger, changed in mid utterance to yells of agonising fear, or to the mute gasp of heart-stopping horror: and then a frantic rush was made for the doorway.

For the calm, smiling doctor, and his quiet, black-clad companion, and the polished platform which upbore them, had vanished before their eyes!

Chapter 2

How an Esoteric Story Became Possible

A SILVERY-foliaged willow by the side of a mere. Out of the cress-spangled waters below, rise clumps of sedge-blades, and among them glows the purple fleur-de-lys, and sapphire vapour of forget-me-nots. Beyond is a sluggish stream of water reflecting the intense blue of the moist Fenland sky; and beyond that a low osier-fringed eyot. This limits all the visible universe, save some scattered pollards and spear-like poplars showing against the violet distance. At the foot of the willow reclines the Author watching a copper butterfly fluttering from iris to iris.

Who can fix the colours of the sunset? Who can take a cast of flame? Let him essay to register the mutations of mortal thought as it wanders from a copper butterfly to the disembodied soul, and thence passes to spiritual motions and the vanishing of Dr. Moses Nebogipfel and the Rev. Elijah Ulysses Cook from the world of sense.

As the author lay basking there and speculating, as another once did under the Budh tree, on mystic transmutations, a presence became apparent. There was a somewhat on the eyot between him and the purple horizon—an opaque reflecting entity, making itself dimly perceptible by reflection in the water to his averted eyes. He raised them in curious surprise.

What was it?

He stared in stupefied astonishment at the apparition, doubted, blinked, rubbed his eyes, stared again, and believed. It was solid, it cast a shadow, and it upbore two men. There was white metal in it that blazed in the noontide sun like incandescent magnesium, ebony bars that drank in the light, and white parts that gleamed like polished ivory. Yet withal it seemed unreal. The thing was not square as a machine ought to be, but all awry: it was twisted and seemed falling over, hanging in two directions, as those queer crystals called triclinic hang; it seemed like a machine that had been crushed or warped; it was suggestive and not confirmatory, like the machine of a disordered dream. The men, too, were dreamlike. One was short, intensely sallow, with a strangely-shaped head, and clad in a garment of dark olive green, the other was, grotesquely out of place, evidently a clergyman of the Established

Church, a fair-haired, pale-faced respectable-looking man.

Once more doubt came rushing in on the author. He sprawled back and stared at the sky, rubbed his eyes, stared at the willow wands that hung between him and the blue, closely examined his hands to see if his eyes had any new things to relate about them, and then sat up again and stared at the eyot. A gentle breeze stirred the osiers; a white bird was flapping its way through the lower sky. The machine of the vision had vanished! It was an illusion—a projection of the subjective—an assertion of the immateriality of mind. "Yes," interpolated the sceptic faculty, "but how comes it that the clergyman is still there?"

The clergyman had not vanished. In intense perplexity the author examined this black-coated phenomenon as he stood regarding the world with hand-shaded eyes. The author knew the periphery of that eyot by heart, and the question that troubled him was, "Whence?" The clergyman looked as Frenchmen look when they land at Newhaven—intensely travel-worn; his clothes showed rubbed and seamy in the bright day. When he came to the edge of the island and shouted a question to the author, his voice was broken and trembled. "Yes," answered the author, "it is an island. How did you get there?"

But the clergyman, instead of replying to this asked a very strange question.

He said "Are you in the nineteenth century?" The author made him repeat that question before he replied. "Thank heaven," cried the clergyman rapturously. Then he asked very eagerly for the exact date.

"August the ninth, eighteen hundred and eighty-seven," he repeated after the author. "Heaven be praised!" and sinking down on the eyot so that the sedges hid him, he audibly burst into tears.

Now the author was mightily surprised at all this, and going a certain distance along the mere, he obtained a punt, and getting into it he hastily poled to the eyot where he had last seen the clergyman. He found him lying insensible among the reeds, and carried him in his punt to the house where he lived, and the clergyman lay there insensible for ten days.

Meanwhile, it became known that he was the Rev. Elijah Cook, who had disappeared from Llyddwdd with Dr. Moses Nebogipfel three weeks before.

On August 19th, the nurse called the author out of his study to speak to the invalid. He found him perfectly sensible, but his eyes were strangely bright, and his face was deadly pale. "Have you found out who

I am?" he asked.

"You are the Rev. Elijah Ulysses Cook, Master of Arts, of Pembroke College, Oxford, and Rector of Llyddwdd, near Rwstog, in Caernarvon."

He bowed his head. "Have you been told anything of how I came here?"

"I found you among the reeds," I said.

He was silent and thoughtful for a while. "I have a deposition to make. Will you take it? It concerns the murder of an old man named Williams, which occurred in 1862, this disappearance of Dr. Moses Nebogipfel, the abduction of a ward in the year 4003 — "

The author stared.

"The year of our Lord 4003," he corrected. "She would come. Also several assaults on public officials in the years 17,901 and 2."

The author coughed.

"The years 17,901 and 2, and valuable medical, social, and physiographical data for all time."

After a consultation with the doctor, it was decided to have the deposition taken down, and this is which constitutes the remainder of the story of the Chronic Argonauts.

On August 28th, 1887, the Rev Elijah Cook died. His body was conveyed to Llyddwdd, and buried in the churchyard there.

Chapter 3

The Anachronic Man

INCIDENTALLY it has been remarked in the first part, how the Reverend Elijah Ulysses Cook attempted and failed to quiet the superstitious excitement of the villagers on the afternoon of the memorable twenty-second of July. His next proceeding was to try and warn the unsocial philosopher of the dangers which impended. With this intent he made his way from the rumour-pelted village, through the silent, slumbrous heat of the July afternoon, up the slopes of Pen-y-pwll, to the old Manse. His loud knocking at the heavy door called forth dull resonance from the interior, and produced a shower of lumps of plaster and fragments of decaying touchwood from the rickety porch, but beyond this the dreamy stillness of the summer mid-day remained unbroken. Everything was so quiet as he stood there expectant, that the occasional speech of the haymakers a mile away in the fields, over towards Rwstog, could be distinctly heard. The reverend gentleman waited, then knocked again, and waited again, and listened, until the echoes and the patter of rubbish had melted away into the deep silence, and the creeping in the blood-vessels of his ears had become oppressively audible, swelling and sinking with sounds like the confused murmuring of a distant crowd, and causing a suggestion of anxious discomfort to spread slowly over his mind.

Again he knocked, this time loud, quick blows with his stick, and almost immediately afterwards, leaning his hand against the door, he kicked the panels vigorously. There was a shouting of echoes, a protesting jarring of hinges, and then the oaken door yawned and displayed, in the blue blaze of the electric light, vestiges of partitions, piles of planking and straw, masses of metal, heaps of papers and overthrown apparatus, to the rector's astonished eyes. "Doctor Nebogipfel, excuse my intruding," he called out, but the only response was a reverberation among the black beams and shadows that hung dimly above. For almost a minute he stood there, leaning forward over the threshold, staring at the glittering mechanisms, diagrams, books, scattered indiscriminately with broken food, packing cases, heaps of coke, hay, and microcosmic lumber, about the undivided house cavity; and then, removing his hat and treading stealthily, as if the silence were a sacred thing, he stepped into the apparently deserted shelter of the Doctor.

His eyes sought everywhere, as he cautiously made his way through the confusion, with a strange anticipation of finding Nebogipfel hidden somewhere in the sharp black shadows among the litter, so strong in him was an indescribable sense of perceiving presence. This feeling was so vivid that, when, after an abortive exploration, he seated himself upon Nebogipfel's diagram-covered bench, it made him explain in a forced hoarse voice to the stillness—"He is not here. I have something to say to him. I must wait for him." It was so vivid, too, that the trickling of some grit down the wall in the vacant corner behind him made him start round in a sudden perspiration. There was nothing visible there, but turning his head back, he was stricken rigid with horror by the swift, noiseless apparition of Nebogipfel, ghastly pale, and with red stained hands, crouching upon a strange-looking metallic platform, and with his deep grey eyes looking intently into the visitor's face.

Cook's first impulse was to yell out his fear, but his throat was paralysed, and he could only stare fascinated at the bizarre countenance that had thus clashed suddenly into visibility. The lips were quivering and the breath came in short convulsive sobs. The un-human forehead was wet with perspiration, while the veins were swollen, knotted and purple. The Doctor's red hands, too, he noticed, were trembling, as the hands of slight people tremble after intense muscular exertion, and his lips closed and opened as if he, too, had a difficulty in speaking as he gasped, "Who—what do you do here?" Cook answered not a word, but stared with hair erect, open mouth, and dilated eyes, at the dark red unmistakeable smear that streaked the pure ivory and gleaming nickel and shining ebony of the platform.

"What are you doing here?" repeated the doctor, raising himself. "What do you want?"

Cook gave a convulsive effort. "In Heaven's name, what are you?" he gasped; and then black curtains came closing in from every side, sweeping the squatting dwarfish phantasm that reeled before him into rayless, voiceless night.

The Reverend Elijah Ulysses Cook recovered his perceptions to find himself lying on the floor of the old Manse, and Doctor Nebogipfel, no longer blood-stained and with all trace of his agitation gone, kneeling by his side and bending over him with a glass of brandy in his hand. "Do not be alarmed, sir," said the philosopher with a faint smile, as the clergyman opened his eyes. "I have not treated you to a disembodied spirit, or anything nearly so extraordinary… may I offer you this?"

The clergyman submitted quietly to the brandy, and then stared perplexed into Nebogipfel's face, vainly searching his memory for what occurrences had preceded his insensibility. Raising himself at last, into a sitting posture, he saw the oblique mass of metals that had appeared with the doctor, and immediately all that happened flashed back upon his mind. He looked from this structure to the recluse, and from the recluse to the structure.

"There is absolutely no deception, sir," said Nebogipfel with the slightest trace of mockery in his voice. "I lay no claim to work in matters spiritual. It is a bona fide mechanical contrivance, a thing emphatically of this sordid world. Excuse me—just one minute." He rose from his knees, stepped upon the mahogany platform, took a curiously curved lever in his hand and pulled it over. Cook rubbed his eyes. There certainly was no deception. The doctor and the machine had vanished.

The reverend gentleman felt no horror this time, only a slight nervous shock, to see the doctor presently re-appear "in the twinkling of an eye" and get down from the machine. From that he walked in a straight line with his hands behind his back and his face downcast, until his progress was stopped by the intervention of a circular saw; then, turning round sharply on his heel, he said:

"I was thinking while I was … away … Would you like to come? I should greatly value a companion."

The clergyman was still sitting, hatless, on the floor. "I am afraid," he said slowly, "you will think me stupid — "

"Not at all," interrupted the doctor. "The stupidity is mine. You desire to have all this explained … wish to know where I am going first. I have spoken so little with men of this age for the last ten years or more that I have ceased to make due allowances and concessions for other minds. I will do my best, but that I fear will be very unsatisfactory. It is a long story … do you find that floor comfortable to sit on? If not, there is a nice packing case over there, or some straw behind you, or this bench—the diagrams are done with now, but I am afraid of the drawing pins. You may sit on the Chronic Argo!"

"No, thank you," slowly replied the clergyman, eyeing that deformed structure thus indicated, suspiciously; "I am quite comfortable here."

"Then I will begin. Do you read fables? Modern ones?"

"I am afraid I must confess to a good deal of fiction," said the clergyman deprecatingly. "In Wales the ordained ministers of the sacraments of the Church have perhaps too large a share of leisure — "

"Have you read the Ugly Duckling?"

"Hans Christian Andersen's—yes—in my childhood."

"A wonderful story—a story that has ever been full of tears and heart swelling hopes for me, since first it came to me in my lonely boyhood and saved me from unspeakable things. That story, if you understand it well, will tell you almost all that you should know of me to comprehend how that machine came to be thought of in a mortal brain... Even when I read that simple narrative for the first time, a thousand bitter experiences had begun the teaching of my isolation among the people of my birth—I knew the story was for me. The ugly duckling that proved to be a swan, that lived through all contempt and bitterness, to float at last sublime. From that hour forth, I dreamt of meeting with my kind, dreamt of encountering that sympathy I knew was my profoundest need. Twenty years I lived in that hope, lived and worked, lived and wandered, loved even, and at last, despaired. Only once among all those millions of wondering, astonished, indifferent, contemptuous, and insidious faces that I met with in that passionate wandering, looked one upon me as I desired ... looked — "

He paused. The Reverend Cook glanced up into his face, expecting some indication of the deep feeling that had sounded in his last words. It was downcast, clouded, and thoughtful, but the mouth was rigidly firm.

"In short, Mr. Cook, I discovered that I was one of those superior Cagots called a genius—a man born out of my time—a man thinking the thoughts of a wiser age, doing things and believing things that men now cannot understand, and that in the years ordained to me there was nothing but silence and suffering for my soul—unbroken solitude, man's bitterest pain. I knew I was an Anachronic Man; my age was still to come. One filmy hope alone held me to life, a hope to which I clung until it had become a certain thing. Thirty years of unremitting toil and deepest thought among the hidden things of matter and form and life, and then that, the Chronic Argo, the ship that sails through time, and now I go to join my generation, to journey through the ages till my time has come."

Chapter 4

The Chronic Argo

DR. NEBOGIPFEL paused, looked in sudden doubt at the clergyman's perplexed face. "You think that sounds mad," he said, "to travel through time?"

"It certainly jars with accepted opinions," said the clergyman, allowing the faintest suggestion of controversy to appear in his intonation, and speaking apparently to the Chronic Argo. Even a clergyman of the Church of England you see can have a suspicion of illusions at times.

"It certainly does jar with accepted opinions," agreed the philosopher cordially. "It does more than that—it defies accepted opinions to mortal combat. Opinions of all sorts, Mr. Cook—Scientific Theories, Laws, Articles of Belief, or, to come to elements, Logical Premises, Ideas, or whatever you like to call them—all are, from the infinite nature of things, so many diagrammatic caricatures of the ineffable—caricatures altogether to be avoided save where they are necessary in the shaping of results—as chalk outlines are necessary to the painter and plans and sections to the engineer. Men, from the exigencies of their being, find this hard to believe."

The Rev. Elijah Ulysses Cook nodded his head with the quiet smile of one whose opponent has unwittingly given a point.

"It is as easy to come to regard ideas as complete reproductions of entities as it is to roll off a log. Hence it is that almost all civilised men believe in the reality of the Greek geometrical conceptions."

"Oh! pardon me, sir," interrupted Cook. "Most men know that a geometrical point has no existence in matter, and the same with a geometrical line. I think you underrate … "

"Yes, yes, those things are recognised," said Nebogipfel calmly; "but now … a cube. Does that exist in the material universe?"

"Certainly."

"An instantaneous cube?"

"I don't know what you intend by that expression."

"Without any other sort of extension; a body having length, breadth, and thickness, exists?"

"What other sort of extension can there be?" asked Cook, with raised eyebrows.

"Has it never occurred to you that no form can exist in the material universe that has no extension in time? … Has it never glimmered upon your consciousness that nothing stood between men and a geometry of four dimensions—length, breadth, thickness, and duration—but the inertia of opinion, the impulse from the Levantine philosophers of the bronze age?"

"Putting it that way," said the clergyman, "it does look as though there was a flaw somewhere in the notion of tridimensional being; but …" He became silent, leaving that sufficiently eloquent "but" to convey all the prejudice and distrust that filled his mind.

"When we take up this new light of a fourth dimension and reexamine our physical science in its illumination," continued Nebogipfel, after a pause, "we find ourselves no longer limited by hopeless restriction to a certain beat of time—to our own generation. Locomotion along lines of duration—chronic navigation comes within the range, first, of geometrical theory, and then of practical mechanics. There was a time when men could only move horizontally and in their appointed country. The clouds floated above them, unattainable things, mysterious chariots of those fearful gods who dwelt among the mountain summits. Speaking practically, men in those days were restricted to motion in two dimensions; and even there circumambient ocean and hypoborean fear bound him in. But those times were to pass away. First, the keel of Jason cut its way between the Symplegades, and then in the fulness of time, Columbus dropped anchor in a bay of Atlantis. Then man burst his bidimensional limits, and invaded the third dimension, soaring with Montgolfier into the clouds, and sinking with a diving bell into the purple treasure-caves of the waters. And now another step, and the hidden past and unknown future are before us. We stand upon a mountain summit with the plains of the ages spread below."

Nebogipfel paused and looked down at his hearer.

The Reverend Elijah Cook was sitting with an expression of strong distrust on his face. Preaching much had brought home certain truths to him very vividly, and he always suspected rhetoric. "Are those things figures of speech," he asked; "or am I to take them as precise statements? Do you speak of travelling through time in the same way as one might speak of Omnipotence making His pathway on the storm, or do you—ah—mean what you say?" Dr. Nebogipfel smiled quietly. "Come and look at these diagrams," he said, and then with elaborate simplicity he commenced to explain again to the clergyman the new quadridimensional geometry. Insensibly Cook's aversion passed away, and seeming impossibility grew possible, now that such tangible things as diagrams and models could be brought forward in evidence. Presently he found himself asking questions, and his interest grew deeper and deeper as Nebogipfel slowly and with precise clearness unfolded the beautiful order of his strange invention. The moments slipped away unchecked, as the Doctor passed on to the narrative of his research, and it was with a start of surprise that the clergyman noticed the deep blue of the dying twilight through the open doorway.

"The voyage," said Nebogipfel concluding his history, "will be full of undreamt-of dangers—already in one brief essay I have stood in the very jaws of death—but it is also full of the divines' promise of undreamt-of joy. Will you come? Will you walk among the people of the Golden Years? … "

But the mention of death by the philosopher had brought flooding back to the mind of Cook, all the horrible sensations of that first apparition.

"Dr. Nebogipfel … one question?" He hesitated. "On your hands … Was it blood?"

Nebogipfel's countenance fell. He spoke slowly.

"When I had stopped my machine, I found myself in this room as it used to be. Hark!"

"It is the wind in the trees towards Rwstog."

"It sounded like the voices of a multitude of people singing … when I had stopped I found myself in this room as it used to be. An old man, a young man, and a lad were sitting at a table—reading some book together. I stood behind them unsuspected. 'Evil spirits assailed him,' read the old man; 'but it is written, "to him that overcometh shall be given life eternal." They came as entreating friends, but he endured through all their snares. They came as principalities and powers, but he defied them in the name of the King of Kings. Once even it is told that in his study, while he was translating the New Testament into German, the Evil One himself appeared before him… ' Just then the lad glanced timorously round, and with a fearful wail fainted away …

"The others sprang at me… It was a fearful grapple… The old man clung to my throat, screaming 'Man or Devil, I defy thee … '

"I could not help it. We rolled together on the floor … the knife his trembling son had dropped came to my hand … Hark!"

He paused and listened, but Cook remained staring at him in the same horror-stricken attitude he had assumed when the memory of the bloodstained hands had rushed back over his mind.

"Do you hear what they are crying? Hark!"

Burn the warlock! Burn the murderer!

"Do you hear? There is no time to be lost."

Slay the murderer of cripples. Kill the devil's claw!

"Come! Come!"

Cook, with a convulsive effort, made a gesture of repugnance and strode to the doorway. A crowd of black figures roaring towards him in the red torchlight made him recoil. He shut the door and faced Nebogipfel.

The thin lips of the Doctor curled with a contemptuous sneer. "They will kill you if you stay," he said; and seizing his unresisting visitor by the wrist, he forced him towards the glittering machine. Cook sat down and covered his face with his hands.

In another moment the door was flung open, and old Pritchard stood blinking on the threshold.

A pause. A hoarse shout changing suddenly into a sharp shrill shriek.

A thunderous roar like the bursting forth of a great fountain of water.

The voyage of the Chronic Argonauts had begun.

12:01 P.M.

12:01 P.M.

THERE was the echo of that single, loud sound resembling the crashing implosion of air into a shattered vacuum tube or the report of a small-caliber firearm. The clock on the Grand Central Tower said 12:01, as it always did at resumption time, and Castleman knew that the dateline on the newspapers being hawked at the corner of Lexington and 46th would be the same that it always was.

He waited for the familiar grime-crusted, green-and-silver bus to make its turn onto short Vanderbilt Avenue, dodged the usual yellow taxi while crossing Vanderbilt himself, and passed between the two Cadillac limousines waiting at the curb for their passengers to return from whatever errand detained them.

On the west side of Madison he stopped in front of Finchley's and waited for the middle-aged window dresser to set up the full-length mirror at the back of the display, as he did every time, and perfunctorily inspected himself in its shiny surface. Same tweed suit, striped button-down shirt and modishly broad tie, same haircomb with one stubborn lock sticking out above his left ear. He put a hand to his chin and rubbed vigorously, but there was no particular evidence of stubble.

Not that he could have grown much stubble in an hour, but if the effect of the hours was cumulative for him, it should become apparent after a dozen or two resumptions.

Strolling casually toward the West Side, he decided to stop at the first convenient restaurant and get himself a snack. The sky was blue and unusually clear for midtown, the air warm and slightly moist with the moisture of a balmy spring day rather than the sticky humidity that used to come later in the year. A good thing, Castleman thought, that the resumptions had come on such an afternoon rather than in the middle of a midwinter cold snap with the streets full of dirty slush and everyone sneezing and coughing flu bugs at one another.

He stepped into Hamburger Heaven and surveyed the situation vis-a-vis seating. There were no vacancies but only a handful of people waited ahead of him. No point in waiting in a long line or trying to dine in a fancy restaurant where a fancy lunch could take two hours to consume. If he couldn't get served and finish his meal by one o'clock, it was a waste.

Which is not to say that it wasn't one anyhow. At the next resumption he'd be back on the sidewalk gazing up at the Grand Central Tower anyway; he'd have a pleasant appetite anyway; if he took off his tie and flushed it down the toilet in the basement washroom of Hamburger Heaven, he'd find it back knotted around his neck, clean and dry. Or at least he was confident that he would; that might prove an interesting experiment to try sometime, but the result was pretty well a foregone conclusion.

The hostess had come over to the small group of customers waiting for seats and was holding up two fingers in a V sign. Castleman looked beside him and found, to his surprise, that he had reached the head of the line. He turned to the person beside him and asked if she would mind sharing a table.

"It'll save time," he said, stifling an urge to laugh at his own line.

The woman nodded agreement, and the hostess showed them to a tiny wooden table near the back of the restaurant. They contorted themselves onto the fixed wooden seats and received oversized ketchup-and coffee-stained menus. Castleman decided quickly what he wanted and lowered his menu, letting his eyes take in his impromptu companion.

She was obviously a working girl—or woman, more accurately. Slightly overage and overweight for the blouse and modish-length skirt she affected, with her hair done up in an elaborately curled style that almost suited her oval face. She put her menu down, clearly having made her own choice of food, and looked at Castleman.

"Do you eat here often?" she said.

Castleman said, "Not very."

"I didn't think so. I come here every day. There are so many regulars, so many transients. As soon as I didn't recognize you, I knew who you were."

"Makes sense," Castleman said. He looked around the room for a wall clock, wishing that he'd had a watch at resumption time, knowing that he could get one easily enough now but that it would be gone at the end of the hour anyway.

There was a clock at the back of Hamburger Heaven. It was nearing half past. Castleman wished that the resumptions came further apart, really an hour wasn't long enough to do much. But then, he thought philosophically, it could be a lot worse. Hung up at a period of five minutes, he'd never get *anything* done. And if it were *really* short—say, a second or less—it would be a living hell.

You could get a fair amount done in an hour. In fact, in some ways, it was an ideal situation to be in. Anything you do, you can mess up, anything, and get another chance in an hour. On the other hand it wasn't so ideal to do something worthwhile knowing that it would be totally wiped out, but then the positive and negative aspects of reality often balanced that way.

He looked at the plump woman sitting opposite him at the little wooden table. "Say, my name is Myron Castleman," Castleman said. "I work for Glamdring and Glamdring up in the Stoebler Building on Forty-ninth."

The plump woman looked at him, surprised at the breach of Manhattan anonymity. Then she seemed to decide that he was all right, that she could give him information without his using it in some unspecified way to take advantage of her. "Dolores Park," she said. "I'm a legal secretary. Sometimes I have lunch with friends, but I came out alone today."

A waiter arrived and they ordered. Castleman nodded in self-confirmation when Dolores asked for French fries with her Roquefort-baconburger. He also noted that she wore no ring on her left hand, not that that meant much nowadays.

"Do you live in the city, ah, Miss Park?" he asked her.

She shook her head. The flesh on her cheeks and neck, although excessive, was still firm. It did not wobble as she moved. "No, I come in on the Long Island. I live in Roslyn." She paused as if surveying Castleman closely. "With my mother."

Castleman said, "Oh."

"And you?" Dolores Park asked.

"Oh," Castleman said again, "yes, I live up in the Seventies, East Seventy-third." He looked at the clock again. This was getting him nowhere, and his stomach was beginning to gnaw at him. It was already twenty minutes to one.

Dolores Park said, "What do you do for Glamdring and Glamdring, Mr. Castleberg?"

"Man," said Myron.

"Man? I don't understand."

"Castleman. Not Castleberg."

"Oh, I'm sorry," Dolores said. She seemed to wilt.

"It's all right," Myron comforted her. "Don't think of it, names aren't important, you'll forget all about it in a few minutes anyhow.

"I'm a personnel manager. In charge of corporate recruiting and career development."

"Oh," said Dolores, "that sounds very exciting."

"A daily bacchanal," Myron said, "look, here comes our food."

The waiter dropped Myron's cheeseburger in the middle of the table, threw Dolores' lunch at her, and dropped a single check into the jar of piccalilli relish that festered in the middle of the table.

"Ooh," squealed Dolores, "that waiter was terrible! I ought to report him to the manager. I've never had such rude service in this place."

"Never mind," Myron told her. "Better eat your food quick or it'll be too late." He dumped a glob of ketchup onto his cheeseburger and took a large bite of it. He savored the mixture of flavors, the toasted bun, the spicy seasoning, the rare meat and hot, melted cheese. As he chewed he let his eyes rove the room.

A cake tray on the counter held a delicious-looking devil's food cake with dazzling white icing and mahogany-brown chocolate shavings scattered across the top. Maybe I should have ordered cake instead, Myron thought. Maybe I'll have the cake instead of the cheeseburger next time I come in here. Maybe on the next resumption, maybe not, but soon.

He swallowed his cheeseburger and smiled at Miss Park. She was chomping on a length of raw carrot. "Enjoying your food?" Myron asked.

She nodded yes.

"Good," Myron said. He began to hear the familiar crackling, splitting sound that preceded each resumption. "I'm glad you like it. Dolores, since you'll get to have it again. Good-by," he said.

Dolores looked at him, surprised and puzzled by his remark.

There was a single, loud sound resembling the sound made by the implosion of air into a shattered vacuum tube or the report of a small-caliber firearm. Castleman experienced a confusing instant during which he was never able to tell whether there was a flash of light or of darkness, a rush of sound or an instant of total silence, a full-capacity loading of all the senses of a total deprivation of sensation.

Then there was the echo of that single, loud sound. The clock on the Grand Central Tower said 12:01, as it always did at resumption time, and Castleman knew that the dateline on the newspapers being hawked at the corner of Lexington and 46th would be the same as it always was.

He checked his personal appearance briefly, using a plate-glass window in a House of Cards shop as an impromptu looking-glass; as he expected, it was the same as always. He licked the heel of his left hand to get a little moisture onto the skin, then used it to try and make that stubborn lock of hair lie down.

The day being as pleasant as it was, he decided that it would be pleasant to spend his hour strolling down to the library and relaxing on the steps in the warm sunshine.

He walked toward Fifth, planning to stroll down to 42nd Street that way. A little past Madison Avenue he stopped and looked in through the front window of a Hamburger Heaven. Inside, a short line of patrons waited for seating. He could see a familiar figure standing at the end of the line, a woman slightly overdressed and overweight, but still fairly smart looking. Hi there, Dolores, he thought to himself.

For a moment the notion of entering the restaurant and making conversation with her flitted through his mind, but he rejected it with hardly a moment's consideration and walked on toward Fifth. As far as Dolores Park was concerned, she'd never laid eyes on him in her life. She would be puzzled at the stranger's talking to her, calling her by name. It would only spoil her hour, and even though it would be wiped out at the next resumption, Castleman didn't have the heart to do that to an innocent stranger.

He reached Fifth Avenue and walked downtown toward the library. He went past the Israel Bank, stopped and examined the window display at Record Hunter, then waited for the lights to change and made his street crossings, to the downtown side of 42nd and then to the west side of Fifth.

He glanced at the newspapers on sale at the corner. There was the *Times* with its staid front page, the *News* with its screaming headline and a photo of a train wreck near New Brunswick, and the first edition of the *Post* with a blue banner proclaiming another chapter in the inside biography of Yosef Tekoah. The news stories of all three dealt with the prediction of Nathan Rosenbluth that a disfiguration of time would shortly take place, with the entire world snapping backwards for the period of an hour, to resume normal progress as if nothing had ever happened.

Castleman laughed bitterly at the front pages and their different approaches to the story, then ambled down the broad sidewalk, stopped in front of the giant neo-Grecian library and began to ascend the long flight of steps toward its portico.

Near the top of the stairs a small group of young people were seated, talking. An intense young man was holding forth, his eyes glaring through tiny, wire-rimmed glasses as he waved his arms with each sentence.

Castleman stopped a couple of steps below the group and listened.

"Rosenbluth is absolutely right," the young man was saying. "The world has come to a state of affairs where things cannot go on any longer. We have to repair the social order to get things going again, or we'll soon be stopped at one place; we'll have to go back. The administration in Washington...."

He got no further, cut off by another young man, a round-faced individual sitting patiently with a spiral notepad and pencil in his lap. "You don't understand, Oswald," he interrupted the intense man with the beard. "Rosenbluth isn't talking about the social order at all. He's a physicist, and he's talking about purely physical phenomena."

"Besides," put in a slim, short-haired girl with faded jeans and a moderate case of acne, "LIU, I mean, a physicist from LIU. If he was from Columbia or even City College...."

"With imperialist forces threatening all people's progressive movements on every continent," the first speaker resumed, "how can you waste your energy quarreling about physics? Radical and revolutionary elements in every stratum of society...."

The round-faced man said, "If you'll just stop emoting and listen for a minute, I have the figures right here." There was a brief silence as he brandished his notebook. Castleman saw that the page was indeed covered with finely penciled mathematical calculations.

"From LIU," the girl in jeans said.

"Look," the round-faced man said, "Rosenbluth claims that the total energy content of the universe we live in is mirrored by a counteruniverse made of antimatter, coexisting with our universe in terms of three-dimensional space but separated from us by a fourth dimension or vibrational plane."

"Betrayal of laboring masses by yellow-dog sellout trade union bosses," put in the intense man.

"Yes, Oswald," the round-faced man continued. "Rosenbluth claims that by random but not acausal processes the two universes, moving in opposite temporal directions, attempt to emerge from their states and merge. If this should come about, they would cancel each other because of their opposite energy polarities, but the phenomenon of opposing time-vectors prevents this, and they will instead rebound from each other, each universe snapping backwards into its own past—that is, the other universe's *future*—and...."

"How far?"

"Hah?"

The girl in jeans said, "How far will it bounce?"

"Oh," said the round-faced man, "Rosenbluth claims an hour."

"Just like daylight-savings," said the girl. "We bounce back an hour then. Or do we go forward an hour?"

"Spring ahead in spring, fall back in fall," Castleman put in, inserting himself into the conversation.

"Yeah, thanks, mister," the girl said.

Castleman hunkered down on the step between the girl and the intense man with the beard, facing round-face. "You don't think Rosenbluth is right?" Castleman asked the mathematician.

"No, I don't. If Rosenbluth were right, what would happen after the bounce? We'd resume normal temporal processes and so would the counteruniverse. But since our bounce into our own past would put us in their future and their bounce would put them in our future, what would happen next?"

"What do you think?" Castleman asked.

The round-faced man studied the math on his lined papers before replying. Castleman used the time to lean over toward the girl with acne and examine the old watch pinned like a brooch to her blouse. It was very nearly one o'clock.

"Better think fast," Castleman told the round-faced man. He was already hearing the familiar crackling sound. It was hard to tell just what the sound reminded him of—a hard-boiled egg being peeled? Chinese sizzling-rice soup?

The round-faced man said, "If that happened, why, after the hour was up again the two universes...."

There was a single, loud sound resembling that made by the implosion of air into a shattered vacuum tube or the report of a small-caliber firearm.

Castleman looked up at the clock on the Grand Central Tower. It was 12:01.

Castleman sighed once, took a deep breath and started to walk briskly toward the West Side. Just before crossing Vanderbilt Avenue he stepped down from the curb, dodged a yellow taxi halfway across the street, and passed between two Cadillac limousines waiting at the curb.

He headed up Madison Avenue to 49th Street and entered the Stoebler Building, took the elevator up to Glamdring and Glamdring and pushed open the heavy glass doors that marked the entrance to the company's headquarter's suite.

"Back so soon, Mr. Castleman?" asked the receptionist as he strode past her desk.

"Decided to skip lunch today," Castleman told her.

"But it's so lovely out today, hardly any smog, and it's warm for early spring. I think I'd just take a walk even if I didn't have an appetite."

"Another time," Castleman said.

He walked down the corridor to his own department, went into his private office and sat down behind his desk. He looked at the digital clock beside his note box. It was 12:09 P.M.

He picked up the telephone, punched local and got his own secretary on the line. "Stephanie," Castleman said, "do me a favor. Would you get information, find out the number of Long Island University, and call a Professor Nathan Rosenbluth. I'm not sure what department he's in, probably physics or math."

Stephanie's voice came back briefly.

"Yes," Castleman said, sighing, "Rosenbluth the time-bounce man. Oh, he was on TV this morning? Fine. Yes, see if you can reach him. Yes, ring me back."

He hung up the telephone and reached for a copy of this morning's *Times* lying on a low table near the couch in his office. He reread the small story near the bottom of the front page, about the professor—ah, it was physics—who had predicted the odd time-bounce phenomenon. As far as Castleman could figure out—but his telephone rang.

"I have Professor Rosenbluth's secretary," Stephanie said. "But she claims he's swamped with calls and not taking any."

"Ahah," said Castleman, glancing at the digital clock on his desk. It was 12:17. "Look, Stephanie, I can understand how the guy feels but this is really urgent. Pull rank—tell his secretary that it's a big shot in Glamdring and Glamdring, pull out the stops. Yes, the works. Thanks." He hung up.

He threw down the *Times* and picked up the *Wall Street Journal*. There was a one-paragraph summary of the Rosenbluth story in the *Journal's* world news roundup column. It gave the same information that all the other versions gave. Castleman dropped the *Journal* in his wastebasket and looked at the clock again. It was 12:27. In thirty-three minutes he knew that he'd be outside near the Grand Central Tower again and that the *Journal* would be back on the coffee table along with the *Times* in his office. He pushed his chair back from the heavy desk provided by Glamdring and Glamdring, pushed himself out of his seat and strode around his office impatiently, glancing out the window toward the East River and the factory smokestacks of Long Island City beyond.

His phone rang and Stephanie's voice said, "Professor Rosenbluth on the line, Mrs. Castleman."

Castleman gripped the receiver tightly to his ear, looked at the digital clock again—it was 12:31—and heard his own voice say quiveringly, "Professor? Listen Professor Rosenbluth, about your theory of time snapping backwards...."

"Yes, yes," the voice came back from the receiver, "I know about that, it is my theory, everyone knows that, you do not have to tell me about it. What does Glamdring and Glamdring want of me? I am available on a consulting basis. They can hire me day by day. My rates are very reasonable."

"Professor, listen please. I happen to know that your theory is absolutely correct, but the bounce has already taken place."

"Nonsense, nonsense. Are you a mathematician? Are you a scientist? How can you claim to understand my theory? Have you read my papers? What is your name, young man?"

Castleman swallowed.

"Hah?" asked Professor Rosenbluth.

"My name is Myron Castleman."

"Of Glamdring and Glamdring? Yes? Yes? That's a very good firm. I am not prepared to resign my professorship as yet, but I am available on a consulting basis. What precisely do you require, Mr. Castleberry?"

"Professor, what I want to know is, once the bounce happens, when we get back up to the moment we, ah, bounced from, what happens then? Won't we just bounce again? Won't we get stuck at one point and just keep repeating that hour?"

"No no no, Castleberry. No, no. The energy of the temporal redisplacement will be dissipated, and we will pass through the point of intersection with the counteruniverse and no one will ever even notice it. That is the beauty of my theory. That is its greatness, its elegance. Do you understand scientific elegance? Economy of detail? Parsimony? How can you comprehend me?"

Castleman looked at his clock. It said 12:51. "Professor," he said desperately, "once the bounce takes place, everything is restored to its previous condition. The world is set back exactly where it was. Only nobody notices because their minds are set back too. Don't you see?"

"What are you trying to do, Castleberry, horn in on my theory? I don't think I can talk to you any more. You are trying to steal ideas. If you want my services, you have to hire me. I cannot afford to give away my thoughts. How can I support myself? How can I support my family, Castleberry?"

"Everybody bounces back and forgets everything that happened during the bounce, but I don't. I don't! Do you understand me, professor? The whole world is stuck here, recycling this single hour!"

He looked at his clock. 12:52.

"Professor Rosenbluth," he said. "in precisely eight minutes the world is going to flash one hour into the past. From one o'clock it's going to go back to one minute after noon. Everything will be restored to its condition at 12:01. You'll be back doing what you were doing. I'll be back outside my office, standing near Grand Central.

"Nobody will remember this hour. It will, uh, unhappen. But I remember! I've relied this one hour over and over!"

"Mr. Castleberry," the professor's voice came sharply, "I am a very busy man, but I will give you a few more minutes. Here is what you must do. Stay there on the telephone. When the time is up, I will still be here as well. That will disabuse you of your silly notion."

Defeated, Castleman said. "Very well." He looked at his clock, waiting for the digital neons to flash 1:00. They did. There was a familiar crackling sound followed by a single, loud report.

With the echo of that crack still in his ears, Castleman looked up at the Grand Central Tower clock. It said 12:01. He turned ninety degrees and sprinted west, bouncing off startled pedestrians and recklessly dodging cars and buses as he crossed the avenues.

At Madison he turned and continued uptown, his sprint slowing to a dogged trot as his breath came with increasing difficulty. At 49th Street he entered the Stoebler Building, mopped his sweating forehead with a soft handkerchief while he waited for the elevator to arrive, rode up to his office and snatched up the telephone after brushing past the receptionist and his secretary with breathless grunts.

"Stephanie," he gasped, "get me Rosenbluth back!"

"Back, Mr. Castleman? I don't understand."

"I was just talking to—him." Castleman stopped, held the receiver away from his ear and looked at it as if to discover some secret in the official Glamdring and Glamdring beige plastic piece. "No, of course not. I'm sorry, Stephanie." He looked at the digital clock on his desk. It said 12:06.

"Will that be all, Mr. Castleman?" Stephanie asked.

He thought for a few seconds. "I want you to call Long Island University, physics department, and get me a Professor Nathan Rosenbluth. This is extremely urgent, Stephanie. I'll stay on the line while place the call."

He dragged in a deep lungful of air while he waited. His eyes roamed to the low table where the morning *Times* and *Wall Street Journal* lay. In the telephone earpiece he heard Stephanie calling information, then placing the call to Rosenbluth's office, wheedling a line to the professor from his own secretary.

Then Rosenbluth's voice came over the line. "This is Rosenbluth. What is it? Who is calling from Glamdring and Glamdring? Don't you realize that I am a very busy man? What do you want?"

Castleman moaned. Well, give it a try anyway, he thought. "Professor," he said, "this is Myron Castleman at Glamdring and Glamdring. We were talking on the phone just a few minutes ago, do you remember that?"

"Nonsense," Rosenbluth's voice came sharply. "I never heard of any Castleton, never spoke with you, and besides I just arrived here from conducting a doctoral seminar. So I could not have spoken with anyone on the telephone."

"I'm very sorry to have disturbed you, sir," said Castleman. Slowly and carefully he hung the receiver back on to the telephone desk set.

His digital clock said 12:22.

He stood up and walked around his office again, stopping to gaze out the window at the grime of industrial Long Island City. Of course, for all that Rosenbluth was the one to discover the time-bounce phenomenon, he was as much subject to its influence as someone who'd never heard of it. Castleman could talk to him all he wanted, could possibly even convince him of what was happening during the hour-long period of a resumption, but once the bounce took place and time resumed its progress — for a single hour — Rosenbluth would be back at 12:01 just like everybody else.

What frustration, Castleman thought, if he ever did succeed in making Rosenbluth realize that the strange phenomenon he had theorized was an actuality, had taken place, and was recurring at one-hour intervals. At the end of the hour the next resumption would find Rosenbluth as ignorant as ever—and Castleman back at his familiar post looking up at the Grand Central Tower, the place where he'd happened to be at one minute after noon. Resumption time.

He picked up the phone again and buzzed his secretary. "Stephanie," he said to her, "I want to do some heavy thinking for the next few minutes. Please don't put though any calls or visitors until one o'clock."

He hung up, paced, started out the window, paced some more and flung himself onto the couch. The peculiarity of the time bounce, as he mulled it over, was that the resumption of the earlier state of being not only set physical objects back to their former positions, it actually wiped out the events of the lost hour. Like daylight saving indeed!

With the lost hour *unhappened*, even memories of the time were obliterated. As far as anyone else was concerned, the hour hadn't been spent and then undone—it seemed never to have happened at all! Thus no one was aware of the bounce. They might be reliving a given moment for the fifth time, the fiftieth, the five millionth, and never notice it! And never get past one o'clock this afternoon, either....

The entire universe hung up on a single sixty-minute period, eternally repeating the events of that hour. As Castleman contemplated the prospect his head spun.

Strangest of all was the fact that he — and so far as he could tell, no one else in the world— retained his memory of the lost hour even after the bounce. He had already piled up a whole series of memories of that hour, and by recalling those experiences and by understanding the phenomenon, he could vary his behavior each time, while everyone else simply repeated the same hour over and over — except when Castleman influenced them.

Once Miss Dolores Park had a different luncheon companion at Hamer Heaven.

Once the trio on the library steps had a fourth member for part of their debate.

Once — no, twice — Professor Rosenbluth himself had had odd phone calls when he got back to his office from conducting his graduate seminar.

But those aberrations no longer existed even as memories for the persons they had happened to. Only Castleman retained those events in his mind.

It was a curious sort of immortality. Everyone in the world would repeat one hour, forever, and never realize that time had come to a quivering halt at that point. And Myron Castleman would be permitted to live forever, piling up experiences and memories, but each of only an hour's duration, each resumed at 12:01 P.M. on this balmy spring day in Manhattan, standing outside near the Grand Central Tower.

He looked at the clock on his desk and sighed. It was nearly one o'clock. He closed his eyes and folded his hands behind his head, waiting for the crackling sound.

A few minutes later — or perhaps it was an hour earlier — he found himself standing in midtown, looking up at the clock. He ran to the corner United Cigar Store, hurled himself into an unoccupied phone booth, dropped a dime in the slot and dialed his own office.

"This is Myron Castleman speaking," he began as soon as he heard his secretary's voice. "Now, listen, this is extremely urgent. I want you to telephone Long Island University, physics department. Get hold of Professor Nathan Rosenbluth."

A query.

"R-o-s-e-n-b-l-u-t-h. Right. Tell him that I'm a big shot at Glamdring and Glamdring, that I have to talk to him immediately about his time-bounce theory. That I'm on my way now, and please to be ready for me in the lobby.

"Tell him that it's a vital matter, and we must complete our conversation by one o'clock or all is lost."

A few words in response.

"Fine. Good."

He pulled open the door and vaulted from the booth, leaving the telephone hanging by its reinforced cord. He ran from the store, into Grand Central, fishing for a subway token as he ran. When he reached the lower level, he jammed the token into its slot, shoved through the turnstile, saw an express at the platform just closing its doors and managed to wedge an arm between the rubber seals.

Reluctantly the doors rolled open again, and Castleman collapsed into a vacant seat on the half-empty noontime train. He sat gasping for breath, feeling sharp pains in his chest and shoulder. With his right hand he pulled a handkerchief from his hip pocket and ran it around the inside of his collar.

When he reached his stop, the pains had partially subsided and he had his breath back. He climbed the stairs laboriously, crossed the wide plaza and pushed his way into the building where he hoped to find Nathan Rosenbluth.

Inside the lobby was a receptionist's desk manned by a bored-looking student. Castleman gasped his name and asked if Professor Rosenbluth was expecting him.

The student jerked a casual thumb over his shoulder, indicating a shabby-looking figure examining a wall plaque nearby.

Castleman staggered to the man and introduced himself. It was Rosenbluth. Castleman said, "We only have a few minutes." He looked frantically for a clock in the wall, saw one high on the wall behind the desk. It was eight minutes until one. He put his head into his hands and began to sob.

Rosenbluth said, "What's the matter? What kind of thing is this? Are you really the man from Glamdring and Glamdring? What's going on here? I'm a busy man!"

Castleman tried to explain his situation to Rosenbluth, tried to make him understand that the time bounce had occurred, was continuing to occur at hourly intervals. Rosenbluth seemed a mixture of disinterest and hostility.

Castleman's chest pains were growing worse. He could feel a cold sweat on his brow, feel perspiration dripping down his sleeves from his armpits. He pulled off his jacket and threw in onto the floor, pleading with Rosenbluth to find a way to get time flowing normally again.

"I don't want immortality," Castleman wept, "not this way, anyhow! Everybody else has it, but they don't know it! I know it and it's unbearable. I can't go on living this hour over and over!"

Rosenbluth demanded to know what evidence Castleman could give him.

Castleman looked at the clock. It said 12:56. The pain in his chest and shoulder became excruciating; a hot wave seemed to pass through his entire body, and he couldn't breathe.

He pitched forward onto the floor of the room; but before he ever felt the impact of his body on the dirty terrazzo, a roaring filled his ears, a red film seemed to cover his eyes, and then everything went black.

Death! Death was Castleman's last thought. Death, oblivion would help him to escape from the maddening trap he found himself in, would bring him dissolution and release from the terrible form of immortality that fate had thrust upon him.

There was total oblivion.

For Castleman, time was meaningless, but for the rest of the world just over three minutes ticked away while Rosenbluth and the student receptionist worked over Castleman's inert form, massaging the chest and forcing air futilely in and out of Castleman's lungs.

Oblivion.

There was the echo of a single loud sound resembling the report of a small-caliber firearm. Castleman found himself looking up at the clock on the Grand Central Tower. His tweed jacket was back on his body, and an unruly lock of hair stood out over his left ear.

It was 12:01 P.M.

12:02 P.M.

12:02 P.M.

HOW MANY TIMES?

HOW many times had he awakened—if that was the right word, awakened—on this same street corner, wearing the same button-down shirt and quiet-patterned necktie, carrying the same tan leather attaché case with his initials stamped on it in *faux* gold, MC?

MC.

Myron Castleman.

The same brilliant sun beat down on the midtown traffic. Castleman watched the parade of Fords and Chevys, Plymouths and Nash Ramblers and little Volkswagens scuttling along like shiny-backed beetles. Horns blared, cops blew their whistles, shoppers on their errands and workers on their lunch hours jostled on the sidewalk.

He fought his way through the pedestrian crush on Vanderbilt Avenue to even busier Forty-Second Street and stopped at a newsvendor's kiosk to buy a copy of the *Daily Mirror.* The front page featured a photo of Richard Nixon and Leonid Brezhnev standing side by side in the Oval Office admiring a shiny shotgun.

Castleman looked at his wristwatch.

It was 12:02 P.M.

How many times, he asked himself again. How many times had this happened? For the first few repetitions he'd been able to remember. Each instance was a discrete event. But after a while they'd started to run together. He bought a pocket notebook and started to record them, but of course every time time snapped back, the notebook disappeared and he had to buy another one and start over.

That was the end of that plan.

He had an appetite. He always did when time snapped back and he was whisked from wherever he'd been, whatever he'd been doing, to this time and place. He thought of the many meals he'd consumed in the endlessly repeating lunch hour that made up his life. There was the soup and salad he'd shared with that woman, Dolores Park, with whom he'd sat in a Hamburger Heaven restaurant. The seafood and Bloody Mary in the Oyster Bar in Grand Central. The hot dog and sauerkraut that he'd bought from a Puerto Rican vendor's pushcart. The fancy meal at Longchamps that he'd finished just in time to avoid paying the bill when the time bounce had whisked him back to his spot on Vanderbilt Avenue.

The time bounce. That was what he called it. That was what the professor at Long Island University called it. Nathan Rosenbluth, that was the professor's name. He'd written a journal article on the phenomenon and the daily papers had picked it up as a novelty story, he and a gaggle of colleagues, but Rosenbluth was clearly first among equals. The problem, Rosenbluth had pointed out, was that when the universal clock reset itself each hour, every scrap of evidence that the past hour had transpired would disappear. Including the memory of that hour in every person in the world.

Except, Myron Castleman realized, except for one. Except for Myron Castleman.

Why? How? Castleman had no idea. And Rosenbluth himself had been unable to offer any help when Castleman, after a frantic dash, had reached the professor's office in Brooklyn. It took Castleman most of the hour to reach the DeKalb Avenue building and get to Rosenbluth's office. By the time he could talk Rosenbluth into believing that the time bounce was real, not just an amusing theoretical conceit, time was up.

Castleman was back on Vanderbilt Avenue. Rosenbluth's memory would have been wiped, along with everyone else's except for Castleman's. There was no way out of the trap.

Or was there?

For the moment, there was one thing Castleman felt like doing. It might not make much difference, and he knew that the next time time reset, it would be wiped out. But it might lift his spirits at least for the moment.

He found a telephone booth, dropped a dime in the slot, and dialed his office at Glamdring and Glamdring. The receptionist answered the phone.

"Stephanie, put me through to Mr. Armanino, would you?"

"Mr. Armanino? The boss? Why would he want to take a call from you? You'll be back here after lunch. I could make an appointment for you if he's not too busy."

"No, I want to talk to him. Now."

"I don't know."

The petulant whine in her voice grated. She always acted as if she was doing you a favor when she just did her job. But—he glanced at his wristwatch again. It was 12:20 P.M. Plenty of time. Of course. If there was one thing Myron Castleman had plenty of, it was time.

"Please, Stephanie," he tried again, "this is important. It's very urgent."

Moments later he heard Armanino's voice. Cold, efficient, passionless. Scuttlebutt held that Armanino knew the company manual by heart and had a prepared answer, right out of its pages, for any question, any situation.

"What is it, Castleman? You're due back here in," Castleman could visualize Armanino squinting at his wall clock, "thirty-eight minutes. Can't this wait?"

Castleman ground his teeth. "No, Mr. Armanino, it can't wait. And I won't be back in thirty-eight minutes. Or ever. I quit. You can take this stupid, boring job that I've been doing for Glamdring and Glamdring for seventeen years and blow it out your bung-hole!"

Armanino said, "Obviously you're very upset, Mr. Castleman. It is imperative that you consult the company psychiatrist immediately. I'll have Stephanie set up an appointment for you. She'll have that taken care of by the time you get back here from lunch."

Castleman slammed the receiver back on its hook.

He crossed Forty-Second Street and made his way to the Public Library at Fifth Avenue. He trotted toward the main entrance, smiled at the sculpted lions flanking the steps as he passed between them, and checked his watch again as he headed for the information desk.

He talked to a young librarian, picked up a call slip, turned away, and found a writing surface where he filled out the slip.

He checked his watch. It was 12:39 P.M.

He paced nervously, waiting for a response to his call slip. Finally the librarian signaled to him. He started toward the desk once more. There was a clock on the wall behind the desk. It read 12:54 P.M. He laid the call slip on the counter in front of the librarian.

The librarian said, "That would be in the periodicals room. We can't get those up here and you can't take them to the main reading room, but you can read anything you like, in the periodicals room."

Castleman looked at the clock. The time was 12:56 P.M.

He said, "Never mind. I don't have enough time right now. I'll come back just after twelve o'clock."

The librarian frowned, a look of confusion on his features. He turned away from Castleman and looked up at the clock. The time was 12:59. "Don't you mean one o'clock?" the librarian asked.

"No." Castleman smiled. "Look up there. Just keep your eye on the second hand. As soon as it reaches —"

There was the echo of that single, loud sound resembling the crashing implosion of air into a shattered vacuum tube or the report of a small-caliber firearm.

Castleman was standing on the sidewalk beside Vanderbilt Avenue, his attaché case in his hand. The sun beat down. Traffic raced by on Forty-Second Street. A cop was blowing his whistle. Cars and trucks were honking. Shoppers on their errands and workers on their lunch hours jostled on the sidewalk.

Castleman looked at his watch. The time was 12:03 P.M., same as it was every time time reset. He headed for Fifth Avenue and Forty-Second Street and jogged up the steps of the Public Library, tossing a jaunty wave to the stone lions as he passed between them.

In the lobby he spotted the same librarian with whom he'd spoken earlier. This time he was ready for the encounter.

"I need a copy of the latest edition of *Proceedings of Theoretical Temporal Physics*. The one with Professor Nathan Rosenbluth's paper on the time-bounce phenomenon. I know it's in the periodicals room. Please direct me there."

The librarian said, "Of course. But you'll need a call slip. Here's a blank form you can use."

Castleman already had his Parker 51 out of his pocket. He adjusted the cap on the barrel, took the half-sized sheet of foolscap, and filled in the required spaces. The librarian glanced at the form, nodded approval, and directed Castleman to the periodicals room.

Striding across the marble-floored lobby, Castleman checked the time. It was 12:26.

He handed in his call slip when he reached the periodicals room. Another librarian, this one middle-aged and tired looking, accepted the slip and offered Castleman a grimace.

"We've had a run on this today. Can't figure out why. Most months we're lucky to get any calls at all for it. New issue has been here three days. No action. Now, all of a sudden, must have had twenty requests today alone."

The librarian was five feet tall. She wore her gray hair chopped off at the level of her earlobes. No makeup. Gray sweater, black skirt. Stocky build. A Norman Thomas button on her chest, soliciting anyone's vote for the Presidential election of 1938. The librarian also wore a pin that said, "Miss Kleinman."

Castleman said, "There's an odd article in it about the nature of time. All the daily papers did a takeout on it. Must have got people interested."

Miss Kleinman grunted. She reached under the counter, emerged with a paperbound magazine with nothing but typography on the cover. It was indeed the *Proceedings of Theoretical Temporal Physics.* Miss Kleinman said, "It just came back. See that weird individual with the hair and the Che Guevara shirt? He took it out, looked it over, and handed it back to me without reading it. They shouldn't let that kind in here. They don't take showers. They're a disgrace to the movement."

She shoved the magazine across the counter, looking Castleman up and down. "Here," she grunted.

Castleman scanned the front cover, skipping over the volume and issue number and the date to the table of contents. There was the article he needed. He found a seat at a long table, pulled the bead chain to turn on the reading lamp, and breathed a sigh when the light actually blazed on.

Aspects of Opposing Temporal Displacement Phenomena and Five-Dimensional Symmetry, with Theorems and Analyses, by Rosenbluth, N., Feinberg, J., Horowitz, B., and Hirsch, H.

Castleman glanced back at the counter, where Miss Kleinman was deeply engrossed in conversation with a tweed-jacketed individual sporting a square-cut gray beard, a maroon beret, and a bow tie. He kept pulling a curved-stem briar pipe out of his jacket pocket, chewing on the mouthpiece, taking the pipe out of his mouth and studying the bowl as if he expected to find a wonderful surprise there, and dropping it back into his pocket.

Castleman returned his attention to the journal. There was an abstract on the first page of the paper by Rosenbluth et al., giving the essence of the paper in a single lengthy paragraph. The type was small enough to strain Castleman's eyes but not too small for him to read.

Based on the abstract, Rosenbluth and Company had pretty well figured out what was happening. They had started with the idea that everything in the universe was balanced. Past and future, up and down, big and small. Atoms were made of positive protons and negative electrons. Whoever wrote the abstract even mentioned that the Buddhists believed in a balance of good and bad karma. And when you carried the concept out to the grandest possible scale, the entire universe was balanced with a mirror image of itself. In the counter-universe past was future, positive was negative, dark was light.

If the two versions of the universe should ever collide, what would happen? Rosenbluth et al. decided that each would bounce off the other, like one of those children's toy Superballs dropped from a tall building. Each one would bounce back, then fall forward again, then they would collide and each would bounce back again, endlessly.

At least that was the theory. And when that happened, if it happened, time would flow backward in each universe as far as the energy of the bounce would drive it, then reverse its course as the universes started forward again, racing toward each other and toward another collision.

Castleman had to laugh, drawing a nasty glance from Miss Kleinman and her pipe-chewing friend and the weird character in the Che Guevara tee shirt. Castleman's Uncle Izzy, a diamond in the rough if ever there was one, had preached a similar doctrine. He looked like an overweight, out-of-condition version of Victor Mature and spoke with a perpetual whiskey slur. He'd never gone past grammar school, and yet he seemed to have a remarkable intuitive grasp of physical reality.

"Myron," he used to say, "everything has a positive and a negative. That's the way of the world. A positive and negative." Izzy had always taken a shine to Myron. Izzy had been married an unspecified number of times and had fathered an uncertain number of children. He might have been the black sheep of the family, but he and Izzy had always got along well. Izzy used to take Myron to Coney Island, buy him candy and hot dogs, furnish him with coins to operate the game machines. He'd even taken Myron on the parachute ride.

"Positive and negative, Myron. Don't forget that. Positive and negative. The parachute goes up. The parachute goes down. It all balances."

Castleman was surprised to discover that he had tears in his eyes. He wiped them away and checked the time. 12:55 P.M. He made a quick attempt at reading the body of the Rosenbluth paper but there was no way he was going to make head or tail of it. The graphs were meaningless to him and the equations weren't even in numbers, just Greek letters.

"It's all Greek to me," he muttered to himself. He permitted himself a quiet chuckle. He closed the journal and walked back to the counter, returning it to Miss Kleinman.

To Castleman's surprise, the librarian thanked him with a nod and a smile. She said, "I'd like you to meet my friend and comrade —" but before she could tell Castleman her bearded man's name —

There was the echo of that single, loud sound resembling the crashing implosion of air into a shattered vacuum tube or the report of a small-caliber firearm.

Castleman was standing on the sidewalk on Vanderbilt Avenue just above Forty-Second Street.

He had an appetite.

He bought a copy of the *Daily Mirror,* made his way to a cafeteria, and purchased a cup of coffee and a slice of apple pie. The coffee was cold and the pie was stale. He left them on his table and walked out. No need to worry about wasting the price of a meal. He knew that he'd have exactly as many bills in his wallet and coins in his pocket as ever, next time time reset.

And he knew that he'd have his appetite back, exactly the same appetite he had every time.

He looked up at the bright blue sky and glaring sun, then back down at the roaring traffic, the whistling cop, the scurrying pedestrians. He looked at his wristwatch. It was 12:04, same as always.

He started east on Forty-Second Street, past the Hotel Roosevelt. He paused to check his appearance in a large mirror in the window of an optometrist's shop. He patted down a stray lock. To his mild surprise he noticed a touch of gray around his ears. It actually looked distinguished, he thought. There were a couple of character lines around his mouth.

Well you can't stay young forever.

But—wait a minute! Every time time reset everybody in the world went back to the way he'd been an hour ago. Nobody ever aged more than that one hour. On one occasion Castleman had bluffed his way into the critical care ward at Beth Sinai Hospital. He stood at the bedside of a wizened, transparently thin woman. She must have been close to 100 years of age and was clearly breathing her last.

A bedside monitor beeped and the jagged green line skittering across its face had flattened. Her breathing had been so shallow that it was almost undetectable but now it ceased altogether.

Nothing happened for a few minutes, then some medical personnel and an orderly had appeared and disconnected the woman from the monitor, from an oxygen feed, from an array of intravenous tubes. She lay unmoving, uncaring.

What had he expected? Castleman wondered. Next time he'd know better.

Next time he bluffed his way into the critical care ward the woman was still alive. He read her name off a placard attached to the foot of her bed.

She was still breathing.

He took her hand. It was cold and papery thin. She did not respond. He touched her cheek gently. To his surprise she turned her head toward him and smiled faintly.

"Mrs. Hirschhorn," he said, "Mrs. Hirschhorn. I need to ask you this. Did you see anything? Was there a—was there a there, there, Mrs. Hirschhorn? Was there anyone there at all?"

She frowned. She moved her lips but no sound emerged. She sighed and her breathing ceased and the green line on the bedside monitor stopped its jagged dance and went flat.

Castleman left the room.

He turned away from the optometrist's window and walked briskly eastward on Forty-Second Street, heading toward Lexington Avenue. He felt a sudden pain in one knee. It was sharp but not severe. He stopped walking and rubbed his knee. He continued until he reached the Chrysler Building. His friend Morris Burke nee Berkowitz had an office on the seventy-seventh floor. He paid a fortune in rent, Castleman knew, but his practice was prosperous and he loved showing his clients the view.

Castleman rode the elevator to the top floor of the building. Burke's receptionist recognized him and told him that Mr. Burke had spent the morning in court but was expected back momentarily. If Mr. Castleman would like to wait....

There was a clock on the receptionist's desk. It indicated that the time was 12:12. Castleman sat gratefully, favoring his new trick knee. He set his black leather attach6 case on the floor beside his chair. His initials were embossed on the leather in *faux* gold: MK.

Wasn't that odd? MK. Castleman—or Kastleman—had always spelled his last name with a capital C. He looked again at the attach6 case. Sure enough, MK. He shifted his weight so he could reach his back pocket and extracted his leather wallet. He opened the wallet and examined his driver's license. *Myron Kastleman,* it read. *Kastleman* with a capital K.

He opened his attaché case and extracted one of his business cards. *Myron Kastleman, Deputy Assistant Manager, Claims and Investigations,* it read, *Glamdring and Glamdring,* and the familiar street address.

Or was it familiar? Suddenly Castleman—no, he reminded himself, *Kastleman*—felt a cold chill of uncertainty. "Martha," he said.

Burke's receptionist, Martha Trout, looked up from her typewriter. "Yes, Mr. Kastleman?"

Kastleman shook his head. "Nothing, I just—could I have a cup of water, please? I'd get it myself but I seem to have hurt my knee and I'd rather not, ah ...... He let his voice trail away.

The receptionist said, "Oh, I'm so sorry. My husband has a trick knee so I know what it's like. Just you stay where you are, I won't be but a jiffy."

She crossed to the water cooler, filled a paper cup, and carried it to him.

As he was finishing the drink Morris Burke arrived. He spotted Kastleman and bent to shake his hand. "What a surprise! Myron, how are you? What are you doing in this neck of the woods? I thought you never left the Glamdring preserve."

Kastleman stood up. His knee sent a hot knife of pain up through his leg. He said, "Something strange is going on and I need to talk to you about it."

Burke ushered him into his private office. Once Kastleman was situated comfortably Burke opened a walnut cabinet and brought out a bottle and two glasses.

"I don't normally believe in this until after office hours, but you look as if you need a pick-me-up, Myron." He poured a healthy shot of amber liquid for Kastleman, a token dribble for himself.

"L'chayim!"

They emptied their glasses.

Kastleman looked at his wristwatch. It was 12:29. He said, "Morris, promise you won't think I'm crazy."

"Okay, you're not crazy. Now what?"

"You've heard of the time-bounce? Professor Rosenbluth at LIU, the time bounce theory, it's been in the papers."

"I've heard of it." Burke nodded. "Even the *Wall Street Journal* did a squib on it. All that hocus-pocus about Superballs bouncing off each other." He was tan and muscular. Kastleman knew that Burke spent his summers working on a kibbutz in Israel. He brought back a skin like leather and arms like iron rods. "What about it?"

"It's real, Morris. It's real and it's happened. It's happening right now. Nobody notices when it happens because their memories are reset along with everything else."

"So Yogi was right."

Now it was Kastleman's turn to frown. It was 12:34. "Yogi?"

"Yogi Berra. Used to catch for the Yanks. Holy smoke, Myron, what planet do you live on these days? Yogi said, 'It's déjà vu all over again.' Brilliant line."

Kastleman rubbed his forehead, then looked at his hand. His knuckles seemed to be swelling a little bit, as if he was in the early stages of arthritis. "That's exactly right," he said. "The same hour keeps happening over and over and over again. Only it isn't an hour. Not really. It seems to be getting shorter. Shorter each time. I think. It's hard to keep track."

Burke gestured. "It's those Superballs. Myron, I'm no physicist, I'm just a humble old country lawyer from Essex Street, but I know that no system is one hundred percent efficient. Those balls are losing their energy. Every time they bounce, they lose a little height. Eventually they'll come to rest."

Kastleman pushed himself to his feet and crossed the room to walk to the window. Burke had it open to let in fresh air. The building management kept talking about putting in central air conditioning, he'd told Kastleman, but they hadn't got around to doing it yet.

In the distance, Kastleman could see the famous skyscrapers farther downtown. The Empire State Building, the Woolworth Tower, the twin towers of the World Trade Center. He looked down at Forty-Second Street. Cars and buses moved like toys. Pedestrians were barely visible, mere specks.

"What do you think," he asked Burke, "would happen if there was a little English on one of those Superballs?"

"English?"

"You know. Spin. If you're such a baseball fan, surely you know what happens when a pitcher puts some spin on the ball as he releases it."

"That I do. I got to play a little baseball on the kibbutz last year. Couldn't hit a curve when I was a kid and I can't hit one now."

"Look, if I dropped a Superball out your window and it landed on the sidewalk it would bounce straight up, wouldn't it?"

"Better not, Myron. You could kill a pedestrian that way."

"I mean, just theoretically."

"I told you, I'm no physicist, but I suppose it would."

"But if I put a little English on it, a little spin, what would happen?"

"Huh!" Burke leaned forward, laced his fingers together under his chin, put his elbows on his desk. "It would bounce back, ah, off-line."

"That's what I'm thinking, Morris. And then when it fell again, it wouldn't land on the same spot, would it? It would be off to the side a little bit. And as it kept bouncing it would keep moving off to the side. If there were two Superballs coming from opposite directions, they would only collide once. If they both had English on them, or even on one of them. They'd get farther and farther apart. They'd fly past each other and keep on going forever and time would flow normally again."

Burke got up and crossed to Kastleman. "Fascinating, Myron, fascinating. Maybe you should go talk to this Professor Whatsizname."

"Rosenbluth."

"Right. At NYU, right?"

"LIU. Brooklyn campus."

"Right. I bet he'd love to hear your theory." After a brief pause Burke said, "And this only happens to you, is that right?"

Kastleman said, "Right."

Burke tilted his head, an odd expression on his face. "You know, Myron, that sounds like classic paranoia. I know I promised not to think you were crazy, but you know, you're not acting very rational."

Kastleman said, "I can't help it. Those are the facts."

"Only you?" Burke asked again. "Only you, out of the billions of people in this world? Why would that be, Myron?"

Now it was Kastleman's turn to shake his head. "I don't know, Morris. I've thought about that, believe me, and I can't figure out why. Maybe God is mad at me. I just don't know."

Kastleman looked at his wristwatch. Time was key. Timing was everything. It was 12:59 P.M. He watched the second hand tick around. THE moment was coming. It was coming.

Timing was everything.

If he jumped too soon he'd hit the sidewalk before the time bounce hit and he'd wind up on Vanderbilt Avenue again. And if he waited too long to jump he'd never get to jump at all, he'd still be in Morris Burke's office when time reset and—and he'd also wind up on Vanderbilt Avenue.

But if he timed it just right....

He tossed his attaché case at a startled Morris Burke, launched himself over the parapet and plummeted toward the sidewalk. While he fell he remembered a crazy joke he'd heard as a college student. Man falls out a seventy-seventh-story window. As he passes the thirtieth floor somebody leans out and yells, "Are you all right?"

First guy shouts back at him, "I don't know, but so far so good!"

Kastleman twisted. He twisted his body, he twisted his mind, he exerted every bit of concentration to put English on himself.

He saw the sidewalk rushing up to meet him, panic-stricken pedestrians scurrying to scramble out of the way, to avoid being killed by the human missile roaring down from the sky to destroy them. He

There was the echo of a sound, a single tone made of every sound in the universe, the shattering of crystal and the reverberating throb of a gong a million miles across, a flash of blackness and of light swirling together in mad coitus.

He looked around. He was standing in Bryant Park behind the New York Public Library. The grass had been recently cut and the delicious odor was still in the air. The sky was a glorious shade of blue and the sun was a brilliant white disk overhead.

He looked for his attaché case but he couldn't see it anywhere. Oh, oh, that's right, he'd left it in Morris Burke's office in the Chrysler Building. Well, no harm in that. He wouldn't need it again. He was never going back to Glamdring and Glamdring anyway.

He checked his wristwatch. The time was 1:00 P.M. He watched the second hand circle deliberately around the dial—twice, just to be certain—and then it was 1:02 P.M. He collapsed onto the grass, sitting cross-legged like a child beside a campfire, weeping, weeping with relief and with joy.

He realized that he had a hearty appetite. He wiped his face with his handkerchief and rose to his feet, careful to avoid re-injuring his trick knee.

He wondered if Dolores Park was eating at Hamburger Heaven today. It was a little bit late for lunch, but what did he have to lose? He started walking, and whistling.

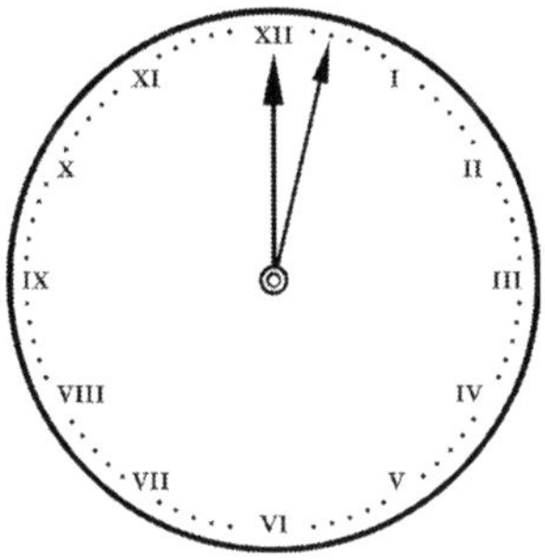

12:03 P.M.

12:03 P.M.

IT didn't look like a psychiatrist's office.

No dark wood panels. No bookshelves filled with thick leather-bound volumes. No heavy wooden desk. No comfortable chaise for the customer to lie on.

In fact, it looked like a kitchen out of one of those slick 1950s magazine ads. Cheerful yellow walls, an electric clock shaped like an ocean liner humming away on a small shelf, a Formica-topped table with chromium-plated legs and a couple of matching chairs. There was even a tiny stove and sink in one corner of the room.

The psychiatrist didn't fit the model, either. No sign of a shaggy-haired pipe-smoker wearing a salt-and-pepper spade-shaped beard and a tweed jacket. Nope. Just a pleasant-looking, thirty-five-ish woman. She wore her light-brown hair modishly short, daringly frosted at the tips, and a modest, comfortable-looking outfit. In fact, with the addition of a frilly apron she could have fit right into that 1950s kitchen.

The only book in the room lay on the table: a battered paperback romance by Barbara Cartland. An AM-only Philco radio in a jade-green bakelite case would have completed the scene, but here a touch of modernity intruded. Instead of the radio, a state-of-the-art tablet computer cast a faint light on the psychiatrist's face.

"Well, what brings you to see me today, Mr. Castleman?" The psychiatrist cast a quick glance at the tablet's screen.

Although he could not see it at the moment, Castleman knew that the computer was displaying his personal page. "The same thing as last time," Castleman said.

"I don't understand." The psychiatrist frowned. "Have we met before?"

Castleman managed a wry smile. Actually, it was more like a grimace. "We have indeed, Dr. Monroe. Many times. Many."

"I'm sorry. I have no record here. See for yourself, Mr. Castleman." She turned the tablet so Castleman could see the screen.

He knew exactly what it would say but he pretended to look at it. A small courtesy. He really liked Dr. Monroe. "Please," he said, "if we're going to work together, please call me Myron."

That elicited a smile. "Very good. And you may call me Isabella. Or simply Bella, if you'd like."

After a brief silence she continued. "Would you like to tell me why you think we've met before?"

"Oh, we haven't merely met before." He glanced toward the room's homelike window. The day outside was bright and pleasant. He'd noticed a light breeze on his way into the building.

"We haven't merely met before," he repeated. "We've had this very conversation, not once but many times."

"There's a name for that feeling," Dr. Monroe said. "It's called *déjà vu.*"

"I know that. And I knew you were going to say it. You do every time."

"It's a common experience," the psychiatrist continued. "There are several theories as to its cause, but I don't think it's anything to be very worried about."

"But you see, it isn't just *déjà vu,*" Castleman said. "I really have lived this moment before. So have you, Dr. Monroe. Bella. So have you. But you don't remember it, and I do."

"I wonder why you think your experience is different from that of anyone else, Mr. Castleman."

"Myron."

"Yes."

"You mean, out of all the thousands—I suppose millions—of people who experience this odd feeling of *I've been here before, I've lived this moment before*—of all those people, it's just a mental aberration for everybody else, but an objective reality for me. That would mark me as a megalomaniac, wouldn't it? Or a paranoid. Or both. *I'm superior, I'm unlike anyone else, I am destiny's child—and everyone else, all the ordinary folk, are out to get me.* Is that what you mean?"

"You put it remarkably well." She smiled. "I wonder, then, if there is any way you could support your claim. Any evidence you could show me? Oh, and would you like a cup of coffee or tea? A glass of water?"

"Coffee would be nice, thank you. Cream and sugar or whatever is convenient."

She poured coffee for them both and returned to her chair. They appeared for all the world like a pleasant, middle-aged, middle-class couple sharing a cup of coffee.

"Do you know what's across the street from this building?" Castleman asked.

"Of course."

"This is a lovely enclave, Bella. The giant city is bustling around it. A pedestrian makes his way through the canyons, jostling busy citizens left and right. He turns the corner and he's on a quiet little street with low building and shady trees. It's like stepping back into the Dwight Eisenhower era. Or the Teddy Roosevelt era. Don't you agree?"

"I do. That's one of the reasons I took this office space."

"You've walked past those establishments many times." He gestured toward the window. Dr. Monroe did not demur, so Castleman went on. "I'd like you to look at something with me."

He walked to the window, carrying his saucer in one hand and coffee cup in the other.

Dr. Monroe said, "We've lived this moment before, have we?"

"Yes."

"And I get up and stand beside you, looking down into Tremaine Place?"

"You do."

Dr. Monroe grinned. "All right then, suppose I don't get up and stand at the window. Suppose I just stay where I am. What would you think of that?"

"I would be very, very surprised." Castleman took a sip of coffee. He bent forward slightly to get a clear view of the street below. "But in fact you will walk over here and stand beside me. You'll take a sip of coffee, put your cup on the saucer, push back your chair, and come to the window."

"Oh, please. I really don't think I'll do that."

"But you will," Castleman smiled.

"All right." She took a sip of coffee, placed her cup on her saucer, pushed back her chair and stood beside him.

"There," Castleman said, "that wasn't so hard, was it?"

"I didn't have to do it," she said.

"But you did."

"Do you mean to say I had no choice?"

"Of course you had a choice. Nobody is compelling you to do anything."

"But I had to do this. Isn't that what you're saying?"

"Not at all. You decided to do it, didn't you? Why, Bella? Why did you do it?"

She made an annoyed face. "Let's just say I was humoring you."

"All right."

"Otherwise...."

"Otherwise, what?"

"Oh, I don't know. We seem to wandering into philosophy. Or maybe physics. Free will versus predestination, causation versus randomness. I'm not a philosopher or a physicist, I'm a psychiatrist."

Castleman pointed downward. Across Tremaine Place in a row of retail establishments, a dry cleaner's and a shoe repair shop flanked a glass-fronted business. The sign above that establishment read, *Webster & Poe, Bookmongers.* Castleman nodded, pointed, uttered an interrogatory syllable.

Dr. Monroe responded. "I know that store very well. I shop there frequently."

"Watch the door."

A woman wearing blue jeans, a patterned sweater and a red beret exited the store. She started to walk slowly away.

"I know her," Dr. Monroe said. "That's my friend Francesca. Francesca di Napoli. We bowl every Friday night. Our team is the Bobby Pins."

"I knew that," Castleman said. "Now watch. Watch. Here he comes."

The door of the shop opened again and a tall, skinny man

wearing a plaid shirt and tan trousers emerged. He looked around, spotted the woman, and ran after her. He took her by the elbow and they exchanged a few sentences, then they returned to the store.

Sounding annoyed, Dr. Monroe asked, "What does this prove, Myron? What's your point?"

Castleman said, "Just wait. She'll be back in a couple of minutes carrying a package."

Shortly, the door opened and the woman in the red beret left Webster and Poe for the second time. She carried a rectangular package wrapped in brown paper.

Dr. Monroe cast an inquiring glance at Castleman.

He said, "That package contains a copy of *Murder at Covent Garden*, by Delia Marston, Chatto & Windus, 1935. Your friend is a fan of Delia Marston's and she's been looking for *Murder at Covent Garden* for the past decade. The copy that she just bought from Jake Webster is in jacket, complete except for a chip out of the base of the spine."

Psychiatrist and patient returned to their chairs and sat down. Dr. Monroe said, "Myron, tomorrow is league night at the alley and the Bobby Pins are going against the Green Hairnets. I'll see Francesca there. I'll ask her about the Marston book. We can get together again next week and if you were wrong about the book that will prove that you haven't lived this afternoon before. Will you agree to that?"

"I always have before," Castleman replied. "Why should I change our arrangement now?"

The little electric clock on its shelf against the bright yellow wall buzzed softly.

"Our time is up," Dr. Monroe said. "I'd like to continue but I have another patient waiting."

Castleman said, "Of course, of course." He stood up and headed for the door. With his hand on the knob he turned and said, "Oh, one more thing, Dr. Monroe. Bella."

She had turned her attention to the tablet computer but she looked up now. "Yes, Myron, what is it?"

He heard the electric clock still making its buzzing sound, and smiled. How often had heard that alarm? He said, "You're going to break two hundred for the first time in your life. I'm afraid the Green Hairnets will come out on top, but you'll have the best game of the night. Enjoy!"

He turned the doorknob, expecting to find himself back in Dr. Monroe's cheerful, kitchen-like office. Instead, he blinked at the sudden, shocking display of every color in the spectrum and the crackle of sound that wasn't sound. He experienced an instant of total blackness and utter nonbeing, and recognized the bedroom of his own three-room apartment on East Seventy-third Street. The doorknob was that of his bathroom. He was clad in pajamas and slippers.

Uh-oh! It was going to be one of those days.

He padded across the blue-carpeted living room, down the short entry hallway to the outer door of the apartment, and bent to pick up the morning newspapers. He always took at least two papers, dreading the day that they would arrive with different dates on them. That had never happened, but he always checked.

The sensational tabloid *New York Post-Herald* had a one-word headline set in end-of-the-world type. It said, simply, *SHOT!* Below this was a photo in lurid color of a familiar face, its eyes wide and mouth open in horror, blood streaming from a gaping hole in the forehead.

Even the conservative daily, the so-called good, gray *Daily Graphic* had broken out its largest font.

Castleman staggered back into his apartment and slammed the outer door shut. He stumbled to the table that also served as his desk and spread the two newspapers. He read the headlines on the *Graphic*. They cascaded down the right side of the page in progressively smaller type.

PRESIDENT ASSASSINATED

LONE GUNMAN KILLS SPIRO T. AGNEW

PRESIDENT WAS IN QUEBEC FOR INDEPENDENCE OBSERVANCE

VICE PRESIDENT NIXON SWORN IN AS CHIEF EXECUTIVE

PRESIDENT LÉVESQUE ACCOMPANIES NIXON ON RETURN FLIGHT TO D.C.

NATION IN SHOCK

FLAGS AT HALF-STAFF

CANADA RUSHES TROOPS TO RESTORE ORDER IN FORMER PROVINCE

The *Graphic* ran a less sensational version of the *Post-Herald* photo. The ruined face was smaller and the injured man was surrounded by startled, obviously shocked others. They had the look of politicians, all of them staring in horror at the bloodied face. One woman, though, seemed to be looking in another direction. A lapel pin on her unobtrusive outfit had caught the day's bright sunlight and reflected a speck of brilliance into the camera's lens.

Castleman automatically attempted to look at his wristwatch, realized that he was still in his pajamas and peered instead at the antique clock on the mantelpiece. Ten o'clock. Brilliant sunlight poured through the eastward-facing window. All right, it was definitely morning. He'd lost something like twenty-two hours. Well, *lost* wasn't exactly the word for it. It wasn't as if he'd blacked out since leaving Dr. Monroe's office and somehow functioned on autopilot for the rest of Thursday and for the night that followed. He'd skipped—bounced—jumped—whatever'd over those hours of time, from the moment he'd turned the doorknob on the office door to the moment he'd turned the doorknob on his bathroom door.

He'd experienced time jumps before. He didn't like them and he kept hoping that he'd find a way to stop them from occurring, or at least learn to control them, but so far they seemed to occur quite at random.

Most often he just lived the hour starting shortly after noon, then when he reached one o'clock he'd simply snap back, like a rubber band that a playful kid had first stretched, then released. He didn't know how long he'd lived that way. How many times had he lived—*relived*—the hour from 12:01 to 1:00 o'clock, only to find himself standing on the same midtown street corner at exactly 12:01 PM?

Finally he'd discovered a way to escape that endless loop. He'd taken the elevator to the thirty-third floor of the Chrysler Building, had stopped to chat briefly with Mrs. Hirschhorn, had visited his childhood friend Morris Berkowitz, now doing legal business as Morris Burke. And then he'd seen his solution, his salvation, his escape-hatch from that single, eternal hour.

* * * * *

He scrambled a couple of eggs and downed them with a glass of orange juice and a slice of toast. He rode the IRT to Grand Central and walked east on Forty-second Street to the Chrysler Building. The elevator ride went as quickly as ever. In the suite marked *Morris Burke – Attorney at Law* Mrs. Hirschhorn smiled, "I see you're not limping, Mr. Castleman. Sore knee feeling better?"

He said it was.

She said, "I don't see you on today's calendar but Mr. Burke is just back from court." She pressed a button, murmured into her telephone, looked up and smiled again. "Go right in."

He didn't waste time on any small talk. "Morris, you remember the last time we saw each other?"

Burke was a beefy, muscular individual. He looked more like a linebacker than a lawyer. "Let me see." He wore his courtroom outfit, a conservative suit from Trippler, white shirt, solid tie. Relaxing at his desk, he'd hung the suit jacket on a coat rack and worked in his shirtsleeves. His cufflinks were tiny gold baseballs. "Didn't we have lunch at Le Valois that day? Yes, I remember. We met there. You were on time, I was a few minutes late and you got on my case about it."

"I don't mean that. I mean the other time." Castleman shook his head impatiently. "You were just back from Israel. We talked about baseball. I told you I was stuck in one hour, living it over and over and you stopped just short of saying that I was absolutely crazy."

Burke frowned. "Can't say I remember that, Myron." He tilted his head. "You feeling all right? Is there something going on that I ought to know about?"

Castleman asked if Burke had seen the morning's headlines, read about the dreadful events in Quebec.

"I caught the flash last night. Watched the late news on TV. Terrible, terrible. But I think Nixon can handle it, don't you? Far as I know, they haven't caught the killer, but you have to give the son of a gun credit. Plenty of security in Washington, but who would think of somebody gunning for Agnew up in Quebec?"

"But you don't remember the last time I was actually here in your office?"

"Myron, what's this about?"

"That day I figured out how to escape. We were talking about baseball. Talking about hitting a curve or a screwball. And it came to me. I realized how I could get out of that endlessly repeating hour. I jumped off your terrace and—"

"You what?"

"You tried to stop me but I got away and I jumped off your terrace. I went straight down, like a diver going off a diving board, and I twisted—I *twisted*—on my way down to the street. Not just my body, I twisted my *mind* and when I hit the pavement instead of bouncing straight back through time I bounced through..."

He held his head in his hands.

"Myron, I think you really need to see a head-shrinker."

Castleman looked up, looked into his friend's worried face. He laughed. "I beat you to the punch on that. I'm seeing a shrink. Funny thing is, I think she thinks I'm crazy. I told her about the time bounce and she insists I'm just having *déjà vu.* But I'm not, Morris. I'm not! This is real. It's real!"

Burke leaned across his desk and put his hand on Castleman's arm. "Okay, Myron, we'll work this out."

Castleman shook his head. He managed a feeble smile. "Thank you, Morris. I—I don't have many friends. I—there's Dolores, I think she really cares about me, but it's too soon, she doesn't know me well enough, but you've been my friend since we were boys and..."

Burke said, "All right, Myron." He picked up the phone, told Mrs. Hirschhorn to hold all calls. "All right," he said again, "just tell me what's going on, Myron."

"See, by twisting my mind I was able to change things. I was still stuck in the time bounce, the one that Professor Rosenbluth at LIU wrote about."

"I remember Rosenbluth."

"But once I figured it out, I was able to *twist* just before the bounce. Twist just a little bit. So instead of bouncing straight back for an hour I could—I don't know exactly how to explain it.

Maybe I was able to shift into an alternate time stream. Or, don't laugh, please, maybe by making the smallest change in the universe I made everything change. Rosenbluth was writing about that, too, you know. Chaos theory. I don't understand it, but he says the smallest change can have the biggest results. So maybe I changed the whole universe."

"All right." Burke stood up. "Let's get out of here, Myron." He removed his suit coat from the rack, slipped into it, lifted Castleman by one elbow and guided him toward the door.

"I think I can make things change the way I want them to. I mean, it's an idea. I want to try. I was thinking about that terrible shooting in Quebec. Poor President Agnew! I..."

He reached past Morris Burke and grasped the doorknob. The lights flashed and there was that crackling sound, nearly as sharp as a gunshot, and he clutched the doorknob to keep from falling.

It wasn't enough. He did fall, as if from a height, into the arms of a heavyset man wearing a gray suit and white shirt and red tied. He had barely time to recognize the man. It was Spiro T. Agnew, President of the United States.

Arms and legs jumbled, Castleman and President Agnew tumbled to the ground. No, not the ground. To the polished wooden stage that had been erected on the steps of a marble government building.

There was the sound of a single loud shot.

A band had been playing but stopped suddenly, the sound of horns and drums replaced by the screams of spectators. He felt bodies tumbling across him, rough hands pulling him away from Agnew, blood spurting upon them from someone who had been standing behind Agnew, rough voices shouting in English and in French, and he was lifted, carried bodily away from the scene, manhandled toward a vehicle. As he approached a waiting ambulance he reached for a door handle.

Lights flashed. A sound like a firecracker the size of an oil drum rang out. There was silence, noise, blackness, light, a moment of complete nonexistence, a return to consciousness and utter disorientation.

The door handle he'd reached for became a doorknob and he

was standing in the bathroom of his bachelor apartment on East Seventy-third Street. He turned around and leaned against the edge of the white porcelain sink. He blinked, then peered into the mirror above. He was haggard and unshaven. His thinning hair stood out in all directions. He was wearing a set of rumpled maroon pajamas. For a moment he thought he saw blood on his forehead and cheek but realized that he was mistaken when he stepped back and rubbed his eyes.

He shaved and dressed and went into the kitchen only to discover that there was no way he could eat anything right now.

He padded across the blue-carpeted living room, down the short entry hallway to the outer door of the apartment, and bent to pick up the morning newspapers. He always took at least two papers, dreading the day that they would arrive with different dates on them. That had never happened, but he always checked.

The sensational tabloid *Morning Bulletin* had a one-word headline set in end-of-the-world type. It said, simply, *SHOT!* Below this was a photo in lurid color of a familiar face, its eyes wide and mouth opened in horror, blood streaming from a gaping hole in the forehead.

Even the conservative daily, the so-called good, gray *New York Sun-Journal* had broken out its largest font.

QUÉBEQUISE PRESIDENT ASSASSINATED

LONE GUNMAN KILLS RENÉ LÉVESQUE

SOLON WAS IN QUÉBEC FOR INDEPENDENCE OBSERVANCE

QUÉBEQOISE PREMIER SWORN IN AS CHIEF EXECUTIVE

PRESIDENT AGNEW REMAINS IN NEWLY INDEPENDENT NATION

QUÉBEC, CANADA IN SHOCK

WORLD FLAGS AT HALF-STAFF

TORONTO RUSHES TROOPS TO RESTORE ORDER IN FORMER PROVINCE

Castleman groaned. He had intervened with history, all right. He'd set out to save President Agnew's life by moving him out of the path of the gunman's bullet, and he had succeeded, but instead of averting the tragedy he had simply substituted one victim for another.

He turned on the television and clicked to an all-news channel. A perky young housewife was exclaiming to a neighbor over the wonders of a new and improved version of her favorite detergent. Castleman blinked. The pitch woman was either his psychiatrist, Isabella Monroe, or her evil twin. And the ever-so-impressed neighbor was the receptionist at Glamdring and Glamdring, Stephanie Holt.

Commerce would not be denied.

After the commercial block the station went back to news, or what passed for news on TV. People sitting across a table from each other talking about the news. You could tell they were really important because they sat at a table. If they had been mere news readers they would have sat behind a mock desk.

The anchorperson said a word about the disaster in Quebec, gestured, and disappeared as footage of the event filled the screen. There was René Lévesque, newly inaugurated President of the newly fledged *Republique Quebéqoise,* smiling broadly as he accepted the congratulations of Spiro T. Agnew, President of the United States.

Another figure flashed into the scene, a man wearing a dark suit, his back to the camera. He crashed into President Agnew, dragging him aside just as a bullet slammed into Président Lévesque.

The news clip ended and the anchor again faced the camera. "What we've just seen will doubtlessly become as famous and controversial a piece of news footage as the Zapruder film of the assassination of President John F. Kennedy or the dramatic images of the *Hindenburg* disaster."

The anchor reached for a nonexistent pair of spectacles, channeling Walter Cronkite's famous gesture as he spoke of the death of President Kennedy, decades before.

He resumed: "The man in the dark suit has become the most

talked about mystery man in the world. Who was he? Where did he come from? He appeared and unquestionably saved the life of one President but inadvertently—we presume inadvertently—caused the death of another."

And after a dramatic pause: "And then he simply disappeared, swallowed up into the milling crowd of confused, horror-stricken witnesses to this international tragedy."

Castleman shook his head. He turned off the TV.

He made his way downtown via subway, jostled a path through the crowds and looked up at the great clock in the middle of Grand Central Terminal. It was too early to follow through on his plan, so he exited the building, walked down Vanderbilt Avenue and crossed Forty-second Street at the corner of Fifth Avenue.

He wandered into the reading room of the public library and stood over the newspaper rack. The *Star-Record,* normally an afternoon paper, had put out an extra covering the events at the independence ceremony in Quebec. There were a few more photos but Castleman could find nothing useful beyond what he'd already seen. The accompanying text had little to offer beyond what he'd got from the TV. There would certainly be reams of copy written about the mystery man in the dark suit. Probably a *Tempus Weekly* cover story headed by a silhouetted male face and teaser line: *Have You Seen this Man?* Odds on there would be mystery man tee shirts and posters in a matter of days.

He checked his wristwatch, left the library and strolled through Bryant Park. The whole city seemed subdued, chastened into silence by the events of the past twenty-four hours.

Only one person in the world knew the identity of the mystery man of Quebec, and he wasn't talking.

He re-crossed Forty-second Street, stopped to watch an argument between the driver of a spiffy new Tucker Torpedo and a battered DeSoto Airflyte, and shouldered through the crowd of shoppers, workers, students, and tourists.

He found the Hamburger Heaven where he and Dolores Park met so often for lunch. The restaurant was crowded. Castleman stood inside the doorway, absorbing the sights and sounds and odors. A manager was controlling the flow of customers. Castleman spotted Dolores Park. She was taking her meal alone. Castleman pushed his way past the manager and sat down opposite Dolores.

She looked up at him and he smiled at her. She had the same pleasant, informal manner he'd grown so fond of. Her hair was done in the current style and her outfit made her slightly overweight figure attractive. She cocked her head to one side.

"Do I know you?"

Castleman gasped. He hadn't thought of this. Ever since he'd started this latest phase of his strange life, he'd assumed that the rest of the world was going about its business unaware of the changes he made.

But what if he was wrong about that? Maybe some Chinese peasant or Chilean gaucho or Saudi oil field worker had discovered that he or she had the same peculiar faculty that Castleman had? What if somebody else was changing Castleman's reality just as Castleman was changing everybody else's reality?

If the time-bounce was working the way it had at first, for the first ten times or the first ten million times—Castleman had long since lost count of the repetitions—then when he introduced himself to Dolores she should regard him as a perfect stranger.

This time, such seemed not to be case.

Dolores Park was frowning at him, her expression not one of anger so much as of puzzlement. "Do I know you?" she asked. She had been eating a steaming bowl of red clam chowder but now she laid down her spoon and gazed into Castleman's face.

He didn't know how to reply.

Dolores said, "It's very strange. You look familiar to me, and yet..." She smiled, "If this is a pick-up, I'm afraid I'm reading from the wrong script."

A waiter had appeared with pad and pencil in hand. Castleman looked up and stammered, "I'll have what she's having."

The waiter departed.

Dolores laughed. "That's the right line, but I thought it always happened in the bar, not a hamburger joint. At least, that's the way it works in all the old gangster movies I've seen."

Castleman finally managed to put a couple of sentences together. "My name is Myron Castleman and yours is Dolores

Park. Yes, we've met before. The first time we met it was right here, right in this restaurant. I told you I was a personnel recruiter for Glamdring and Glamdring and you told me you were a legal secretary and we became very good friends."

"I guess so," Dolores said. She picked up a cellophane-wrapped packet of saltine crackers and nervously broke the seal and crumbled the crackers into her chowder.

The waiter reappeared with Castleman's order and set it before him.

Dolores said, "I don't think this is a pick-up. You don't look like the kind of man who plays that kind of game."

"I'm not," Castleman said.

"But how did you know my name? How can you remember our being friends when I'm not even sure we've met before. I have the strangest feeling of—oh, darn, I know there's a term for it, now what was that...?"

Castleman said, *"Déjà vu."*

"Exactly."

"But this is different, isn't it? I mean, to me it might be—"

"Déjà vu."

"Yes, I keep forgetting that, isn't that strange? But if it's just *déjà vu* for me, it's something else for you, isn't it? You didn't just have a feeling that we'd met before. You remembered all about it and you remembered my name. So it must have been real, don't you think?"

"I do. Dolores—please don't be angry with me. Don't think I'm being forward."

"What do you mean?"

"I need someone to talk to. Someone like you. Someone I can tell things to, things that will seem absolutely crazy, and you won't think I'm crazy, you'll pay attention and take me seriously."

"Of course."

"I tried talking to my old friend Morris and he wanted me to see a shrink. I even went out to Long Island to talk to Professor Rosenbluth but that didn't work either. He was interested as long as it was just a theory but as soon as I told him this was really happening he just shut down. He just shut down. So—so,

Dolores—will you have dinner with me tonight, and we'll talk. You'll let me talk. You'll take me seriously and you won't just think I'm crazy. Will you do that?"

"Myron," she smiled, "that is the most creative, most irresistible pick-up line I have heard in all my forty-seven—I mean, thirty-seven—years. Will eight o'clock be good? I want to get home and change after work. Where shall we meet?"

He suggested a little Italian place he knew on Second Avenue and she agreed. They got separate checks and paid for their lunches and outside the restaurant in the middle of the bustling crowd she reached up and kissed him on the cheek and then disappeared into the mass of pedestrians.

He stood there feeling the wondrous electrical sensation that he hadn't felt since his first schoolboy romance. He went back to his apartment and spent the afternoon surfing the internet for articles on time travel and parallel universes and multiplex realities. He wandered into a network of academic sites and found a long essay on something called Uchronias, alternate versions of the real world. There was even a bibliography of the things:

What if the assassin's bullet had missed Kennedy?

What if the Trinity test had fizzled?

What if Lincoln had caught influenza and had to skip the theatre?

What if the meteor that crashed into the Gulf of Mexico and killed all the dinosaurs (maybe) had collided with the moon instead?

Those alternate timelines surely existed as theories, but what if they really existed, separated from our own reality by the thinnest of boundary layers but as unreachable as the faintest star in the farthest galaxy? Or — what if they were reachable as easily as thinking the right thoughts as you reached for a doorknob?

* * * * *

The restaurant was called Pasquale's 840. Castleman hadn't been there in years, in decades, and he had the chilling thought as he walked down Second Avenue that it might have gone out of business and Dolores would arrive and think that he'd stood her up, that the whole meeting at Hamburger Heaven and the *Yes we've met before and I really, really need someone to talk to* routine, had been some elaborate, cruel, practical joke.

But Pasquale's 840 was there, a modest establishment in a less than fashionable section of Manhattan. He stopped and looked at a newspaper vending machine. There was a blown-up photo on the front page of the evening paper. It showed the dark-suited back of the mysterious interloper who had saved President Agnew's life beneath a bold tag-line: WHO IS THIS MAN?

The longer caption under the photo recapped the story of the mystery man who had muscled the President aside, saving his life from an assassin's bullet at the expense of the new President of Quebec.

Castleman had made it his business to arrive at the restaurant fifteen minutes early so as to make sure that he was waiting when Dolores arrived, and when she came through the doorway he felt his heart leap.

She'd arranged her hair in a softer style that framed her features, and chosen a blouse that showed her ample figure just to the boundary of good taste without crossing the so-subtle line into vulgar display.

She approached his table and he stood up and barely avoided knocking the table over, like an over-eager schoolboy on his first real date. She held both her hands toward him and he took them and leaned forward and kissed her, briefly and gently but on the lips.

She smiled and they sat down and the waiter brought the bottle of wine that Castleman had already selected. "I hope you don't mind," Castleman said, "I've always had a weakness for Valpolicella."

Dolores took a sip and said, "I don't mind." She smiled across the lip of her wine glass, managing to look simultaneously flirtatious and ironic. She took another sip of the wine. "In fact it's very good."

Castleman gestured around them. Pasquale's was a small establishment, holding just half a dozen tables. Tonight they were nearly all filled. The patrons were mostly in couples, mostly youthful, mostly with the look of the upwardly-mobile, not yet arrived but definitely on their way.

Me ten years ago, Castleman thought. *Or twenty.*

Dolores said, "It's amazing. I've lived here all my life and this city is still full of marvelous places I didn't even know existed."

Castleman said, "I hope it's not too corny."

Dolores raised her eyebrows. "Corny?"

"Oh, candles in Chianti bottles on the tables," he gestured. "Travel posters of Tuscany and Venice and Rome. Italian music."

"Locatelli," Dolores said. "I love Locatelli." She had a lovely smile. The candle light glinted off a tiny gem that rested on her bosom, suspended from a fine gold chain.

They ordered dinner. While they waited for the food Castleman munched nervously on a breadstick. Conversation from other tables floated in and out of the recorded baroque music. Talk of the business world, the theater, the latest novel, but always the topic turned to the Mystery Man of Quebec.

Dolores Park read Castleman's mind. "I know who he is," she said.

Castleman was unable to reply before the waiter arrived with their dinners. Castleman had ordered sole piccata with seedless grapes and capers. Despite his distracted state of mind he couldn't keep his attention off his dinner. The presentation was simple and the odor was irresistible.

Dolores had only a Caesar salad. "The menu was tempting but I'm really trying to slim."

Castleman waited for her to sample her dinner before starting on his own. A gentleman to the last. "Who is he?"

Dolores laid down her fork, swallowed wine, lowered her glass. "You."

"How did you know?"

"Myron, of course I know."

He couldn't help following her gesture as she lowered her chin to glance at the glittering gem on her bosom.

"We all know."

"What do you mean 'we'—who are 'we'?"

"You wouldn't believe it if I told you, Myron. You'd think it was some kind of practical joke. Something out of an Ian Fleming novel or one of those spooky movies where shadowy figures sneak around changing reality."

She paused.

Then, "Just—just trust me that we're grateful for everything you've done or tried to do. I'm personally..."

She shook her head. "I'm sorry, Myron. We haven't treated you at all well."

"All right, if you won't tell me who you are, at least tell me how you picked me, and what you're doing."

"Myron, we're the good guys. Can you believe that? You've known me for a long time and you've known me very well."

"You didn't act that way a few hours ago. 'Do I know you?' 'Is this just *déjà vu?*' And I swallowed it, hook line and sinker!"

"I'm sorry. Myron, there's a struggle going on in this world. You must know the story of the past century. The monsters, the wars, the horrors."

He waited for her to continue.

"It didn't just happen that way. I didn'thave to happen that way."

He nodded, waited.

"Countries get rid of their tyrants and they only get worse ones in their place. The Russians got rid of the Czar and wound up with Stalin. The Germans got rid of the Kaiser and wound up with Hitler. It happens over and over again. It's happening today, all over the world." She let out a breath. "Why do you think that's happening?"

Castleman clutched the edge of the linen tablecloth, his thumbs and forefingers like twin vises. "You're telling me that this planet is just a giant chessboard and we're all pieces being moved around by—by invisible hands? By *you?"*

"Not just by me. Hardly just by me. But yes, that image is not inaccurate. The world *is* a giant chessboard, and you are—"

"A pawn!" he interrupted angrily. He crashed a fist onto the tablecloth. Their glasses jumped. A pair of intense young business types stared, then conspicuously looked away.

The manager approached their table. “Is everything all right?”

Castleman was going to answer but Dolores murmured something to the manager, something inaudible to Castleman, and he bowed, somehow produced a cheese grater and a slab of hard white cheese and ground a coating of it onto Dolores’s salad.

“Not a pawn,” Dolores told Castleman finally. “Not a pawn at all. Look around this room, Myron. Look at the people around us, the ambitious ones wondering if they’ll get the promotion they’re after, the lustful ones wondering if they’ll get the sex they’re hoping for, the discouraged ones who just want to finish their meals and go home and go to bed. They’re the pawns, Myron. Not you. Believe me, not you.”

“What am I then? And what are you, Dolores? Are you a chess player or are you a game piece?”

“You know chess?”

“I’m no expert.”

“The pieces, the moves.”

He nodded.

“I suppose I’m a bishop. I can move diagonally. I can slay with a nod or a glance. But always on the bias. Anything straightforward is beyond my power.”

“And I? If I’m not a pawn, what am I?”

“I suppose you might consider yourself a knight.”

“My armor is pretty rusty and my lance is getting battered.”

“You can move ahead and strike to the side. Only the knight can do that. Of all the pieces, only the knight can do both in a single move. That’s why we need you, Myron. The rooks and bishops may be more powerful and the pawns more numerous, but we need your ability, Myron. Only you can do what must be done. We need your talent.”

* * * * *

They wound up at Castleman’s apartment. They sat in his living room, Dolores in a wing chair, Castleman alternately pacing nervously and sprawling in a matching chair, stamping from the room and returning.

"You have a talent, Myron. You have a rare talent. It is not unique, believe me, but it is far from common. We have our talented workers and they have theirs."

They went around and around on that notion, until finally Castleman laughed. "I guess I should be flattered, but I'm not."

"I don't blame you. Sometimes I think the pawns are happier. But we can't help being who we are."

He'd been sitting opposite her but now he stood up once more and walked in a circle, watching the nap in the blue woolen carpet bend with each step, then spring back behind him. He felt as if that was the way he was effecting reality. Step, down goes the nap, step away, up it comes. But was it ever quite the same afterwards?

He plunged back into his chair, face to face with Dolores. She seemed to have waited patiently for him to reach a decision, but he was not ready to commit himself.

"What if I just refuse?" he asked. "What if I just say, 'I don't like your game and I'm not going to play'?"

She heaved a sigh, then reached out and took his hands. "Myron, we don't always have a choice."

"We do!" he interrupted. "We always have a choice!"

"All right." Her expression showed exasperation but she contained her feelings and spoke calmly. "I said we were like chess pieces but that isn't completely accurate. Chess pieces have power but they have no will."

"You're damned right about that. And I'm no chess piece and neither are you!"

"Now wait, wait. I can tell what you're going to say next."

"Really? You really can?" There was no way she could have known about his last conversation with Bella Monroe but he felt as if she did, or else this was a remarkable coincidence because she was turning the tables on him. "And what if I choose not to say it?"

"You can choose, Myron. I'm not telling you that you have to do anything, but I know what you're going to choose to say."

"All right. Just hold it one second." He stamped to his desk, snatched up a yellow pencil and a lined notepad. He brought them back to her, almost threw them into her lap. "Okay, write it down, write it down, and put it right there on the coffee table. Face down. Go ahead!"

She did.

He said, "If we're chess pieces, who are the players?"

Dolores pointed at the sheet of notepaper.

Castleman picked it up and turned it over. He read aloud. "If we're chess pieces, who are the players?"

Dolores shook her head slowly from side to side. "I don't know, Myron."

* * * * *

By morning he knew what he had to do and why he had to do it. But he wasn't ready to give up, wasn't ready to accept everything that Dolores had told him in their hours-long dialogue. He knew that he could bounce from one time to another, from one place to another. There was nothing magic about doorknobs, either, but somehow the act of grasping one and turning it acted as a trigger in setting off the bounce.

He stood at the bathroom door, grasped the doorknob and turned.

He was standing at a window in a psychiatrist's office on a strangely rustic street, a street that could have been out of another era. He turned and noticed a book lying on the psychiatrist's desk. It was a battered copy of a mystery novel by Agatha Christie. His psychiatrist was standing beside him. Across the street he saw a row of small retail businesses, a dry cleaning establishment, a bookshop, a shoe repair service.

The psychiatrist has just asked him what point he was trying to make.

Castleman said, "Just wait. She'll be back in a couple of minutes carrying a package."

Shortly, the door opened and a woman in the blue beret left the bookshop, Hawthorne and Twain. A portly man incongruously dressed in a cowboy shirt came running after her, caught her by the elbow and escorted her back to the shop, chattering silently all the time.

Shortly the woman left the shop for the second time. She

carried a rectangular package wrapped in yellow paper.

Dr. di Napoli cast an inquiring glance at Castleman.

He said, "That package contains a copy of *Romance at Pirate Cay*, by Frederica Fontaine, A. L. Burt, 1932. Your friend is a fan of Frederica Fontaine's and she's been looking for *Romance at Pirate Cay* for the past decade. The copy that she just bought from David Hawthorne is in jacket, complete except for a chip out of the base of the spine."

Psychiatrist and patient returned to their chairs and sat down. Dr. di Napoli said, "Myron, tomorrow is our bridge night. I'll see Isabella there. I'll ask her about the Fontaine book. We can get together again next week and if you were wrong about the book that will prove that you haven't lived this afternoon before. Will you agree to that?"

"I always have before," Castleman replied. "Why should I change it now?"

The little electric clock shaped like an art deco airliner buzzed softly on its shelf against the bright yellow wall.

"Our time is up," Dr. di Napoli said. "I'd like to continue but I have another patient waiting."

Castleman said, "Of course, of course." He stood up and headed for the door. With his hand on the knob he turned and said, "Oh, one more thing, Dr. di Napoli. Francie."

He turned the doorknob and collided with a man wearing garb identical to his own. Dark suit, white shirt, button-down collar, conservative regimental striped tie. He had only a fraction of a second to take in the man's countenance. Still, it was long enough for him to recognize himself.

He reached for the figure beside him. At the same time he saw his counterpart duplicate the gesture. They took down two others, two middle-aged men dressed more or less as they were. Out of the corner of his eye he thought he recognized a woman seated on the platform where they all stood jostling one another, a tiny jeweled pin glinting on the lapel of her jacket.

He recognized the wooden platform, the government building backdrop, the crowd of dignitaries milling and jostling for the spotlight and the attention of news cameras.

He turned his back on the clustered politicians, took two quick steps to the edge of the platform, launched himself like a football tackle at an unassuming individual in the audience, an individual holding something that looked like a camera but that Castleman knew was not a camera.

In a timeless instant he saw an expression of startled rage flood the individual's face, saw the thing that was not a camera flash, heard a sudden, deafening crash.

Something smashed into the very center of Castleman's forehead and he felt himself lifted out of his body, his immaterial psyche flung away from the reality of the surroundings. He saw the colors and heard the sound that went with his transitions, was immersed in the absolute blackness and silence. Yet he detected another presence, still another avatar of himself.

He merged with the other Castleman, circling through non-space. For a fleeting moment he caught a glimpse of the scene he had left, of people swirling in confusion, of two identical dark-suited men, unmoving, their heads smashed, their faces covered with blood. Uniformed and business-suited security had hustled the two Presidents from the scene. Video cameras pointed at the platform, news-gatherers fighting like football linemen for access to the VIP area.

Castleman saw the blue rug of his bedroom rush up to meet him. He felt himself crash, bounce, then lie still. He felt warm, competent hands on his shoulders, hands lifting him and helping him back to his bed.

He looked into a familiar face. He recognized the concerned, caring features of Dolores Park. He managed a feeble grin. He tried to speak but the words wouldn't come and he realized what the reason was, that his thoughts were so confused that he couldn't formulate a simple sentence.

Dolores leaned closer to him. "What is it, Myron? What is it?"

He shook his head. Breathed deeply. Smiled up into Dolores Park's face. "My shrink," he said.

"Yes. Myron, what about your shrink?"

"She'll never believe this. She'll never believe my story." He found himself wishing he had a mirror because he wanted to see the expression on his own face. Was he laughing or crying? He couldn't tell. He squeezed his eyes shut and tried to decide but he couldn't and he gave up and opened his eyes again.

He tried to read the expression on Dolores Park's face. "You're a hero, Myron. Did you know that? An authentic hero."

He tried to shake his head but the pain was unbearable and he stopped, panting, waiting for Dolores to go on.

She said, "I don't know whether this will be good news, Myron, or bad news. But this is only the beginning of your story."

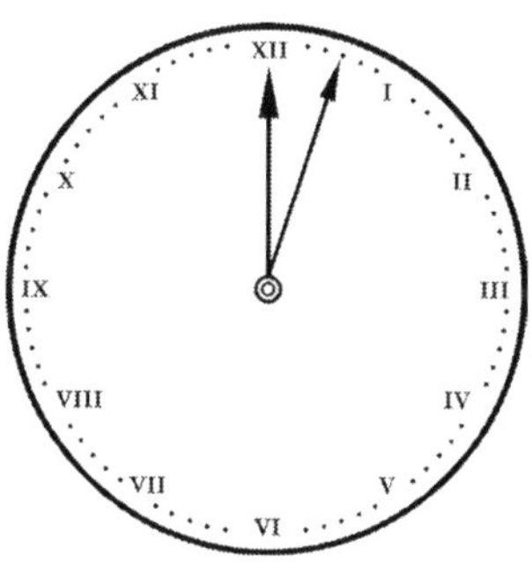

RAMBLE HOUSE's

Harry Stephen Keeler Webwork Mysteries

(RH) indicates the title is available ONLY in the RAMBLE HOUSE edition

The Ace of Spades Murder
The Affair of the Bottled Deuce (RH)
The Amazing Web
The Barking Clock
Behind That Mask
The Book with the Orange Leaves
The Bottle with the Green Wax Seal
The Box from Japan
The Case of the Canny Killer
The Case of the Crazy Corpse (RH)
The Case of the Flying Hands (RH)
The Case of the Ivory Arrow
The Case of the Jeweled Ragpicker
The Case of the Lavender Gripsack
The Case of the Mysterious Moll
The Case of the 16 Beans
The Case of the Transparent Nude (RH)
The Case of the Transposed Legs
The Case of the Two-Headed Idiot (RH)
The Case of the Two Strange Ladies
The Circus Stealers (RH)
Cleopatra's Tears
A Copy of Beowulf (RH)
The Crimson Cube (RH)
The Face of the Man From Saturn
Find the Clock
The Five Silver Buddhas
The 4th King
The Gallows Waits, My Lord! (RH)
The Green Jade Hand
Finger! Finger!
Hangman's Nights (RH)
I, Chameleon (RH)
I Killed Lincoln at 10:13! (RH)
The Iron Ring
The Man Who Changed His Skin (RH)
The Man with the Crimson Box
The Man with the Magic Eardrums
The Man with the Wooden Spectacles
The Marceau Case
The Matilda Hunter Murder
The Monocled Monster
The Murder of London Lew
The Murdered Mathematician
The Mysterious Card (RH)
The Mysterious Ivory Ball of Wong Shing Li (RH)
The Mystery of the Fiddling Cracksman
The Peacock Fan
The Photo of Lady X (RH)
The Portrait of Jirjohn Cobb
Report on Vanessa Hewstone (RH)
Riddle of the Travelling Skull
Riddle of the Wooden Parrakeet (RH)
The Scarlet Mummy (RH)
The Search for X-Y-Z
The Sharkskin Book
Sing Sing Nights
The Six From Nowhere (RH)
The Skull of the Waltzing Clown
The Spectacles of Mr. Cagliostro
Stand By—London Calling!
The Steeltown Strangler
The Stolen Gravestone (RH)
Strange Journey (RH)
The Strange Will
The Straw Hat Murders (RH)
The Street of 1000 Eyes (RH)
Thieves' Nights
Three Novellos (RH)
The Tiger Snake
The Trap (RH)
Vagabond Nights (Defrauded Yeggman)
Vagabond Nights 2 (10 Hours)
The Vanishing Gold Truck
The Voice of the Seven Sparrows
The Washington Square Enigma
When Thief Meets Thief
The White Circle (RH)
The Wonderful Scheme of Mr. Christopher Thorne
X. Jones—of Scotland Yard
Y. Cheung, Business Detective

Keeler Related Works

A To Izzard: A Harry Stephen Keeler Companion by Fender Tucker — Articles and stories about Harry, by Harry, and in his style. Included is a compleat bibliography.

Wild About Harry: Reviews of Keeler Novels — Edited by Richard Polt & Fender Tucker — 22 reviews of works by Harry Stephen Keeler from *Keeler News.* A perfect introduction to the author.

The Keeler Keyhole Collection: Annotated newsletter rants from Harry Stephen Keeler, edited by Francis M. Nevins. Over 400 pages of incredibly personal Keeleriana.

Fakealoo — Pastiches of the style of Harry Stephen Keeler by selected demented members of the HSK Society. Updated every year with the new winner.

Strands of the Web: Short Stories of Harry Stephen Keeler — 29 stories, just about all that Keeler wrote, are edited and introduced by Fred Cleaver.

RAMBLE HOUSE's Loon Sanctuary

A Clear Path to Cross — Sharon Knowles short mystery stories by Ed Lynskey.
A Jimmy Starr Omnibus — Three 40s novels by Jimmy Starr.
A Niche in Time and Other Stories — Classic SF by William F. Temple
A Roland Daniel Double: The Signal and The Return of Wu Fang — Classic thrillers from the 30s.
A Shot Rang Out — Three decades of reviews and articles by today's Anthony Boucher, Jon Breen. An essential book for any mystery lover's library.
A Smell of Smoke — A 1951 English countryside thriller by Miles Burton.
A Snark Selection — Lewis Carroll's *The Hunting of the Snark* with two Snarkian chapters by Harry Stephen Keeler — Illustrated by Gavin L. O'Keefe.
A Young Man's Heart — A forgotten early classic by Cornell Woolrich.
Alexander Laing Novels — *The Motives of Nicholas Holtz* and *Dr. Scarlett*, stories of medical mayhem and intrigue from the 30s.
An Angel in the Street — Modern hardboiled noir by Peter Genovese.
Automaton — Brilliant treatise on robotics: 1928-style! By H. Stafford Hatfield.
Away From the Here and Now — Clare Winger Harris stories, collected by Richard A. Lupoff
Beast or Man? — A 1930 novel of racism and horror by Sean M'Guire. Introduced by John Pelan.
Black Hogan Strikes Again — Australia's Peter Renwick pens a tale of the 30s outback.
Black River Falls — Suspense from the master, Ed Gorman.
Blondy's Boy Friend — A snappy 1930 story by Philip Wylie, writing as Leatrice Homesley.
Blood in a Snap — The *Finnegan's Wake* of the 21st century, by Jim Weiler.
Blood Moon — The first of the Robert Payne series by Ed Gorman.
Bogart '48 — Hollywood action with Bogie by John Stanley and Kenn Davis
Calling Lou Largo! — Two Lou Largo novels by William Ard.
Cornucopia of Crime — Francis M. Nevins assembled this huge collection of his writings about crime literature and the people who write it. Essential for any serious mystery library.
Corpse Without Flesh — Strange novel of forensics by George Bruce
Crimson Clown Novels — By Johnston McCulley, author of the Zorro novels, *The Crimson Clown* and *The Crimson Clown Again.*
Dago Red — 22 tales of dark suspense by Bill Pronzini.
Dark Sanctuary — Weird Menace story by H. B. Gregory
David Hume Novels — *Corpses Never Argue, Cemetery First Stop, Make Way for the Mourners, Eternity Here I Come*. 1930s British hardboiled fiction with an attitude.
Dead Man Talks Too Much — Hollywood boozer by Weed Dickenson.
Death Leaves No Card — One of the most unusual murdered-in-the-tub mysteries you'll ever read. By Miles Burton.
Death March of the Dancing Dolls and Other Stories — Volume Three in the Day Keene in the Detective Pulps series. Introduced by Bill Crider.
Deep Space and other Stories — A collection of SF gems by Richard A. Lupoff.
Detective Duff Unravels It — Episodic mysteries by Harvey O'Higgins.
Diabolic Candelabra — Classic 30s mystery by E.R. Punshon
Dime Novels: Ramble House's 10-Cent Books — *Knife in the Dark* by Robert Leslie Bellem, *Hot Lead* and *Song of Death* by Ed Earl Repp, *A Hashish House in New York* by H.H. Kane, and five more.
Don Diablo: Book of a Lost Film — Two-volume treatment of a western by Paul Landres, with diagrams. Intro by Francis M. Nevins.
Dope and Swastikas — Two strange novels from 1922 by Edmund Snell
Dope Tales #1 — Two dope-riddled classics; *Dope Runners* by Gerald Grantham and *Death Takes the Joystick* by Phillip Condé.
Dope Tales #2 — Two more narco-classics; *The Invisible Hand* by Rex Dark and *The Smokers of Hashish* by Norman Berrow.
Dope Tales #3 — Two enchanting novels of opium by the master, Sax Rohmer. *Dope* and *The Yellow Claw.*
Double Hot — Two 60s softcore sex novels by Morris Hershman.
Dr. Odin — Douglas Newton's 1933 racial potboiler comes back to life.

Evangelical Cockroach — Jack Woodford writes about writing.
Evidence in Blue — 1938 mystery by E. Charles Vivian.
Fatal Accident — Murder by automobile, a 1936 mystery by Cecil M. Wills.
Fighting Mad — Todd Robbins' 1922 novel about boxing and life
Finger-prints Never Lie — A 1939 classic detective novel by John G. Brandon.
Freaks and Fantasies — Eerie tales by Tod Robbins, collaborator of Tod Browning on the film FREAKS.
Gadsby — A lipogram (a novel without the letter E). Ernest Vincent Wright's last work, published in 1939 right before his death.
Gelett Burgess Novels — *The Master of Mysteries, The White Cat, Two O'Clock Courage, Ladies in Boxes, Find the Woman, The Heart Line, The Picaroons* and *Lady Mechante.* Recently added is A Gelett Burgess Sampler, edited by Alfred Jan. All are introduced by Richard A. Lupoff.
Geronimo — S. M. Barrett's 1905 autobiography of a noble American.
Hake Talbot Novels — *Rim of the Pit, The Hangman's Handyman.* Classic locked room mysteries, with mapback covers by Gavin O'Keefe.
Hands Out of Hell and Other Stories — John H. Knox's eerie hallucinations
Hell is a City — William Ard's masterpiece.
Hollywood Dreams — A novel of Tinsel Town and the Depression by Richard O'Brien.
Hostesses in Hell and Other Stories — Russell Gray's most graphic stories
House of the Restless Dead — Strange and ominous tales by Hugh B. Cave
I Stole $16,000,000 — A true story by cracksman Herbert E. Wilson.
Inclination to Murder — 1966 thriller by New Zealand's Harriet Hunter.
Invaders from the Dark — Classic werewolf tale from Greye La Spina.
J. Poindexter, Colored — Classic satirical black novel by Irvin S. Cobb.
Jack Mann Novels — Strange murder in the English countryside. *Gees' First Case, Nightmare Farm, Grey Shapes, The Ninth Life, The Glass Too Many, Her Ways Are Death, The Kleinert Case* and *Maker of Shadows.*
Jake Hardy — A lusty western tale from Wesley Tallant.
Jim Harmon Double Novels — *Vixen Hollow/Celluloid Scandal, The Man Who Made Maniacs/Silent Siren, Ape Rape/Wanton Witch, Sex Burns Like Fire/Twist Session, Sudden Lust/Passion Strip, Sin Unlimited/Harlot Master, Twilight Girls/Sex Institution.* Written in the early 60s and never reprinted until now.
Joel Townsley Rogers Novels and Short Stories — By the author of *The Red Right Hand: Once In a Red Moon, Lady With the Dice, The Stopped Clock, Never Leave My Bed.* Also two short story collections: *Night of Horror* and *Killing Time.*
John Carstairs, Space Detective — Arboreal Sci-fi by Frank Belknap Long
Joseph Shallit Novels — *The Case of the Billion Dollar Body, Lady Don't Die on My Doorstep, Kiss the Killer, Yell Bloody Murder, Take Your Last Look.* One of America's best 50's authors and a favorite of author Bill Pronzini.
Keller Memento — 45 short stories of the amazing and weird by Dr. David Keller.
Killer's Caress — Cary Moran's 1936 hardboiled thriller.
Lady of the Yellow Death and Other Stories — More stories by Wyatt Blassingame.
League of the Grateful Dead and Other Stories — Volume One in the Day Keene in the Detective Pulps series.
Library of Death — Ghastly tale by Ronald S. L. Harding, introduced by John Pelan
Malcolm Jameson Novels and Short Stories — *Astonishing! Astounding!, Tarnished Bomb, The Alien Envoy and Other Stories* and *The Chariots of San Fernando and Other Stories.* All introduced and edited by John Pelan or Richard A. Lupoff.
Man Out of Hell and Other Stories — Volume II of the John H. Knox weird pulps collection.
Marblehead: A Novel of H.P. Lovecraft — A long-lost masterpiece from Richard A. Lupoff. This is the "director's cut", the long version that has never been published before.
Master of Souls — Mark Hansom's 1937 shocker is introduced by weirdologist John Pelan.
Max Afford Novels — *Owl of Darkness, Death's Mannikins, Blood on His Hands, The Dead Are Blind, The Sheep and the Wolves, Sinners in Paradise* and *Two Locked Room Mysteries and a Ripping Yarn* by one of Australia's finest mystery novelists.
Money Brawl — Two books about the writing business by Jack Woodford and H. Bedford-Jones. Introduced by Richard A. Lupoff.

More Secret Adventures of Sherlock Holmes — Gary Lovisi's second collection of tales about the unknown sides of the great detective.

Muddled Mind: Complete Works of Ed Wood, Jr. — David Hayes and Hayden Davis deconstruct the life and works of the mad, but canny, genius.

Murder among the Nudists — A mystery from 1934 by Peter Hunt, featuring a naked Detective-Inspector going undercover in a nudist colony.

Murder in Black and White — 1931 classic tennis whodunit by Evelyn Elder.

Murder in Shawnee — Two novels of the Alleghenies by John Douglas: *Shawnee Alley Fire* and *Haunts*.

Murder in Silk — A 1937 Yellow Peril novel of the silk trade by Ralph Trevor.

My Deadly Angel — 1955 Cold War drama by John Chelton.

My First Time: The One Experience You Never Forget — Michael Birchwood — 64 true first-person narratives of how they lost it.

Mysterious Martin, the Master of Murder — Two versions of a strange 1912 novel by Tod Robbins about a man who writes books that can kill.

Norman Berrow Novels — *The Bishop's Sword, Ghost House, Don't Go Out After Dark, Claws of the Cougar, The Smokers of Hashish, The Secret Dancer, Don't Jump Mr. Boland!, The Footprints of Satan, Fingers for Ransom, The Three Tiers of Fantasy, The Spaniard's Thumb, The Eleventh Plague, Words Have Wings, One Thrilling Night, The Lady's in Danger, It Howls at Night, The Terror in the Fog, Oil Under the Window, Murder in the Melody, The Singing Room.* This is the complete Norman Berrow library of locked-room mysteries, several of which are masterpieces.

Old Faithful and Other Stories — SF classic tales by Raymond Z. Gallun

Old Times' Sake — Short stories by James Reasoner from Mike Shayne Magazine.

One Dreadful Night — A classic mystery by Ronald S. L. Harding

Pair O' Jacks — A mystery novel and a diatribe about publishing by Jack Woodford

Perfect .38 — Two early Timothy Dane novels by William Ard. More to come.

Prince Pax — Devilish intrigue by George Sylvester Viereck and Philip Eldridge

Prose Bowl — Futuristic satire of a world where hack writing has replaced football as our national obsession, by Bill Pronzini and Barry N. Malzberg.

Red Light — The history of legal prostitution in Shreveport Louisiana by Eric Brock. Includes wonderful photos of the houses and the ladies.

Researching American-Made Toy Soldiers — A 276-page collection of a lifetime of articles by toy soldier expert Richard O'Brien.

Reunion in Hell — Volume One of the John H. Knox series of weird stories from the pulps. Introduced by horror expert John Pelan.

Ripped from the Headlines! — The Jack the Ripper story as told in the newspaper articles in the *New York* and *London Times.*

Robert Randisi Novels — *No Exit to Brooklyn* and *The Dead of Brooklyn*. The first two Nick Delvecchio novels.

Rough Cut & New, Improved Murder — Ed Gorman's first two novels.

R.R. Ryan Novels — Freak Museum and The Subjugated Beast, two horror classics.

Ruled By Radio — 1925 futuristic novel by Robert L. Hadfield & Frank E. Farncombe.

Rupert Penny Novels — *Policeman's Holiday, Policeman's Evidence, Lucky Policeman, Policeman in Armour, Sealed Room Murder, Sweet Poison, The Talkative Policeman, She had to Have Gas* and *Cut and Run* (by Martin Tanner.) Rupert Penny is the pseudonym of Australian Charles Thornett, a master of the locked room, impossible crime plot.

Sacred Locomotive Flies — Richard A. Lupoff's psychedelic SF story.

Sam — Early gay novel by Lonnie Coleman.

Sand's Game — Spectacular hard-boiled noir from Ennis Willie, edited by Lynn Myers and Stephen Mertz, with contributions from Max Allan Collins, Bill Crider, Wayne Dundee, Bill Pronzini, Gary Lovisi and James Reasoner.

Sand's War — More violent fiction from the typewriter of Ennis Willie

Satan's Den Exposed — True crime in Truth or Consequences New Mexico — Award-winning journalism by the *Desert Journal.*

Satans of Saturn — Novellas from the pulps by Otis Adelbert Kline and E. H. Price

Satan's Sin House and Other Stories — Horrific gore by Wayne Rogers

Secrets of a Teenage Superhero — Graphic lit by Jonathan Sweet

Sex Slave — Potboiler of lust in the days of Cleopatra by Dion Leclerq, 1966.
Shadows' Edge — Two early novels by Wade Wright: *Shadows Don't Bleed* and *The Sharp Edge.*
Sideslip — 1968 SF masterpiece by Ted White and Dave Van Arnam.
Slammer Days — Two full-length prison memoirs: *Men into Beasts* (1952) by George Sylvester Viereck and *Home Away From Home* (1962) by Jack Woodford.
Slippery Staircase — 1930s whodunit from E.C.R. Lorac
Sorcerer's Chessmen — John Pelan introduces this 1939 classic by Mark Hansom.
Star Griffin — Michael Kurland's 1987 masterpiece of SF drollery is back.
Stakeout on Millennium Drive — Award-winning Indianapolis Noir by Ian Woollen.
Strands of the Web: Short Stories of Harry Stephen Keeler — Edited and Introduced by Fred Cleaver.
Summer Camp for Corpses and Other Stories — Weird Menace tales from Arthur Leo Zagat; introduced by John Pelan.
Suzy — A collection of comic strips by Richard O'Brien and Bob Vojtko from 1970.
Tales of the Macabre and Ordinary — Modern twisted horror by Chris Mikul, author of the *Bizarrism* series.
Tenebrae — Ernest G. Henham's 1898 horror tale brought back.
The Amorous Intrigues & Adventures of Aaron Burr — by Anonymous. Hot historical action about the man who almost became Emperor of Mexico.
The Anthony Boucher Chronicles — edited by Francis M. Nevins. Book reviews by Anthony Boucher written for the *San Francisco Chronicle,* 1942 – 1947. Essential and fascinating reading by the best book reviewer there ever was.
The Barclay Catalogs — Two essential books about toy soldier collecting by Richard O'Brien
The Basil Wells Omnibus — A collection of Wells' stories by Richard A. Lupoff
The Beautiful Dead and Other Stories — Dreadful tales from Donald Dale
The Best of 10-Story Book — edited by Chris Mikul, over 35 stories from the literary magazine Harry Stephen Keeler edited.
The Black Dark Murders — Vintage 50s college murder yarn by Milt Ozaki, writing as Robert O. Saber.
The Book of Time — The classic novel by H.G. Wells is joined by sequels by Wells himself and three stories by Richard A. Lupoff. Illustrated by Gavin L. O'Keefe.
The Case in the Clinic — One of E.C.R. Lorac's finest.
The Case of the Bearded Bride — #4 in the Day Keene in the Detective Pulps series
The Case of the Little Green Men — Mack Reynolds wrote this love song to sci-fi fans back in 1951 and it's now back in print.
The Case of the Withered Hand — 1936 potboiler by John G. Brandon.
The Charlie Chaplin Murder Mystery — A 2004 tribute by noted film scholar, Wes D. Gehring.
The Chinese Jar Mystery — Murder in the manor by John Stephen Strange, 1934.
The Compleat Calhoon — All of Fender Tucker's works: Includes *Totah Six-Pack, Weed, Women and Song* and *Tales from the Tower,* plus a CD of all of his songs.
The Compleat Ova Hamlet — Parodies of SF authors by Richard A. Lupoff. This is a brand new edition with more stories and more illustrations by Trina Robbins.
The Contested Earth and Other SF Stories — A never-before published space opera and seven short stories by Jim Harmon.
The Crimson Query — A 1929 thriller from Arlton Eadie. A perfect way to get introduced.
The Curse of Cantire — Classic 1939 novel of a family curse by Walter S. Masterman.
The Devil and the C.I.D. — Odd diabolic mystery by E.C.R. Lorac
The Devil Drives — An odd prison and lost treasure novel from 1932 by Virgil Markham.
The Devil's Mistress — A 1915 Scottish gothic tale by J. W. Brodie-Innes, a member of Aleister Crowley's Golden Dawn.
The Devil's Nightclub and Other Stories — John Pelan introduces some gruesome tales by Nat Schachner.
The Disentanglers — Episodic intrigue at the turn of last century by Andrew Lang
The Dumpling — Political murder from 1907 by Coulson Kernahan.
The End of It All and Other Stories — Ed Gorman selected his favorite short stories for this huge collection.
The Fangs of Suet Pudding — A 1944 novel of the German invasion by Adams Farr

The Ghost of Gaston Revere — From 1935, a novel of life and beyond by Mark Hansom, introduced by John Pelan.
The Girl in the Dark — A thriller from Roland Daniel
The Gold Star Line — Seaboard adventure from L.T. Reade and Robert Eustace.
The Golden Dagger — 1951 Scotland Yard yarn by E. R. Punshon.
The Great Orme Terror — Horror stories by Garnett Radcliffe from the pulps
The Hairbreadth Escapes of Major Mendax — Francis Blake Crofton's 1889 boys' book.
The House That Time Forgot and Other Stories — Insane pulpitude by Robert F. Young
The House of the Vampire — 1907 poetic thriller by George S. Viereck.
The Illustrious Corpse — Murder hijinx from Tiffany Thayer
The Incredible Adventures of Rowland Hern — Intriguing 1928 impossible crimes by Nicholas Olde.
The Julius Caesar Murder Case — A classic 1935 re-telling of the assassination by Wallace Irwin that's much more fun than the Shakespeare version.
The Koky Comics — A collection of all of the 1978-1981 Sunday and daily comic strips by Richard O'Brien and Mort Gerberg, in two volumes.
The Lady of the Terraces — 1925 missing race adventure by E. Charles Vivian.
The Lord of Terror — 1925 mystery with master-criminal, Fantômas.
The Melamare Mystery — A classic 1929 Arsene Lupin mystery by Maurice Leblanc
The Man Who Was Secrett — Epic SF stories from John Brunner
The Man Without a Planet — Science fiction tales by Richard Wilson
The N. R. De Mexico Novels — Robert Bragg, the real N.R. de Mexico, presents *Marijuana Girl, Madman on a Drum, Private Chauffeur* in one volume.
The Night Remembers — A 1991 Jack Walsh mystery from Ed Gorman.
The One After Snelling — Kickass modern noir from Richard O'Brien.
The Organ Reader — A huge compilation of just about everything published in the 1971-1972 radical bay-area newspaper, *THE ORGAN*. A coffee table book that points out the shallowness of the coffee table mindset.
The Poker Club — Three in one! Ed Gorman's ground-breaking novel, the short story it was based upon, and the screenplay of the film made from it.
The Private Journal & Diary of John H. Surratt — The memoirs of the man who conspired to assassinate President Lincoln.
The Secret Adventures of Sherlock Holmes — Three Sherlockian pastiches by the Brooklyn author/publisher, Gary Lovisi.
The Shadow on the House — Mark Hansom's 1934 masterpiece of horror is introduced by John Pelan.
The Sign of the Scorpion — A 1935 Edmund Snell tale of oriental evil.
The Singular Problem of the Stygian House-Boat — Two classic tales by John Kendrick Bangs about the denizens of Hades.
The Smiling Corpse — Philip Wylie and Bernard Bergman's odd 1935 novel.
The Spider: Satan's Murder Machines — A thesis about Iron Man
The Stench of Death: An Odoriferous Omnibus by Jack Moskovitz — Two complete novels and two novellas from 60's sleaze author, Jack Moskovitz.
The Story Writer and Other Stories — Classic SF from Richard Wilson
The Strange Case of the Antlered Man — 1935 dementia from Edwy Searles Brooks
The Strange Thirteen — Richard B. Gamon's odd stories about Raj India.
The Technique of the Mystery Story — Carolyn Wells' tips about writing.
The Threat of Nostalgia — A collection of his most obscure stories by Jon Breen
The Time Armada — Fox B. Holden's 1953 SF gem.
The Tongueless Horror and Other Stories — Volume One of the series of short stories from the weird pulps by Wyatt Blassingame.
The Tracer of Lost Persons — From 1906, an episodic novel that became a hit radio series in the 30s. Introduced by Richard A. Lupoff.
The Trail of the Cloven Hoof — Diabolical horror from 1935 by Arlton Eadie. Introduced by John Pelan.
The Triune Man — Mindscrambling science fiction from Richard A. Lupoff**.**
The Unholy Goddess and Other Stories — Wyatt Blassingame's first DTP compilation.
The Universal Holmes — Richard A. Lupoff's 2007 collection of five Holmesian pastiches and

a recipe for giant rat stew.

The Werewolf vs the Vampire Woman — Hard to believe ultraviolence by either Arthur M. Scarm or Arthur M. Scram.

The Whistling Ancestors — A 1936 classic of weirdness by Richard E. Goddard and introduced by John Pelan.

The White Owl — A vintage thriller from Edmund Snell

The White Peril in the Far East — Sidney Lewis Gulick's 1905 indictment of the West and assurance that Japan would never attack the U.S.

The Wizard of Berner's Abbey — A 1935 horror gem written by Mark Hansom and introduced by John Pelan.

The Wonderful Wizard of Oz — by L. Frank Baum and illustrated by Gavin L. O'Keefe

Through the Looking Glass — Lewis Carroll wrote it; Gavin L. O'Keefe illustrated it.

Time Line — Ramble House artist Gavin O'Keefe selects his most evocative art inspired by the twisted literature he reads and designs.

Tiresias — Psychotic modern horror novel by Jonathan M. Sweet.

Totah Six-Pack — Fender Tucker's six tales about Farmington in one sleek volume.

Trail of the Spirit Warrior — Roger Haley's historical saga of life in the Indian Territories.

Two Kinds of Bad — Two 50s novels by William Ard about Danny Fontaine

Two Suns of Morcali and Other Stories — Evelyn E. Smith's SF tour-de-force

Ultra-Boiled — 23 gut-wrenching tales by our Man in Brooklyn, Gary Lovisi.

Up Front From Behind — A 2011 satire of Wall Street by James B. Kobak.

Victims & Villains — Intriguing Sherlockiana from Derham Groves.

Wade Wright Novels — *Echo of Fear, Death At Nostalgia Street, It Leads to Murder* and *Shadows' Edge*, a double book featuring *Shadows Don't Bleed* and *The Sharp Edge*.

Walter S. Masterman Novels — *The Green Toad, The Flying Beast, The Yellow Mistletoe, The Wrong Verdict, The Perjured Alibi, The Border Line, The Bloodhounds Bay* and *The Curse of Cantire.* Masterman wrote horror and mystery, some introduced by John Pelan.

We Are the Dead and Other Stories — Volume Two in the Day Keene in the Detective Pulps series, introduced by Ed Gorman. When done, there may be as many as 11 in the series.

Welsh Rarebit Tales — Charming stories from 1902 by Harle Oren Cummins

West Texas War and Other Western Stories — by Gary Lovisi.

Whip Dodge: Man Hunter — Wesley Tallant's saga of a bounty hunter of the old West.

Win, Place and Die! — The first new mystery by Milt Ozaki in decades. The ultimate novel of 70s Reno.

You'll Die Laughing — Bruce Elliott's 1945 novel of murder at a practical joker's English countryside manor.

RAMBLE HOUSE

Fender Tucker, Prop. Gavin L. O'Keefe, Graphics

www.ramblehouse.com fender@ramblehouse.com

228-826-1783 10329 Sheephead Drive, Vancleave MS 39565

Printed in Great Britain
by Amazon

58127894R00123